GOODBYE, DOLLY

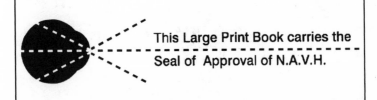

This Large Print Book carries the
Seal of Approval of N.A.V.H.

GOODBYE, DOLLY

DEB BAKER

WHEELER PUBLISHING
An imprint of Thomson Gale, a part of The Thomson Corporation

Detroit • New York • San Francisco • New Haven, Conn. • Waterville, Maine • London

THOMSON
GALE
™

LIBRARY OF CONGRESS CATALOGING-IN-PUBLICATION DATA

Baker, Deb, 1953–
   Goodbye, Dolly / by Deb Baker.
      p. cm. — (Wheeler Publishing large print cozy mystery) (A dolls to die for mystery)
   ISBN-13: 978-1-59722-656-1 (pbk. : alk. paper)
   ISBN-10: 1-59722-656-4 (pbk. : alk. paper)
   1. Dolls — Collectors and collecting — Fiction. 2. Murder — Investigation — Fiction. 3. Large type books. I. Title.
   PS3602.A586G66 2007
   813'.6—dc22   2007033370

Published in 2007 by arrangement with The Berkley Publishing Group, a member of Penguin Group (USA) Inc.

Printed in the United States of America on permanent paper
10 9 8 7 6 5 4 3 2 1

GOODBYE, DOLLY

Jennie H. Graves created the Ginny doll in the late 1940s. Her small home business quickly grew to become the Vogue Doll Company. Ginny's popularity sent other companies racing to emulate the eight-inch plastic play doll. The most innovative feature of the new doll was its separate clothing. Ginny came wearing underwear, ready to dress in costumes designed by her creator. And what wonderful costumes they were.
— From *World of Dolls* by Caroline Birch

Gretchen Birch stood next to the flatbed trailer parked in the driveway leading to the house and eyed the mounds of dolls. Howie Howard, the auctioneer, worked the crowd like a harmonica tongue slap, all swinging elbows and agile, fluid mouth movements. Gretchen had a first-timer's knot of nerves in her stomach the size and weight of a

Sunkist grapefruit.

"Do I hear twenty? There's a two oh. Thirty. Forty. Fine box of dolls." Howie's head bobbed like one of the swivel-head dolls boxed up in Gretchen's doll repair workshop. "Fifty? No. Forty going once . . . Sold for forty dollars."

The smell of popcorn from a portable concession stand wafted through the air, catching the attention of a group of neighborhood kids. Cars filled with potential buyers searching for curbside parking edged slowly past the auction site.

Gretchen glanced at the stucco-and-tile house where Chiggy Kent, the once-vibrant founder of the Phoenix Dollers Club, had lived. Dragging an oxygen tank connected to her nostrils, Chiggy had finally succumbed to the persistence of her concerned neighbors and the ravages of lung disease and now resided at Grace Senior Care. But if she'd had the breath to resist, she would have forced them to haul her out kicking and screaming.

Chiggy's doll-making skills hadn't improved with experience or with advanced age. At least six hundred handmade dolls cluttered the open-bed truck, and Gretchen winced at the poor workmanship. Dolls' eyebrows wisped in unlikely directions, painted with heavy, awkward strokes. Eye-lashes that would have impressed the legendary Tammy Faye, notorious queen of eye art.

The doll clothes were worth more than the dolls that wore them, but many of the shoppers who bellied up to the truck weren't serious collectors and couldn't tell the difference between an original and a poor reproduction.

Howie Howard wasn't about to clue them in. "Here's a priceless imitation of a German Kestner. Full of character. Who could resist? Do I hear ten?" The words melded together, strung without the briefest pause, and Gretchen smiled at his singular ability to sell certifiable junk.

A man beside her lifted a doll from a heap and made space on the flatbed to prop it up. He smoothed the doll's bright blue gown and rearranged the curls framing her face, then stepped back and snapped a picture. Gretchen watched him move along the truck from doll to doll as he repeated the process again and again.

His camera, a Leica digital, looked expensive — too expensive, considering his gaunt, unshaven face and the faded T-shirt stretched over his protruding stomach.

The sun beat down on Gretchen.

She glanced around for a shady spot to stand in. The last day of September was hot and dry, and Gretchen needed a respite from the intensity of the Phoenix sun. One lone palm tree cast a pencil-thin shadow across Chiggy's now barren yard, not nearly enough for protection.

Where did I put it? Gretchen dug through her purse for the list of dolls her mother had wanted her to bid on. She must have left it at home. *Now what?* She didn't have time to search for it. *No choice but to wing it.*

She hoped Howie wouldn't auction off all six hundred of these handmade copies before moving on to the real reason she stood here suffering from the heat. Chiggy's private collection. The real dolls.

Gretchen recognized several serious collectors in the crowd and a few impatient doll dealers looking for bargains. She edged closer to Howie.

"Change of pace," he shouted, as though reading Gretchen's mind. "We can't sell everything one at a time, or we'll be here through Sunday. Let's dig out something new. What've we got, Brett?" He turned and accepted a cardboard box from his assistant. "Box of Kewpie dolls." He held one aloft. "Cute little things. Whole bunch made by the same talented doll artist, Chiggy Kent."

10

Howie held up a three-inch Kewpie. "Who wants to start . . . ?" And he was off and running.

Bidding on the box of Kewpies started low. Gretchen watched with interest, because her turn was coming. She was fascinated by the speed with which Howie flew through the bidding process and the different ways the registered bidders had of alerting the auctioneer to their bids.

She had sorted through the Kewpie dolls before the auction and noticed that most had been repaired in some way. Almost all were bad reproductions. Gretchen saw imperfections in the molded bodies, amateurishly shaped topknots, and tufts of babyish hair.

Someone was actually bidding on this mess?

"Sold for thirty dollars." Howie's voice slammed through the group, and Gretchen craned her neck to see the successful bidder.

Him again. She'd watched the shriveled old man bid several times. Who could miss his stooped shoulders, full head of white hair, and Groucho Marx eyebrows? He waved his registration number with gleeful abandon and slapped his knee in delight.

Howie's assistant, Brett, continued to

bring items to the auction block. A collection of paper dolls, then an Ashton-Drake Little Red Riding Hood.

Gretchen tried to imagine the list her mother had composed. No paper dolls. She was sure of it. Or was she?

Why do I have to be so forgetful and disorganized?

Howie, appreciating the scope of his mission, began to clump groups of dolls together to step up the pace. Brett continued lugging boxes out of the garage.

". . . Ginny dolls."

Gretchen snapped back to the call of the auctioneer. Ginnys were on the list. Here goes. Her reason for standing out in the desert sun for . . . how long? . . . two hours and counting. Her body felt clam-baked, and her hair, hard to manage on a good day, frizzed out from her damp scalp.

Someone pushed past her, another bidder positioning for the same round. Gretchen's palms felt sweaty, and she grasped her number firmly, waiting for the opening volley. *Calm down. This is like a horse race. You don't have to start out in the lead to win.* She remembered her mother's coaching. *Don't look desperate. Lay low. Wait for the right moment.*

Gretchen gulped and felt the thrill of

competition. Right this minute she wanted that collection of Ginny dolls more than anything in the world. Is this how it always felt? What a rush of adrenaline! No wonder her mother always covered the auctions and left her to handle repairs.

The dolls that Gretchen lusted after were eight-inch Vogue vintage dolls from the late forties and early fifties, all in their original boxes. They came with a variety of costumes: hats, dresses, purses, and snap shoes.

Howie's voice sliced the sun-scorched air. "This is it," he said, his words coming fast. "The finest of the fine . . ."

Gretchen's heart sank into her stomach and settled next to the grapefruit-sized nervous lump. Why did he have to call special attention to the dolls she was interested in?

Her eyes never left his as his voice rang out.

"Who'll give me fifty?"

Gretchen raised her number against her sweat-laden halter top. So much for her mother's sound advice to lay low. Howie trained his eyes on her, acknowledged the bid, and worked it up. From the rapid sweep of his head, she guessed that three or four others were placing bids.

"One hundred. We have a cool, crisp bill."

Howie kept going, and Gretchen felt the sting of impending defeat.

One of the bidders dropped out, and Gretchen held up her number again.

Another bidder dropped out.

Yes. Gretchen slapped an internal high five at the dwindling competition.

The Ginny dolls whispered her name, and she did the math in her head. Twelve dolls. She could sell them at the doll show for at least fifty each. That would be a total of six hundred dollars.

She still had some leeway.

The current bid shot past two hundred.

But some of the dolls needed work. Her mind flicked through the supplies in the repair workshop. She was sure she had extra Ginny doll parts. Arms and legs, even some original dresses, a wig or two.

Someone behind her was still bidding, but Gretchen didn't dare turn around. Next time she would take a position in the back of the crowd so she could watch the action.

"We have two eighty."

Gretchen signaled.

"Three hundred." Howie's red face beamed in anticipation of his growing commission. "Do I have three fifty?" His eyes darted behind Gretchen, his eyebrows one big question mark.

14

Silence.

Howie waited a millisecond, then shrugged.

"Sold," Howie shouted, pointing at Gretchen.

Brett, standing behind Howie holding the next box, managed to give her a thumbs-up.

She felt like she'd won a million-dollar lottery.

Howie didn't miss a beat, intent on pounding through the remaining items as quickly as possible. Gretchen worked her way out of the crowd and stood at the back. She'd spent all her money on twelve dolls, but she couldn't help grinning. They were worth it.

Had she paid too much? Her mother's request included at least six or seven different dolls. Even if she hadn't forgotten the list, she wouldn't be able to bid on any others.

After Gretchen paid for the dolls, Brett had her box ready at the side of the truck. He slapped her shoulder. "Good job."

Gretchen tuned out Howie's theatrical voice when he presented another round of Chiggy's badly painted dolls to the crowd. She sat down on a white plastic lawn chair and placed the box beside her. Her registration number and the word *Ginny* were sprawled across the top in black magic marker, the handwriting almost illegible.

The photographer strolled her way, camera strapped at his side, and his hand stretched out to her. Gretchen accepted the business card and glanced at the name. Peter Finch.

"I'm putting together a collection of doll photographs and selling them on eBay," he said. "Photo gallery, you know. A hundred and fifty pictures for thirty bucks. A steal."

"You're including photos of Chiggy's handmade dolls?" Gretchen was incredulous.

"Check it out," he said, moving off, offering his card down the line.

Gretchen tucked the business card in her white cotton purse embroidered with black poodles and red bows, a gift from Aunt Nina.

She bent over the box and opened the cover.

A heap of poorly produced Kewpie dolls grinned impishly up at her astonished face.

Just great.

The boxes had been mixed up. The stooped man with the bushy eyebrows who won the Kewpies must be walking around right now with her Ginnys.

Grabbing the box, she hurried back to the truck and scanned the crowd.

Then she heard tires squeal and a car horn blare. Someone screamed. Gretchen, along with everyone else in Chiggy Kent's yard, rushed toward the street.

"Back up. Quick." A man's voice sounded panicked.

Gretchen scooted between two parked cars, still holding the box of Kewpies.

She saw a woman get out of a Ford Explorer that had stopped in the middle of the street. "I didn't see him," she said to the people gathering around. "He flew right out between the cars. I didn't even have time to brake."

Several people crouched in front of the SUV.

Gretchen gasped and almost dropped the fragile Kewpie dolls.

Howie's assistant, Brett Wesley, lay crumpled in the road.

2

The ambulance pulled away slowly, without the need for wailing sirens and flashing lights. The police finished questioning possible witnesses and released the remaining auction attendees. People stood in small groups, talking quietly. Cars began to pull away. Everyone would drive with extra care for the rest of the day.

The auction came to an abrupt close. Howie Howard had lost his business partner and close friend and was incapable of continuing. No one seemed interested in dolls anymore. Gretchen watched Howie get into a blue pickup truck, his face the color of Arizona adobe. She guessed he would follow Brett's body to the morgue.

She felt a wave of nausea each time she thought of Brett lying dead in the street. How quickly life can be snuffed out by a misstep between parked cars. An image of the car's tire slamming across Brett's torso forced its way into her thoughts, and she tried to block it from her mind.

One of the registration workers slapped a sign on the side of the flatbed trailer. All remaining handmade dolls would sell for ten dollars each. Help yourself. Pay at the register.

The notice reminded Gretchen that she still carried the wrong box of dolls. She looked around for the stooped man but didn't see him.

A chunky woman with brassy blonde curls sat at the registration table. Gretchen approached. "I know this isn't really important, considering what just happened," she said. "But I have the wrong box of dolls."

"Nothing I can do about it, sweetheart." A single sob escaped from the woman, but she quickly composed herself.

"I think I know who I need to contact," Gretchen said. "Can you check the records and tell me who bought a box of Kewpie dolls?"

"I suppose." The woman scanned the registration sheet. "That would be Gretchen Birch."

"Well, I'm Gretchen Birch, but I bought Ginny dolls, not Kewpies. Can you tell me who the list says bought the box of Ginny dolls?"

"Name's Duanne Wilson. Lives on Forty-third Street. You'd better write that down now."

Gretchen dug in her purse for a pen and paper and copied the name and address.

"Shame about Brett. I can't hardly believe it," the woman said, tears in her eyes. "He was a good man."

Gretchen nodded, close to crying herself. Other people's sorrows always set her off. If she caved in now, she'd be a basket case for the rest of the day. "Thanks for the information," she said, in a hurry to get away.

Most of the cars in front of Chiggy's house had cleared out. Gretchen didn't see the Ford Explorer or the woman who had hit Brett. *That poor driver. How awful.* She stowed the box of Kewpie dolls in the trunk of her car and eased away.

Though she'd only met him once before, Brett had been kind. He had smiled and given her a thumbs-up. She fought back tears and considered the accident. Apparently no one had seen him step in front of the car. Amazing, considering the number of people mobbing the trailer, but of course, everyone's attention had been riveted on Howie and the auction. The driver of the SUV had insisted that Brett literally flew into the street. Why had he been in such a hurry? Shouldn't he have been working beside the auctioneer?

Brett had probably been the one who mixed up the boxes. Gretchen sighed heavily. At the moment, the last thing she cared about was the doll mix-up. But three hundred dollars was a lot of money. She had to correct the mistake.

As she drove along Lincoln Drive, Gretchen glanced up at Camelback Mountain, Phoenix's monolithic landmark. The mountain dominated Sun Valley, and Gretchen felt comfort in its solid presence.

The boulevards exploded with colorful plantings, and red bougainvillea covered privacy walls, but Gretchen hardly noticed as she made her way toward what she hoped was Forty-third Street. Two months in Phoenix, and she still couldn't find her way around.

After asking for directions twice, she turned onto the street and searched the buildings for the number she had written down. She drove around the block and tried again.

No number matched the one she'd been given.

Gretchen frowned in annoyance.

Had she written it down wrong? Not an improbability after the tragic accident. But no. She remembered double-checking the numbers with the teary blonde.

She pulled to the curb in front of the only apartment complex within several blocks. This had to be where the man lived. She pulled open the first set of doors, entered, and tried the second set. Locked.

She scanned the names on the mail slots. No Duanne Wilson.

She waited, hoping someone would come along and open the door. Maybe a manager's office inside would give her the correct apartment number.

No one came.

Standing on the sidewalk, she looked up and down the street. *What now?* She had three hundred dollars invested in those dolls.

Then she noticed a sign announcing a vacancy in the building. Gretchen dug her cell phone from her purse and dialed the number.

After a few holds and redirections, she had her answer, and she didn't like it.

No such person. No such place.

Duanne Wilson had vanished along with her Ginny dolls.

3

"Brett came sprinting past like he was train-ing for one of those triathlons," she says, looking up from her seat behind the registra-tion table, studying the man and wishing she'd brushed her hair and powdered her nose. Some women can cry their hearts out and still look good.

Not her.

She runs fingers from both sweaty hands under her blonde curls, hoping to give them more bounce.

She must look a fright, all puffy and red-eyed.

Everybody had gone home after the ac-cident except her, or so she thought. Just a few more things to pack up if she can find the energy.

She still sat in the same position at the registration table, numb all over except for the tears running down her face.

But then this man appeared out of nowhere, and she tried to straighten herself up.

"I was working the registration desk. Howie was off in the corner of the truck working his usual magic on the crowd. Right over there."

She points and imagines going back in time to that precise moment when Brett ran past her. If she had it to do over, she'd stop him somehow and change his future. Maybe give him one of those long, passionate kisses she remembers so well.

Her lower lip quivers.

"Don't forget to write that all down now," she says. "Anyway, he tripped over his own feet he was in such a hurry, and he almost dropped the box."

"You don't say? What kind of box?"

" 'Bout this big," She raises her hands parallel like she's showing off the length of a Gila monster she might spot in the desert near her home. Or a good-sized fish from the Verde River.

" 'Oh damn,' Brett said, all panicked-like, and I was surprised because he is . . . or was . . . one of those Promise Keepers. You know, that men's Christian group with the seven promises? I never heard him utter a cuss word before."

She swipes a finger under her eye, sure

that she has mascara smudges showing; after all, she's cried a bucketful. "Maybe he was trying to catch up with that woman who came by later and said some boxes were switched."

"Woman?"

"She said she had the wrong box."

"Do you remember her name?"

"Is that important?"

"You never know." He shrugs.

"Gretchen something. Let's see. Like a tree. Oak, maple, uh . . ." She snaps her fingers. "Gretchen Birch. That's it. Write that down now."

She pauses and watches him scribble in the notebook.

"Next thing I hear are tires squealing and people screaming." She looks out over the empty yard where the auction had been held. It seems so long ago. "Brett and I were engaged once, you know, when we were younger. I should have stuck with him. He was a good man."

"How much time would you say elapsed between the time you saw him and the time you heard the tires squeal?"

"Oh, I don't know. I guess maybe it was one or two minutes after he ran by that I found out it was Brett in the street." She sniffs. "Don't forget to write that down, too."

A loud sob escapes from her throat.

4

The biggest doll show of the year, and Gretchen had to handle it alone. *But that's life.* Like finding yourself in front of a sold-out audience without a script, and just as the curtain rises you realize that you're standing up there stark naked, and there isn't a thing you can do about it, Gretchen thought.

"You can do it," her aunt Nina said, perching like a colorful songbird on a stool next to Gretchen. "You know your mother would be here if she could. It's not her fault." Nina wore an array of bows in her dark hair that matched her outfit right down to the stones in her rings.

Gretchen glanced at a bin of naked dolls and miscellaneous doll parts in her mother's workshop and felt a surge of nervous energy. After weeks of preparation, the countdown was under way. It would be her first doll show, and she hadn't anticipated losing her mother's help at the last minute.

"She could have rescheduled her California book tour," Gretchen complained, feeling unreasonable and not caring. "It certainly is her fault. I've never even done a little show before. How will I get through one this size all by myself?"

"Caroline put a lot of work into her doll book, and she deserves the time off to promote it," Nina scolded her. "Besides, it could be worse. She could have left without arranging for any assistance. Instead, she asked me to help you, so don't worry."

Knowing Nina as well as she did, help*less* would be more accurate. Since her mother's younger sister knew nothing about dolls or doll shows, Gretchen didn't see how helpful she would be. *An excellent reason to worry myself sick.*

Gretchen had that naked-onstage feeling again.

The final week leading up to the show had been a whirlwind of activity — selecting dolls for the show from her mother's large inventory and repairing damaged dolls they hoped to sell, along with helping the Phoenix Dollers Club coordinate last-minute details.

The workshop where Gretchen and Nina sat talking was cluttered with bits and pieces: fabric, clothes, tools, and dolls.

"Here's the list I was supposed to take to the auction," Gretchen said, pulling it from the clutter on the table and surveying the items. "Two Shirley Temples, a Tammy, two or three Ginnys . . ." Gretchen groaned. "I bought twelve Ginny dolls and none of the others she wanted."

"How could you know Howie would offer them all together?"

"I was a complete failure. I didn't bid on anything else on the list, I paid too much, and, worse, I lost the entire investment *and* the doll show profit."

"You're being too hard on yourself. The dolls will show up. And you have a perfectly good excuse. What with the accident and all."

Brett's death the day before still occupied most of Gretchen thoughts. That, and the show she didn't feel prepared for.

She dabbed a doll repair hook with nail polish labeled Poodle Skirt Pink.

"I love the color," her aunt said, observing the splash of pink on the repair hook. "But when I bought the polish for you, I thought you'd wear it on your nails, not waste it on your tools."

"I'm trying to organize my new toolbox." Gretchen picked up a clamp and steadied her polishing hand. "I'll be restringing dolls tomorrow, and I need everything organized."

"That doesn't explain the polish."

"I'm personalizing my tools so they don't disappear. With all the traffic through the exhibit hall, I have to be careful."

"Well, at least color-coordinate your ensemble by painting your toes the same color. And since when are you worried about order?" Nina looked at the surrounding disorder.

"Self-improvement. I'm determined to put some organization into my life. I'm tired of spending so much time looking for things. My mind is scattered, but I'm going to change."

Nina looked skeptical.

Nimrod, Gretchen's black teacup poodle, looked on from his bed in the corner. Wobbles, the three-legged cat Gretchen had rescued a year earlier in Boston after a hit-and-run, cleaned himself in the doorway, running a moistened paw over his face, one watchful eye on the activity in the doll workshop.

"I've inherited a menagerie," Gretchen said, holding the hook in the air to dry.

"You love every minute of it." Nina twirled around in a full circle. "The animals are good for you. Admit it."

Gretchen blew on the wet polish to hasten its drying and considered Nina's observation. Did she enjoy Wobbles and Nimrod? Absolutely. Would she admit it? Never. Her aunt claimed psychic abilities. Let her figure it out on her own.

Nimrod yawned leisurely from his bed, and Gretchen gave him a tender look in spite of her frayed nerves. Thanks to Nina's experienced guidance, the puppy had quickly adapted to his traveling purse and accompanied Gretchen most of the time.

Nina was a purse dog trainer, teaching miniature puppies to ride in their owners' shoulder bags. Leave it to her aunt to come up with a one-of-a-kind occupation that included unlimited freedom of movement, a unique expertise, and a great deal of patience. Purse dogs were now all the fashion among the local doll collectors.

Nina leaned closer to study Gretchen's polishing technique. "Maybe you should go back to graphic design work. Look how good you are."

"Very funny."

"Do you miss it?"

"Not at all. I'll never go back to the corporate world. This . . ." Gretchen looked

31

around the workshop, ". . . is where I belong."

It took all her willpower to keep her hand steady, her heart rate even, and her words light. As if the pressure of her first show and the abrupt demise of the auctioneer's assistant weren't enough. She had another problem.

"You just missed that clamp and globbed polish on your fingers."

Gretchen jammed the cover on the polish and dropped her chin into her hands. "He's here, you know."

"Who? Who?" Nina said with wide, rounded eyes. She dipped a tissue in polish remover and swiped at Gretchen's fingers.

"Steve Kuchen," Gretchen whispered. She tensed at the thought of coming face-to-face with her former boyfriend. Steve, who had cheated on her. With a summer intern, no less. What a cliché. A very young summer intern, at that.

"It's about time he showed up. For a while I thought he didn't care. How long has it been?"

"Two months." Could it really have been that long since she had packed up and fled from Boston and from him?

"How can you walk away from a seven-year relationship without at least talking it over?" Nina asked. "Even if he *did* deserve it." She caught the look in Gretchen's eyes and made a hasty revision. "Which he did. No doubt about it. The cheating pond scum."

Gretchen stared at the nail polish.

"Not," Nina added, quickly, "that I don't support you in your decision. I love having you here."

"My life certainly has changed since I left Boston."

"That's true. You turned thirty —"

"Don't remind me."

"— and you have a new home and a new job."

Gretchen didn't want to point out that she was, at thirty, living with her mother, or that her mother had offered her a partnership in the doll repair business out of pure pity. Well, that wasn't exactly true. Her mother's business had taken off with the publication of her first doll collecting book, and she'd actually needed Gretchen's help.

The fact remained though: Gretchen was living in her mother's cabana. *How pathetic is that?*

"Now that he knows you're serious, he won't give up," Nina said. "I bet he thought if he waited long enough, you'd come crawling back on your knees. How did he manage to pry himself away from his law firm? No one getting a divorce this week?"

"I don't know, and I don't care." But she did. Very much. She had moved past the angry stage, past the first jolts of anguish. The man she had once loved was long gone, replaced by an ambitious, singularly focused attorney with a roving eye and snappy excuses. "I won't see him."

Nina chuckled. "I bet he's here for the doll show, pretending he likes dolls. You should have taken his phone calls. Now you have to deal with him in person."

"Maybe you can run interference," Gretchen said and instantly regretted the comment. Nina had a tendency to run amok, and planting her in the middle of this dispute wasn't a smart move. In fact, it was a recipe for disaster.

"This isn't a football game." Nina tapped a jeweled hand on Gretchen's knee. "Where's he staying?"

"The Phoenician." *No turning back now.* Nina was involved.

Her aunt raised a penciled eyebrow. "That's where our other visitors from Massachusetts are staying. Those Boston bluebloods have upscale taste. I hear the Phoenician has grass tennis courts. How they maintain grass in the desert is beyond me.

Not to mention using precious water for such extravagance."

"If it wasn't for the doll show, I'd take an unplanned vacation and stay away until Steve left," Gretchen said.

Before she could slip into self-pity mode, she was distracted by Tutu, Nina's schnoodle — half schnauzer, half poodle — who chose that moment to prance toward the doorway, stopping abruptly when she discovered Wobbles blocking the way. The cat's ears slicked back against his head, and his tail swished warningly.

"Those two are never going to get along," Gretchen said, rising to referee the combatants and hopefully save Tutu from another clawed nose.

Wobbles's eyes narrowed to slits, and he hissed. Tutu boldly shot past him and ran down the hall, Wobbles in hot pursuit. Nimrod gleefully joined the race, taking up the rear. His black puppy paws slid on the Mexican tile as he rounded the corner.

Gretchen heard Tutu yelp, then a loud bang, and the sound of something breaking.

"Uh-oh," Nina said, hurrying after them.

Gretchen followed slowly, hoping Nina would handle whatever mess the troublemakers had made. Wobbles, the most sensible of the three, had disappeared from sight. Tutu looked sufficiently contrite, tail between her legs, head hanging. Nimrod thought it was playtime, rollicking in circles around Tutu.

Nina stood over a broken doll lying on the tile floor where it had fallen from the bookcase. Gretchen scowled at her forgetfulness. She had taken this one out of the box to study it and left it on the bookcase. Foolish of her.

She bent and picked up the pieces, doll body in one hand, head in the other.

One of Duanne Wilson's Kewpie dolls, a Blunderboo, had broken in two.

5

One night at the turn of the twentieth century, Rosie O'Neill dreamed about tiny imps and began to sketch them from her imagination. Plump, mischievous babies with laughing eyes and wisps of hair standing straight up. She called them Kewpies, short for Cupid, because they did good deeds in amusing ways.

The series began with magazine drawings accompanied by short stories and poems. Next, she designed Kewpie Kutouts, comic pages, and books. At the request of adoring children, she created a special doll. By 1913 Kewpie dolls could be found all over the world.

— From *World of Dolls* by Caroline Birch

The Kewpie's grinning baby face seemed to be showing appreciation for Gretchen's efforts to repair it. She had to look carefully to detect the thin, glued line reconnecting the doll's head with its body. An expert fix, she thought with satisfaction. Her mother couldn't have done much better.

But her fingers could feel the telltale ridge. Her repair wouldn't fool a professional, but she'd done the best anybody could.

Blunderboo was her favorite of all the Rosie O'Neill designs. He was the clumsy Kewpie, always falling, tumbling, or rolling.

Gretchen turned the three-inch doll upside down and examined the fake O'Neill mark on its feet, then studied the red heart label painted on its bare, chubby body.

Why had Chiggy attempted to make her own Kewpies? Based on the woman's vast collection of dolls at the auction, her tastes ran more toward reproductions of rare antique dolls than the fairylike Kewpies.

"I feel bad about the doll," Gretchen told Nina with genuine regret. "Especially since it isn't mine. I hope the elusive Mr. Wilson isn't an expert. Unless he picks it up and runs his fingers along the neck, he won't know that it's been repaired."

"If he had expertise in the field, he wouldn't have purchased the dolls in the first place," Nina said, peering into the box Gretchen had placed on her mother's worktable. "It's a motley lot anyway. Every one of them seems to be broken."

"Or repaired," Gretchen agreed. "Why did Chiggy keep such a box of junk? It looks like a practice batch that should have been thrown out."

"From what you said about her reproductions, the whole auction was filled with garbage."

"Not the box of Ginnys. Those were exquisite. I have to get them back."

Gretchen gently scraped a tiny dot of glue from the doll's neck with her X-Acto knife. "The first doll I ever owned was a Kewpie. I called her Lucy. Dad gave her to me."

Gretchen felt an acute sense of loss. Her father's death had left an immense hole in her life. "I miss him every day."

"The car accident was a horrible shock," Nina agreed. "It's been two years, but it takes a long time to get over something like that. At least *you* survived."

Gretchen laid the X-Acto knife on the table. "Yesterday when Brett stepped out in front of the SUV, it brought back memories of the accident."

Squealing tires, screams, breaking glass, metal collapsing, moans.

It had all come rushing back — the fear, the horror of crawling unharmed out of the rolled car and finding her father lifeless behind the wheel. The screams she'd heard had been her own.

"I wish you hadn't been at the auction when it happened," Nina said.

"I wish the same thing." Gretchen rose and cleaned off the table, returning the glue to its assigned spot.

"Well, we're off for our hair appointment," Nina said, clipping a pink leash to Tutu's collar. "I'll pick you up for lunch in a few hours."

"Is Tutu getting a new hairdo, too?"

"Of course," Nina said, breezing out, leaving a vacuum of silence behind her.

In spite of the heat, it was good to be in Phoenix, away from the complications associated with Boston. Gretchen liked her renewed relationship with her mother and the comfortable presence of the workshop.

Gretchen glanced around her. Dolls had played an integral part in her life. They were the glue that bonded her to her roots and especially to her mother.

Feeling a need to connect, Gretchen picked up the phone. Her mother answered, her voice light and happy.

"A book tour," Caroline said, "is exactly what I needed. I'm meeting new readers, seeing the coast, renewing acquaintances with doll collectors. It's marvelous."

Now was not the time to start whining

and complaining. "That's great," Gretchen said, forcing the same easy tone. "I just wanted to hear your voice. Everything is fine on my end."

Fine? Brett was dead, Steve had turned up in Phoenix, she'd lost three hundred dollars and the Ginny dolls, and she wasn't sure she could handle the doll show by herself.

"Everything's fine," she repeated.

"Okay, what's wrong?"

"Nothing. What makes you think something's wrong?"

"You're part of me. I can tell."

Gretchen sighed. "I'm worried about the show," she said, picking the least complicated of her concerns to share with her mother.

"I have absolute confidence in your ability to handle the doll show," Caroline said. "It's Brett's death that has you upset."

"How did you know about that?"

"I'm not entirely out of touch. California isn't on Mars."

"Nina told you."

"Nina called to ask if I'd received her telepathic signals and if I had been able to decipher them."

"And?"

"Of course I didn't get Nina's unique but

faulty wireless message. I told her I'd felt something special that I couldn't identify just to keep her happy. She suggested that I try harder next time."

Gretchen laughed, feeling her gloomy thoughts dissipating.

She and Caroline chatted a little longer, and after hanging up, Gretchen turned her attention to creating a sign to display at the doll show announcing her restoration service. Making room on the table for a yellow piece of poster board, she went to work with colored Magic Markers.

As she finished the sign, she heard someone clearing his throat behind her.

Startled, she turned quickly.

Steve Kuchen stood a few feet inside the workshop door. He wore an expensive pair of khakis and an air of confidence that only the really rich carried off well. He'd probably leased a Beemer at the airport.

"How did you get in?" she said.

"The door was unlocked."

Thanks, Nina.

She felt her face flush. How long had he been watching her?

"Do you know what day it is?" Steve asked softly, a hesitant smile on his face, a few blond locks falling loosely across his forehead. He was as handsome as ever.

"It's October first." Gretchen laid the marker on the table. "Friday."

"That was a rhetorical question, Gretchen. Today is day number sixty-two since you left Boston. You refused every one of my calls. You can't hide forever."

Why not? Gretchen was a master at dodgeball. Confrontations weren't her specialty. She considered herself more the ostrich head-in-the-sand type.

"You should have knocked at the front door," she said to fill the uneasy void.

"Would you have answered?"

"Another rhetorical question?" Gretchen felt angry, and her anger energized her. She had nothing to explain. She was the injured party, and he wouldn't force her into a conciliatory role, as he'd done so many times in the past.

"There's someone else, isn't there?" he said.

Predictable.

Steve of the inflated ego could never imagine that the end of their relationship might be his fault.

He has the nerve to ask me if there's someone else? "I believe you stole my line." Gretchen saw him blanch, and she felt smug satisfaction. He'd been the one who cheated, not her. And he couldn't claim it

43

was a random moment. It was an affair with someone at his office.

"Nina says you're dating a police officer."

Gretchen wanted to correct him but didn't. Matt Albright was a detective with the Phoenix Police Department. They'd met right after she had moved to Phoenix. His mother presided over the Phoenix Dollers Club.

Not that they were "dating" as Steve believed, thanks to her Chatty Cathy aunt. It had been only two months since her breakup with Steve. She wasn't ready. Still . . .

"Where did you see Nina?" she said. Nina was at it already.

"Outside. She was in a hurry. Some dog appointment, she said."

He *had* been watching her before he announced his presence.

"Nina's truth is like pulled taffy," Gretchen said, carefully. "It looks like a solid mass in the beginning, but as it's pulled, it stretches until in the end the candy undergoes a complete change."

"I'm not sure I followed that," Steve said.

"Nina operates on a different plane than the rest of us."

Gretchen had been up since five o'clock prepping for the show, and a wave of tiredness hit her.

"Is she still seeing auras and tuning in to the universe?" he asked.

"She hasn't changed."

"New Age Nina," he said with a forced laugh.

Steve walked to the table, and Gretchen backed away. If he touched her, she might lose her resolve.

Stay strong. The Birch women's motto.

He ran his hands over the tools she was about to pack up for the doll show. All had been dipped in Poodle Skirt Pink.

Gretchen noted his manicured fingers before she turned away.

"I can't get into a discussion about our relationship right now," she said with an indifference she really didn't feel. "I'm behind on my prep work, and I have a lunch meeting."

Steve, used to pressure in the courtroom, appeared unruffled. *He came across the country to get me back; he must have prepared a grand opening argument.*

The only hint she had that he was unhappy was the way his hand abruptly stopped brushing across the repair tools.

Steve had changed so much since he'd begun his pursuit of the law office's partnership. Late hours. Preoccupation with his job. Where had his passion gone?

Or was she the one who'd changed?

He pulled away from the table. "Of course," he said, civilized beyond all doubt. "Later today, then."

Gretchen waved at the disarray in the workshop. "I still have all this to clean up, and I'll be working at the doll show starting very early tomorrow."

"I'll find you at the show," Steve said, exuding practiced self-confidence.

But his voice held a hint of disappointment, and his eyes seemed to plead for an opportunity to present his case.

Gretchen needed a continuance. She had to postpone the hearing.

Did that mean she wasn't sure of the verdict?

Garcia's was one of Gretchen's favorite restaurants in Phoenix. After a short wait in the crowded bar, she and Nina were escorted to a table.

Nina, believing she could best detect auras emanating from people if she adhered to a strict vegan diet, scooped guacamole onto a tortilla chip and sighed.

"This vegan diet is harder than I thought it would be," she whined. "Are you sure I can't have cheese?"

"It's made with rennet," Gretchen said. "Which is made from animal by-products. Remember, no dairy products at all. Vegans are very strict about their diets."

"I can't even have cheese quesadillas?"

"Nope."

"Ever since I found out that I can see auras better if I don't eat meat, I've lost ten pounds."

Gretchen studied her willowy aunt. "I wish I could lose ten pounds," she said.

Nina glared at her. "I'm starving to death."

"Then eat. Why do you need to see auras anyway?"

"It's important in my purse dog training. I can tell by the color of a client's aura whether or not we are a good match."

"By clients, you don't mean the owners, do you? You mean the dogs?" Gretchen watched Nina nod. "And you agree to train the dogs based on what color surrounds them?"

Nina nodded again and stuffed a chip into her mouth. She took a sip of her margarita. "Thank goodness, I can still drink alcohol." Nina, newly coiffed, sported a teal bow in her hair that matched the one attached to Tutu's head.

Tutu, also freshly shampooed and trimmed, waited indignantly outside in

Nina's red vintage Impala.

"How am I going to explain the missing Ginny dolls and the lost money to my mother?" Gretchen said.

"Caroline will understand."

"The more I think about it, the more I think I was set up. The boxes were switched on purpose."

"Ridiculous."

The waiter delivered Gretchen's Poco Pollo Fundido, and Nina looked longingly at the chicken, ignoring her plate of veggie fajitas.

"You've become very suspicious of people since Steve betrayed you," Nina said.

"What about the false address?"

"A simple mistake."

"I don't think so."

"The dolls will turn up. You have to focus on the good in people."

Nina had made up her mind, and there would be no changing it. Gretchen switched subjects.

"Why did you tell Steve I was going out with Matt?" she said.

"A little competition never hurt. Besides, you two are very close to connecting. I can feel it."

"He's still married."

"A minor detail. He filed for divorce."

Gretchen took a bite of chicken.

"I love a man in a uniform," Nina said wistfully.

The detective wore Chrome cologne, Gretchen's favorite male scent, and he *did* have a buff build. But he was in the middle of a nasty divorce. Gretchen planned on staying clear. She had enough problems with men at the moment without adding another one to her life.

"He's undercover most of the time, Nina. He usually doesn't wear a uniform. I've never even seen him in one."

"He's really sexy, but Steve has the money. It's a tough choice."

Gretchen took a long draw on her lime margarita and chanted the word *patience* several times in her head before responding. "I don't want Steve back. Never, ever. He cheated on me, and I could never trust him again. I'm through, so I don't want you to encourage him in any way."

Although her words were strong, Gretchen still worked to suppress her feelings for Steve. He'd hurt her badly, but she had seven years of memories, and she'd relived many of them since moving to Phoenix. She had to constantly recall her initial anger.

Seeing him for the first time in two months had affected her, as she knew it would. She should have left the city before he arrived and spared herself all the conflicting emotions.

"I hope he doesn't go crazy when he realizes he can't win you back." Nina fiddled absently with the rim of her margarita glass. "Some men go right over the edge."

Gretchen tilted her head and studied her aunt. Nina, divorced after a brief and tumultuous marriage after college, hadn't had a date with the opposite sex for years. Or if she had, she wasn't sharing any details. She seemed content with Tutu and her purse training business and spending time with her small family — Gretchen and Gretchen's mother, Caroline.

"We should fix you up with a hot date," Gretchen suggested. "After we set up for the show, we'll scout around for someone special for you. Since you're my assigned show assistant, meet me at the hall first thing in the morning. That's six o'clock a.m., Nina."

Nina groaned.

"Lovely. Just where I'd expect to find an interesting man. At a doll show."

"Maybe one of those Boston Kewpie doll collectors needs a tour of Phoenix."

Nina snorted. "I'll be on hand to help you, but I'm hoping you won't need me. April called and asked me to share her table. She can't afford it on her own."

"The tables are only thirty-five dollars. She's that short of cash?" Gretchen said, alarmed that her assistant was jumping ship.

Nina slurped the last of her margarita before answering. "April only charges two dollars for a doll appraisal. That's a give-away. She needs to raise her prices to cover her costs and make a little profit. Maybe when those rich Boston Kewpie collectors come along, she can charge them five dollars."

"You don't even collect dolls," Gretchen pointed out. "How are you going to share her table?"

Enthusiastic, Nina leaned forward. "I'm going to show off my special purse dog training techniques and sign up new clients. Doll people love little dogs. We'll bring Nimrod along so I can use him for my demonstrations. A miniature dog always draws a crowd."

Nina, eternally surrounded by an entourage of canines, had made a good point. People gravitated to Gretchen's teacup poodle like hummingbirds to nectar. Nina's table was guaranteed to be the liveliest area of the show.

"You promised to help me. We'll have to

51

get tables close together," Gretchen said.

"Tables are already assigned," Nina said. "But I'll call Bonnie and work it out in case she's positioned you in another area. Don't worry."

Gretchen rummaged in her purse for money to pay the check. Whenever Nina said, "Don't worry," Gretchen began to worry. "I still have so much to do."

"You're in good shape," Nina said. "You just have first-time jitters."

Gretchen straightened a few crumpled bills she found on the bottom of her purse. *Now, if I could only remember where I put the car keys.* She patted her pockets and drew them out.

"What's this?" Nina said, extracting a paper napkin from between the bills Gretchen had thrown on the table.

"Just garbage. I'll throw it away." Gretchen reached for it.

"Wait. Something's written on it."

Nina held up the napkin with Garcia's imprint, and Gretchen stared at the handwritten word.

"Pushed!"

"Pushed?" she said.

"Is this yours?" Nina asked.

"It's a cocktail napkin." Gretchen glanced at the next table. "They're everywhere." She moved her empty margarita glass and picked up the napkin that had been under it. "This one's mine. I must have swept that one in by accident."

"It may have been in there since last time we dined at Garcia's," Nina said, looking at Gretchen's purse. "I don't know how Nimrod fits with all the stuff you carry around."

"I'm working on it," Gretchen said, taking the napkin from Nina. "Pushed?" she said again.

Nimrod bounced around her heels, squealing with pleasure, and Gretchen couldn't help smiling down at the puppy. Had anyone ever been this excited to see her before? Wobbles never greeted her with such enthusiasm, and she had rescued him from certain death. She'd also nursed him back to health. A little gratitude from him was in order.

She picked up Nimrod, and he wiggled in the crook of her arm, struggling to climb higher and lick her face. She hated leaving him home, but he needed to learn that he couldn't go *everywhere* with her.

Besides, she reminded herself; he wasn't entirely alone. He had Wobbles.

"No sloppy doggie kisses," she warned him. "You should be washing yourself like Wobbles does instead of trying to clean me."

She saw the tomcat eyeing her from the kitchen and stooped to rub his head before heading for the workshop.

She deposited Nimrod on his little comfy bed. He promptly jumped off and bolted for the back door, which led to the pool. She heard him slip through the pet door she'd installed for him, so he could come and go whenever he wanted to.

Gretchen loved the view from the workshop window. Majestic Camelback Mountain rose before her as an earthy reminder of the vastness of the Arizona landscape. Reaching for her binoculars, she watched a few hikers climbing the mountain's steep trails. She wished she had time to join them.

What she needed to do was focus on tomorrow and finish packing up for the doll show. She had to arrive several hours early to allow for setting up the table. Three boxes of dolls were already loaded in her trunk, but she still had to sort through a few more and decide what else to take along.

She gathered Chiggy's Kewpies and returned them to their original box. The restorer in her had no choice but to evaluate each one. Chipped paint, damaged clay, cracks. The one that her pets had broken wasn't the only Kewpie with unsightly cracks. Gretchen, frowning over the awful replication attempts, once again wondered why Duanne Wilson would bid on such a sorry bunch of fake dolls.

Gretchen sighed heavily. He'd gotten the better end of the deal. The Ginnys were worth a lot more, and she'd miss adding them to the group of Ginnys her mother had already collected for the big show. She still thought she'd been the victim of a scam, in spite of Nina's naive comments.

Her repair tools were scattered on the table, and she began to gather them up and organize them in the new toolbox her mother had designed especially for Gretchen's first doll show.

S hooks, pliers, stringing hooks, dowel rods, clamps. Gretchen ticked off the required restringing tools as she added them to the box, each tool accessorized with the pink nail polish. She added a box of standard number eleven X-Acto knife blades and looked around on the table for the hobby knife.

"Where did I put it?" she asked no one in particular. She noticed that since taking in Nimrod, she talked aloud more. It couldn't be a good sign.

Nimrod, returning from outside, perked up at her voice. He cocked his head, and his tiny tail wiggled back and forth wildly.

Gretchen couldn't find the knife.

She needed the utility knife for all kinds of repairs. How would she set doll eyes without it? She needed a pointed blade to remove excess wax or plastic. The knife was a critical tool for her. It couldn't be missing.

Where had she put it?

She remembered using it to wipe glue from the Blunderboo Kewpie, so it had to be here.

After a thorough search of the worktable and the surrounding area, Gretchen gave up.

The knife was gone.

6

"She's answered so many questions already," her husband says. "Can't this wait?"

"I'm afraid it can't."

"I keep reliving the feeling of my tires hitting that poor man's body," she says, her voice dry and flat as the Arizona desert. She doesn't hear her husband's frustration with all the red tape and what he calls badgering. "Gawd, I haven't slept since."

The pills prescribed by her physician ease the emotional pain of killing another human being, but they don't help her sleep. Nothing helps her sleep.

She desperately needs to shut down and wake up later to find out that the accident has all been a bad dream. But that isn't going to happen.

Her husband slides a protective arm around her waist.

"It's all right," she says.

But it isn't.

She has replayed the accident how many times? Dozens? Millions? Everywhere she looks, she sees it again. The man's stunned face, the surprise registering in his eyes.

"There isn't much to tell," she says by rote. "It happened so fast. I was looking for a parking spot. Probably not going over twenty miles an hour. I noticed a man sitting on the curb, and I think I was looking at him. He seemed to be dressed in layers of clothing, none too clean, I thought at the time, and I wondered what he was doing in that neighborhood. If I hadn't been distracted, hadn't been watching him . . ."

"You don't have to do this," her husband says gently. She sees him glare at her inquisitor.

She tries to smile at her husband, reassure him, but the corners of her mouth won't turn up. The pills, she is sure. They have numbed her emotions, but not enough to ease the pain deep inside.

"He came from the same side of the street, a little in front of the man on the curb, and he literally flew at me. I saw his startled face, and then he must have realized what was happening, because I saw his expression of horror." She leans against her husband. "That's it. I slammed my foot on the brake, but he was already under . . .

under the tire. People started screaming, 'Back up. Back up.' And I did."

She covers her face and struggles for composure. Her husband hands her a tissue and protests again.

"Really," he says. "This is too much."

"Getting out and seeing him like that was the hardest part," she continues. "All those people gathered around trying to help him. And he twitched and then lay motionless, and I knew. I knew he was dead."

"Did you see a box?" The man looks up from his notepad where he has been taking notes, and she notices how intense his eyes are. Watchful, studying, calculating. Perhaps hoping for some inconsistency in her side of the story, a plausible reason to arrest her for manslaughter.

Her arrest is a possibility, even though her husband doesn't believe it will happen.

"A box?" She shakes her head, wishing to be helpful. "No, he wasn't carrying anything that I recall." She frowns and concentrates. "I think . . . uh . . . no, sorry . . . no box that I remember."

"This is the last time," her husband says, anger in his voice. "I mean it. She's repeated the story for the last time."

7

Curves for Women literally hopped with activity. When Nina and Gretchen arrived, almost all the stations were in use. Gretchen spotted April and the rest of the doll collectors who made up their exercise group on the far side of the room, exercising away. Nina and Gretchen found space and jumped into the routine.

"Change stations now," a voice boomed every thirty seconds from a recorded message overhead. Women of all sizes and shapes moved around the circle, running on platforms and using pieces of equipment. Gretchen worked on the stepper while Nina ran in place on a platform next to her, arms slightly bent, her feet barely moving.

"Hey!" The greeting came from April, whose long gray-streaked hair was pulled back in a ponytail. She wore an extra large muumuu over her enormous torso and beat-up sneakers. Sweat ran down her puffy face in streams that she blotted at with a wad of tissues clutched in one chubby fist.

Gretchen wondered if anyone in the room knew CPR. Just in case. She waved and greeted each of the collectors she'd come to know in the past two months.

"All set for your first show tomorrow?" April asked.

"Change stations now."

"It's more work than I thought," Gretchen said, moving to the next station on command. "But I'm as ready as I'll ever be."

"You'll do fine. I'm only selling a few of my miniatures at the show, so I can help you." April attempted a squat on a hydraulic machine but became wedged in a crouched position. She edged out sideways and glared at the machine. "And I have all my books together for appraisals. After a few hundred shows, packing is easy."

"You have to increase the price of your appraisals," Nina told her. "You've been charging the same rate for years now."

"I'm thinking about it. I guess it depends if I have any competition and what they're charging."

"I hear Steve's in town to take you home," Bonnie said. The president of the Phoenix Dollers wore her standard red flipped wig and a face full of colorful makeup.

Gretchen couldn't see any physical resemblance between Bonnie Albright and her son, Matt.

Fewer cups of coffee, and her makeup lines might be a little straighter, Nina had commented to Gretchen. Bonnie drank several pots of coffee every day, which accounted for the caffeine-induced tremors.

"I'm not going anywhere with Steve," Gretchen answered carefully, aware that the club's president was also the club's biggest gossip. "Phoenix is my home now."

"Good for you," April shouted, and the group applauded. "I feel sorry for him, though. He sounds devastated."

"How do you know?" Gretchen said.

"He called me." April bent forward, huffing.

"Me, too," Bonnie said.

"But he doesn't even know either of you," Gretchen said. "How did he get your names and numbers?"

Gretchen noticed Nina was exceptionally quiet. "You're helping him, aren't you, Nina? How else would he know about April and Bonnie?"

"I'm not helping him. I'm on your side."

"I'd hate to have you on the other side."

"He asked for their numbers. How could I refuse?"

"By saying no."

"He just wanted to bend my ear," April said. "He needs someone to talk to."

"He's pathetic, all right," Gretchen said. *Trying to get to me through my friends.*

"I hear you were at Chiggy's auction the other day," Bonnie said, switching subjects.

Gretchen nodded. "I wish I had skipped it."

"Howie's totally distraught," Bonnie said. "How are you holding up?"

"Much better than Howie, I'm sure. And the poor woman who hit Brett." Gretchen finished at a machine. "At the end, they practically gave away the remaining dolls."

"I could have told you you'd be wasting your time," April said. "Chiggy had me over last week to appraise her dolls. Worthless."

"I bought twelve Ginny dolls," Gretchen said. "They seemed okay."

"You're a chip off your mother's block," April said, puffing hard. "They were the only dolls worth anything."

Gretchen told them about the exchange. "Anyone ever hear of Duanne Wilson?" she asked.

No one had. Gretchen's suspicion that she'd been conned increased.

"I don't remember seeing any Kewpie dolls when I was at Chiggy's," April said.

"Maybe she planned on throwing them out," Gretchen said. "They're pretty banged up."

"Chiggy never threw out a thing," April said.

"Did you see Brett get hit?" Bonnie asked.

"No, and I'm glad I didn't."

"Has anyone met that bunch from Boston yet?" Nina said, stopping on a platform to rest, not one bead of perspiration anywhere on her body.

Bonnie scrunched her nose. "I greeted some of them at the airport. I held one of those little signs up so they'd know who I was." She looked around the group. "Four of them came in together. When did your Steve arrive, Gretchen?"

Gretchen sensed Nina looking at her as if expecting her to challenge the possessive pronoun.

"I don't know."

Gretchen threw more energy into the hydraulic machines.

"What are the club members like?" April asked Bonnie.

"Oh, they're very friendly."

"Then why did you scrunch your nose when I asked about them?" April wanted to know.

"They talk funny, is all. I couldn't understand a word any of them said. I could have used a translator." Bonnie looked over at Gretchen and said, "I extended an invitation to them for cocktails at my place after the doll show wraps up. They leave on Wednesday morning after a little sightseeing. Everybody's invited over. You, too, Gretchen."

"Gretchen's part of *everybody*," April said. "Why are you singling her out?"

Bonnie gave a weak little laugh. "I invited Steve to the party when he called me. He sounded so sad."

"Don't worry about Gretchen," said Nina of the questionable loyalty. "She couldn't care less if he's there."

Gretchen almost waved at Nina to remind her that she was in the room.

"I'd much rather see her hitched up with Matty," Bonnie said over Gretchen's head.

Just great.

Gretchen imagined herself as a gray mare hitched to a wagon and Matt slapping the reins across her wide rump. She shook her head to clear the image.

Bonnie bent forward and tried to touch her toes. "We've been talking about her and Matty," she said when she straightened up. "Haven't we, girls?"

Everyone muttered assent, confirming

Gretchen's suspicion that the doll group gossiped unmercifully about each other. She vowed to get to Curves earlier next time to keep her name out of the conversation.

"My son needs to think about something other than detective work," Bonnie said.

"He's got his wife to think about right now," April reminded them, stopping to mop her reddening face. "I'm never going to make it around a whole time. I don't know how you guys go around three times. It'd kill me."

"Your goal is one full circuit," Bonnie said in her upper-management voice. "You can do it. Keep at it, and you'll look like Gretchen in no time."

"Gretchen thinks she needs to lose ten pounds," Nina said.

Bonnie eyed Gretchen up and down. "Humph," she said. "Most women would give anything to have your shape."

"Voluptuous," Nina pointed out, nodding.

Bonnie left the circle of women and grabbed a hula hoop. "Matty's almost divorced from that awful woman," she said, her hips flying and her flip swinging. "She cheated on him and then had the nerve to stalk him when he moved out after he couldn't take it anymore. The poor boy is always hiding."

Gretchen hoped Matt's problems didn't foreshadow her own with Steve. She knew exactly how the detective felt when he discovered the betrayal, because the same thing had happened to her.

And now the woman was stalking him?

Gretchen remembered how Steve had crept into the workshop without warning.

He should have called first, and he definitely should have announced himself at the door.

And why was he trying to enlist her friends?

Maybe she should start looking over her shoulder a little more.

Ronny Beam leaned against Nina's red Impala, ignoring Tutu, who lunged at the closed window in an attempt to sever Ronny's carotid artery with her sharp incisors. Unfortunately, shutting off the blood supply to his brain wouldn't improve his personality.

Ronny was a hopelessly flawed human being, something even a prima donna like Tutu could tell.

Ronny's face looked as if it had been cranked through a vise grip. All his features appeared crushed together in a small skull, with narrow-set, beady eyes and a thin streak of a mouth showing mismatched teeth but no lips.

Gretchen recognized him immediately from the photo that Nina had recently mutilated with an entire set of darts.

"What are you doing touching my car?" Nina yelled, rushing out of Curves. "Get away before I sic Tutu on you."

Ronny sneered at the lunging schnoodle and didn't move.

Gretchen hurried after Nina, hoping to get between them before Nina blasted him with the pepper spray she carried in her purse.

"Who's your girlfriend?" He ogled Gretchen while running his tongue around the outside of his mouth. "She's a looker."

"Hi, darlin'," he said to Gretchen.

"Shut up, Ronny," Nina warned.

"I'm gathering news for next week's edition, and I'd like a quote from you," he said to Nina while leering at Gretchen.

Gretchen saw a recording unit in his shirt pocket and a microphone extended toward Nina. "*Phoenix Exposed* is the hottest paper coming off the press. A quote from you will be read by everybody in town, so make it good."

"You rotten little twerp," Nina said, digging in her purse. "You could have ruined my dog training business with that stupid, lying article."

"Is that your quote? Can you repeat it a little louder please? I'm not sure you were close enough for the mic to pick up those fine, literary words."

"I should sue your brains out — that is, if you have any." Nina continued to dig through her large purse. "It's a good thing you have only two subscribers, your mother and your sister."

"Make fun all you want," Ronny said, "but I'm positioning myself to go mainstream. I just need some compelling, breaking news."

"I'll break you, you . . ." Nina's hand shot out of her purse, pointing the nozzle of the spray at Ronny. "Back off."

Ronny pushed off from the Impala and stepped back. "Whoa, Nellie. You didn't like the article?"

Gretchen was aghast at Ronnie's audacity. Didn't the guy have a conscience? Ever since he launched his weekly newspaper, he'd been slinking around hoping for a legitimate story. In the meantime, he wrote bad pulp fiction using real people's names.

The article that had Nina ready to zap Ronny into the nearest hospital with a full frontal spray attack was about her canine business. According to Ronny, Nina was the supreme commander of an alien group from a distant galaxy called Canial that "sent puppy impersonators to infiltrate Arizonian's homes and study human behavior."

He had snapped a photo of Nina as she came out of a downtown New Age shop. She had a purse dog trainee riding in a purse on her shoulder, and she was cooing to him when Ronny snapped the shot. The caption read "Commander Caught Debriefing Foot Soldier."

"People love that stuff," he made the mistake of saying. "Martians, alien attacks, all that space stuff."

Gretchen couldn't bring herself to stop Nina.

It was a direct hit.

Ronny screamed, while Nina rushed around the car and hurriedly unlocked the Impala's doors.

"You better not show up at the doll show with those peeing, shedding mutts," he screamed at her. "I'll have you arrested for a public health violation. That ought to make a great story."

Nina turned and ran at him again. The pepper spray flew in a long, carefully aimed stream.

Gretchen and her aunt jumped into the car and sped off.

"You think he'll call the police?" Gretchen asked.

"It'll be his word against mine. No one saw it."

Gretchen looked back. Ronny was crouched on the ground. "Are you kidding? Everyone inside Curves was watching through the front window."

"That will be his last alien article," Nina said with confidence. "I hope he doesn't recover soon. If he plans on attending the doll show tomorrow, I'm in trouble."

8

After a little shuffling around and re-arranging on Bonnie's part, Gretchen found herself setting up next to April and Nina's table early Saturday morning.

She arranged the dolls on her assigned table. Nimrod peeked out of Gretchen's white cotton purse with the black poodles and red bows. Named for the biblical mighty hunter, the puppy casually watched the commotion around him from a strategic vantage point, slung from the back of Gretchen's chair.

Gretchn glanced at the next table with amusement.

Leave it to Nina to create a buzz.

Her aunt sported a yellow dress with enormous blue and pink flowers and several matching bows wedged into her hair. Her color scheme appeared to be all the colors of the rainbow. Tutu, leashed to a table leg, wore an enormous, multicolored collar with streaming ribbons.

Nina rushed over and tied a bow into Nimrod's hair as well. It matched her rainbow color scheme.

A third dog — a tiny Yorkshire terrier — was next.

"Color coordination is important," Nina said, catching Gretchen laughing. "Gimmicks and gizmos sell services."

"You look great," Gretchen admitted as Nina scooped the puppy's topknot into her hand and tied it back with a ribbon. "Where did you get the Yorkie?"

"Her name is Sophie. She's my latest client. I worked out a deal with her owner, charging less because Sophie is working the show with me. Nimrod's a wonderful example of my excellent training ability, and Sophie is my unruly example of the importance of discipline."

Prepared to live up to her reputation, Sophie promptly peed on the table, reminding Gretchen of Ronny Beam's health violation threat.

"No, no," Nina said, whipping a tiny pad out of her supply bag and shoving it under Sophie. "You go pee-pee on the wee-wee pad. Gretchen, get Nimrod. He can show her how it works. That's the best way to learn. By example."

Gretchen handed Nimrod over and snuck back to her table. Nina desperately needed a male companion to take her attention away from all those animals.

Gretchen propped her newly lettered repair sign on a stand and opened her toolbox.

April came rushing in, her reading glasses perched on the end of her nose and her arms filled with doll valuation books. A white paper bag dangled from her fist under the pile of books.

"The parking lot's filling up," she said, dropping everything on her table. "The ticket takers are letting them in. I almost didn't get through the mob. Have a donut." She dug in the bag, handed one to Nina, and held one out for Gretchen.

Gretchen shook her head no and glanced at her watch. Ten minutes till showtime. Her stomach was doing little flip-flops. Until the show was under way, she couldn't think about eating anything.

Where did I put the stringing nylon? She dug through the toolbox in a moment of panic, then remembered she had stowed it in a separate plastic bag in her purse. She pulled it out with relief and considered her future as a doll restoration artist if she didn't improve her business and organization skills.

Her new career didn't look promising. At this rate, she'd run the business right into the ground if her mother didn't hurry back.

The large hall was filled with stocked tables and lively exhibitors. She scanned her own collection of dolls marked for sale. Usually her mother sold an eclectic grouping, but since this was Gretchen's first show, she planned to focus on just one type of doll: Ginnys, which were extremely popular at the moment.

She wished again that she could have added the dolls from Chiggy's auction. If she ever saw that guy who had cheated her out of those dolls again, she'd chase him down. She'd keep an eye out for Duanne Wilson. Maybe he'd attend the show, if he was really a doll collector and not a scam artist.

Her mother's hard-plastic Ginny dolls were lined up on small stands, waiting for buyers. Gretchen knew she would have her hands full all day, answering questions about the Ginnys and repairing whatever came her way.

"Look at this," someone said, approaching the table. "A Goldilocks Ginny."

"This one is called Doctor Scrubs," someone else said, reading a tag. "Booties, a mask, green scrubs. Isn't it cute? Can you knock ten dollars off the price of this one?"

The doll show had begun.

Nina's table, as Gretchen had predicted, was a huge hit. Everyone stopped to watch Nimrod ride in his embroidered purse on Nina's shoulder, his tiny face a study in sweetness.

"Nimrod, hide," Nina commanded. And the teacup poodle ducked down inside the purse to appreciative cheers.

Bonnie Albright breezed by with a group of collectors at her heels. She stopped abruptly, as though Gretchen were an afterthought, and circled around to approach the table.

Gretchen lowered the antique ball-jointed doll she was attempting to restring. This one was challenging because of the small holes that the stringing nylon had to pass through, so she was glad for the distraction.

"Gretchen, there you are." A chunk of red lipstick graced Bonnie's front tooth. "This is Helen Huntington, president of the Boston Kewpie Club."

Gretchen rose and shook the older woman's hand.

The contrast between the two club presidents was striking. Bonnie looked like a clown with her harsh red wig and painted features. Although well into her seventies, Mrs. Huntington had a face the texture of a newborn's belly. Plastic surgery, Gretchen guessed. And silver hair expensively bobbed. A Chanel suit. Svelte figure. Probably ate nothing but celery and carrots.

Bonnie continued the introductions.

"Eric Huntingon is accompanying his mother," Bonnie said.

Flabby, with a weak chin, the son had obviously indulged in a few too many pastries, making up for his mother's healthful habits. "What a turnout," he said. "I had trouble parking the car."

Bonnie frowned in concentration, apparently never having heard the often-mimicked "pahk the cah."

"Yes, well," Bonnie said, hesitantly. "Yes. And this is Milt Wood and Margaret Turner."

Milt Wood grabbed her hand and squeezed hard. He was fortyish and built like a linebacker, all shoulders and solid girth. "It's exciting to be here. A few days in Phoenix, then we're headed to Palm Beach on Wednesday," He released her hand. "Margaret's planning a party to announce the season of parties. Isn't that right?"

Margaret Turner looked like a classic

grandmother. Reading glasses hanging from her neck, yellow polo shirt tucked neatly into crisp shorts, and sensible walking shoes.

"You have to be careful these days," the granny look-alike said, leaning forward, speaking in a stage whisper. "The nouveau riche are invading all the old neighborhoods. The announcements have to be given discreetly, or there's no telling who will show up."

Gretchen's smile slid sideways and froze. Looks weren't everything. Perceptions had fooled her before, and Margaret Turner had just reminded her that pretentiousness came in all physical forms, even with support shoes.

These were Steve's kind of people.

"I know your mother," Eric said. "I bought a doll from her years ago, when she still resided in Massachusetts. Lovely woman."

"She's in San Diego," Gretchen said. "I'm sure she will be disappointed to have missed you."

After a few more pleasantries and Gretchen's promise to stop by the visiting club's Kewpie table, the group moved on to watch the next act in Nina's theatrical debut.

"*You* don't have that Eastern accent," Bonnie whispered to Gretchen as they were leaving.

"We moved quite a bit when I was young," Gretchen explained. "That's probably why."

April sidled over. "I thought having Nina at my table would improve business," she said with a scowl.

Gretchen glanced at the crowd. "Business looks good."

"*Her* business, you mean. No one can get through the traffic jam for an appraisal. Even if they manage to fight their way through, they forget why they came over once she starts up."

April adjusted her reading glasses with one finger and looked beyond Gretchen. "Uh-oh," she said. "He looks exactly like his picture."

Gretchen followed April's gaze.

Steve was weaving through the hall.

"Uh-oh is right," Gretchen said.

Steve wasn't alone. As unlikely as it seemed, Matt Albright strolled along next to him, scanning the crowd. Matt had dark, wavy hair and a great build. He wore a white T-shirt that accentuated his tan arms.

Gretchen and Matt's eyes met from a distance. Matt nudged Steve and pointed in Gretchen's direction. She could see beads of sweat glistening on the detective's forehead even from here.

"What's Matt doing at the show?" Gretchen muttered. "I thought he had pedio-phobia."

April shot an angry look at Gretchen. "That's how rumors get started. Detective Albright would never assault little kids."

"Not pedophilia," Gretchen said. "Pedio-phobia. It means he's afraid of dolls."

"Well, that's silly."

"You're afraid of clowns," Gretchen pointed out.

"That's different," April said. "Clowns really are scary. I'm going back to my table. If you need me, holler."

Matt gave Gretchen a wave and turned away. She had noticed a nervous tightness along his jaw.

Steve steamed toward her like a runaway train.

"There you are," Steve said, huffing a little. "This place is enormous. I had to ask that guy to help me."

"Where did you run into him?"

"He was helping little old ladies carry bags of dolls in." Steve laughed. "Must have been a Boy Scout at one time. Got all nervous when we came inside, though. Funny thing."

Gretchen couldn't believe that Matt was even near the doll show.

Steve noticed the shoppers at her table.

"You're doing well."

"I'm amazed at how many people like Ginny dolls. I'll have to pull more stock from storage for tomorrow's show."

She edged toward the center of the table, hoping someone would interrupt. *A question, please. Or buy something,* she pleaded silently to the customers.

A uniformed police officer sauntered past, and Gretchen wanted to call him over to referee.

"We need to talk," Steve said to her. "I know this isn't the best place, but it has to be right now."

"I can't discuss anything now. I'm working."

"You're killing me, Gretchen. I came all this way from Boston to convince you that I need you. You have to listen." Steve grabbed her arm.

"I'm busy." She wrenched away. "Nothing you can say will change my mind."

"I can change your mind." *Steve, the great litigator, thinking I'm a jury he can sway.*

"I'm not interested in changing my mind. I've started a new life." *And you aren't part of it.*

"We'll talk tonight." It wasn't a request. "I'm going to insist, Gretchen."

"This guy bothering you, princess?" came

81

a voice from behind her.

Ronny Beam's narrow Wile E. Coyote face glared at Steve.

Steve looked him up and down, then jabbed a thumb toward Ronny. "You know this character?"

"You're looking at Cupcake's sugar daddy," Ronny said. "Keep your mitts off if you don't want trouble. I could be your worst nightmare."

Gretchen's mouth dropped open. Ronny gave her a wink. Her skin crawled. *Cupcake? Sugar daddy? Puhleese.*

Gretchen saw Steve's nostrils flare. Not a good sign. Flaring nostrils meant trouble. Steve wasn't the overly jealous type, but Ronny could ignite the mildest-tempered soul into a flaming rage.

Ronny reached out with a microphone in his hand and tapped it on Steve's chest. "Take off," he said. "Scram."

Then Ronny made the mistake of pushing Steve. Microphone curled in one hand, the other hand balled into a fist, he thumped Steve on both shoulders and shoved.

Steve stumbled, then grabbed Ronny by his shirt and backed him into the table. Several Ginny dolls fell over. "Take your mic someplace else," he said. "Gretchen doesn't want your company."

People near Gretchen's table backed away from the two men. Others moved closer for better views.

Gretchen heard Nina's voice rise in the background. "Steve and Ronny are fighting over Gretchen," she shouted.

"Let him go, Steve. Ronny's harmless." Gretchen spoke nervously, hoping the police officer she'd seen earlier was on the far side of the hall.

"You better listen to her," Ronny said. "Otherwise, you'll be the feature story on page one. I ought to file a complaint against you for battery. Page one, I'm telling you. That would increase circulation."

Steve didn't release Ronny's shirt. "Gretchen, should I remove him for you?" His eyes never left Ronny.

"I hardly know the man," Gretchen said. "And I don't want any trouble."

"What are you saying?" Ronny said, risking a glance at Gretchen. "Is that all I mean to you? A one-nighter?"

Gretchen felt like braining Ronny with her toolbox while Steve had him cornered and defenseless. Instead, she placed a hand on Steve's arm. "He's a creep," she said. "Let him go."

Steve released Ronny.

Ronny made a big show of rearranging his

clothing, then turned to the crowd that had gathered. He smiled crookedly.

"I'm taking statements over by that door," he said, pointing to a back exit. "Anyone see the whole thing, I'll be waiting to interview you. It's going to be a big story."

Turning to Steve, he said, "You're lucky I'm on a story that's about to blow this place sky high. It's going to be better than those old-time horror flicks about them dolls that come alive and start murdering people. Yup. Even better than killer dolls. Even better . . ." he motioned at Gretchen with his head. ". . . than the story about what just happened here."

"Get lost," Steve said.

Ronny looked at Gretchen. "You'll be sorry you passed up a good thing."

Steve took a step forward.

Ronny scurried away.

"Boy, oh, boy," April said for the third time. "Two guys fighting over you. Wow. That was something."

"Just great," Gretchen said, squirting mustard onto a hot dog with one eye on her table. "My cheating ex-boyfriend and the biggest slime in town. How lucky can a girl get?"

The crowds had thinned at noon as most

visitors filed into an attached room for fast-food lunches. The two puppies were exhausted from the morning's attention and napped inside their respective purses. Tutu curled up under a chair and snored loudly.

"Good thing Ronny was distracted by Steve," Nina said from her table. "Or he would have been after me."

"He has a petition going on the other side of the hall," April said.

Nina paused, a nacho close to her open mouth. "What kind of petition?"

"Ronny wants you thrown out of the doll show. He says all that dog hair can't be good for the dolls. Six vendors have signed already."

"Why didn't you tell me sooner?" Nina said.

April shrugged. "I just heard." She reached in a pocket of her enormous muu-muu and grinned. "Here's the petition. It won't be circulating anymore."

"Someone's going to shoot Ronny one of these days," Nina said, grabbing the paper and reading the names. "I heard he went from table to table insulting the doll dealers with outrageous accusations and comments, trying to rile them."

"He'll do anything to sell papers," April said, working on her third hot dog and her

85

second bag of potato chips. "Even if he has to make things up."

"Don't I know it," Nina said.

Gretchen watched April eat. The woman would have to go to Curves several times a day to work off the huge quantities of food she liked to consume. No wonder she was broke. She spent all her money on unhealthy snack food.

Gretchen took a bite of the hot dog and avoided Nina's eyes, which reminded her of Tutu's when the schnoodle begged at the kitchen table. Nina was bound to fall off her vegan diet by the end of the day.

"At least Steve knows he has some competition," Nina said. "But Ronny? Gag me."

Gretchen stared at her aunt. "I really mean it, Nina. I'm not going back to Steve."

"Even if he wants to fly to Vegas for a quickie wedding?"

"Especially not then."

"Just checking to see if you changed your mind. I saw you talking to him. You seemed cozy."

Cozy?

"He's pressuring me," Gretchen said. "I don't want to talk about him."

Nina broke a nacho chip in half and nibbled. "I know why Detective Albright's helping out at the doll show."

Gretchen raised her eyebrows.

"He's working on his doll problem." Nina looked at April. "Probably for Gretchen's sake."

"He can ask her out anyway," April said. "Who cares if he doesn't like dolls."

"He's off duty today," Nina said. "And he's hiding from his soon-to-be ex. She'll never think to look here. He spends five minutes at a time walking the aisles, looking at the dolls, then he takes a break in the back room to recover."

"He seemed pretty uncomfortable when I saw him last," Gretchen said.

"And hot," April added. "As in sexy hot."

"I heard Matt's wife is a nutcase," Nina said. "His mother has plenty of stories to tell about her. Speaking of, here comes Blabby Bonnie."

Bonnie bustled up, her red wig slightly askew. "Gretchen, I'll watch your table for a few minutes. You have to go see the Boston Kewpie Club's table. You know Kewpies are my specialty, but even I haven't seen anything like their combined collections."

The Bostonians' table overflowed with Kewpie dolls. All had knobs of hair on their crowns and long wisps of hair tumbling over their foreheads. Tiny molded blue wings protruded from bare pink shoulders.

Most Kewpies didn't wear clothes. Some in the Boston collection wore scarves or sunbonnets and clutched bouquets of flowers or waved flags, and the rest performed their spirited deeds fully exposed for all to see.

"Kewpie is short for Cupid," Margaret Turner, of the sensible walking shoes, was explaining to a cluster of curious shoppers.

"This one . . ." Eric selected a Kewpie from the table. ". . . is called Always Wears His Overshoes. And this one is a Kuddle Kewpie. Note the cloth face and soft body."

"I have a Kewpie Dog at home," someone said.

"That would be Doodle Dog," Margaret said. "Or Kewpiedoodle Dog. He was modeled after the original designer's Boston terrier."

"Who was the original designer?" someone asked.

"Ruby O'Neill," Milt Wood replied.

"No, it was Rosie O'Neill," someone else said, correcting him.

"That's right," Margaret said. "Her name was Rosie O'Neill. Let me show you a few more."

Several of the club's members wandered back from lunch. Gretchen, relieved that

Steve was nowhere in sight, nevertheless kept a sharp eye out for him. Nimrod yipped from the purse on her shoulder. She took him out and cuddled him in her hands.

Eric held up another Kewpie for the group. "Kewpie Carpenter," he said. "He uses the hammer in his belt to fix things."

"Here's a Blunderboo," Margaret added. "Note how he's rolling down a hill."

Gretchen considered the Kewpie in Margaret's hand. A far superior design to the one from Duanne Wilson's box. Much more detailed and of higher-quality material. More importantly, it was the real thing, not a badly botched reproduction.

"I have a reproduction Blunderboo Kewpie with me," Gretchen found herself saying to what had now become a large gathering of doll collectors. "It belongs to . . ." The box of Kewpies in her trunk would involve a long explanation she'd rather not get into. Why did she even mention it? ". . . a friend," she said. "It's not nearly as nice as this one."

That was the understatement of the year.

As she finished speaking, she spotted a man moving through the packed hall ahead of her. Something about his stride and his white hair seemed familiar. Could it be Duanne Wilson?

"Excuse me," Gretchen said to the group

89

of collectors. "I need to get back to my table."

Still carrying Nimrod, she turned and followed, weaving through the crowd as fast as she possibly could.

The man ahead of her must have been moving almost as fast, because she wasn't gaining quickly enough.

She walked faster, clutching Nimrod to her chest, his tiny ears flapping wildly.

Determined to catch up with the man, she jostled her way down the aisle. She called his name, but he didn't turn around or give any sign that he'd heard.

That has to be him. I'll get my Ginnys back yet.

He stopped at a table, his back still to her.

Gretchen came up behind him and grabbed his sleeve, cradling Nimrod in her other arm.

The man turned, and Gretchen stared into his eyes.

She'd never seen him before.

9

"Man, those doll collectors in there are a bunch of kooks," Ronny Beam says. He leans against the side of his car, eating a salami sandwich he pulled from a cooler in the trunk. Sandwich in one hand, can of iced tea in the other.

What he really wants is a sip of whiskey from the coffee mug in the front seat, but that will have to wait, considering present company.

" 'Sweet cheeks,' I say to them, 'upchuck some juicy gossip for my paper,' but they're a tight-mouthed bunch. Tight something else, too, if you ask me." He waves the can in his hand. "Look at you, stuck out in this parking lot all day with the sun hotter than a cattle brander. What a job you got, huh?"

Ronny grins and takes another bite. Chews.

"I have it on them, though. Something bigger than anything I got so far. Somebody made a lot of money in the black market during Double-U Double-U Two. The big one. I happen to know there's a treasure hidden away. And guess where?" He nods knowingly and pops the last of the sandwich into his mouth. "Inside dolls, that's where. All's I need is a little more background, and it goes to press," he says through packed cheeks.

Ronny realizes he has raised his voice. He looks all around, hoping no one has overheard.

"That's all the preview I can give you for now. Better subscribe to *Phoenix Exposed* if you want to read a Pulitzer Prize–winning story."

He pushes away from the car. "One thing I know. Hanging around inside doll shows with a bunch of doll nuts sure beats standing in a parking lot all day wearing a uniform like you have to do."

He takes a swig of the iced tea. "Tough job you got. You'd think they could hire a kid to watch the lot for a few bucks instead of wasting taxpayers' money. You should be busting bad guys. Maybe someday I'll write something good about you. Let me get you one of my business cards. Here, hold this."

He pops the last of the sandwich into his mouth and hands over his empty can, then pulls his wallet from a back pocket and picks through it. He extracts a card.

"Here ya go. Whew, it's hot out."

10

When attending a doll show, a repair artist must be prepared for any doll emergency. Aside from standard stringing tools such as elastic cording, rubber bands, and S hooks, it's a good idea to carry baby wipes for washing dirty faces and wig glue for fixing loose wigs. A great deal of patience is also an absolute requirement, especially when several collectors are demanding your expertise at the same time.
— From *World of Dolls* by Caroline Birch

"Here comes a mailman," Nina called from her table. "I didn't know they delivered at doll shows."

"Looking for the doll repairer, whatever that means. Someone over by the door said that's you?" the man said, stopping at Gretchen's table and holding a small package. "The world is filled with weirdoes. No name, and they think I'm a magician." He tipped his head back and looked down the length of his nose at Nina. "And we aren't mailmen anymore, in case you haven't noticed. I'm a postal carrier ever since you women libbers changed everything."

"I guess that's me," Gretchen said, taking the package and looking at the address on the label. "That's all it says. 'Doll repairer' and this address. Who sent it?" "Fragile" had been stamped across the package in bold red lettering.

The postal carrier shrugged. "What you think I got? A crystal ball? I just deliver the stuff."

He walked away.

"Friendly sort," Nina muttered.

"Open it," April said eagerly. "I love presents."

"Must be from Steve," Nina surmised. "A take-me-back gift."

"Too big," April observed.

"Steve would have addressed it directly to me," Gretchen said.

"Oh, right," Nina agreed.

The smell of Chrome cologne distracted Gretchen from the package. She laid it on the floor next to a cardboard box that was quickly filling with damaged dolls in need of repair. She knew before she looked up that Matt would be standing in front of her.

Up close, the blue T-shirt had a darker blue and white dream catcher etched into it.

"I'm investigating an altercation," he said. "It appears that you are the cause of a major disturbance. I'll have to take you down to the station and drill you unmercifully."

Nina sighed loudly from the next table. "You're such a tease," she called to him.

Matt's eyes riveted on Gretchen.

"Drill me instead," April said. "I give in easily."

"Rake her over the coals," Nina said. "She *is* easy."

Therapy must be helping. Gretchen had seen firsthand what the presence of a little doll could do to the muscular cop. He'd been reduced to a pale, sweating shell of the man who stood before her. But the large number of dolls surrounding him hadn't stopped him from walking directly down the aisle today.

"Ronny Beam's on a rampage, Nina," said the new, improved Matt. "He just lodged a formal complaint against you at the same time that he filed one against Gretchen's . . . um . . . friend, Steve."

"A complaint for what?" Nina looked surprised.

"An alleged pepper spray attack yesterday.

Unprovoked, according to Ronny."

"Unprovoked!" Nina fairly shouted. "That worm is spreading rumors about me, and he was leaning on my Impala. I'll have to have it washed to get the crud off."

"Then you admit the charges."

"I admit nothing. His word against mine."

Matt flipped through a notepad. "He went into Curves after the alleged incident, and he's listed thirty-nine witnesses who, he claims, saw the whole thing."

"Oh," Nina said, suddenly subdued. "Are you going to arrest me?"

"I'd gladly haul you in if I was on duty today." Matt closed the notepad. "I covered for you with the responding officer, so you owe me. Now . . ." He turned to Gretchen. "I *did* think about arresting Steve Kuchen. What do you have to say about that?"

Gretchen shrugged. Matt's idea certainly would buy her time. It was an intriguing solution, even if it was only in fun. "Can I think about it for a while?"

Matt attempted a grin. "Sure. In the meantime, I have to get out of here. The dolls are closing in. When I come back, I'll track down Ronny and escort him out before he gets himself hurt. Has anyone seen him?"

Nina shivered. "He's around here someplace. He's like a boomerang, keeps coming back every time you try to throw him away."

Milt Wood leaned his solid body against Gretchen's table. A high school wrestler, Gretchen guessed. And a middle school bully.

"I insist," he insisted again, the gums above his teeth exposed from the stretch of his good-natured smile.

Gretchen's eyes wandered to Nina and April's table in a hopeless appeal for interception, but both women were involved with potential clients. April paged through one of her value books, her reading glasses edging closer to the end of her nose. A Shirley Temple doll lay before her, and a woman and young girl waited patiently. Nina held Sophie while Nimrod entertained several dog-loving fans, including the two waiting for the appraisal.

Gretchen sent a silent plea to her so-called psychic aunt. But Nina was apparently on break from mind reading, because she demonstrated Nimrod's hiding trick without even glancing at Gretchen.

A customer approached, and Milt hovered off to the side as Gretchen sold a Ginny doll.

"Mr. Wood," she said, when the transaction was complete. "I really —"

"Please, call me Milt."

Gretchen forced a smile. "Why would you want to buy a doll that you've never seen?"

"Fine. Fine. I'll take a look at it if that will make you happy, but from your description, I know it's exactly what I need to finish off my collection."

"The Blunderboo isn't for sale," Gretchen repeated, knowing that no collection is ever really finished off. Most likely, Milt Wood was an amateur collector trying to keep up with a group of experts, and his inexperience was showing.

"It doesn't belong to me. Until I speak with the owner, I can't offer it to you."

"Price is no object. I'll pay whatever you ask."

"But as I've explained, even if the owner is willing to sell the doll, it's a reproduction."

"Yes, I heard you. Insignificant." Milt Wood was an expressive talker, his hands keeping time to the beat of his persistence.

"The doll isn't for sale at the moment," Gretchen said firmly. She regretted having mentioned the doll earlier to the collectors gathered at the Boston Kewpie Club table. Who would have guessed that anyone would be interested in an imitation doll?

"Very well," he said, no longer quite as jovial and friendly. His smile remained, but his eyes darkened. "We'll discuss it again later."

Before Gretchen could think of a response that would send Milt Wood away permanently, she heard sirens screaming outside the building. Instead of growing fainter, the sound grew louder.

Bonnie Albright ran by, her red wig more than a little askew. "Ronny Beam's been murdered," she shouted. "Right out in the parking lot."

Behind Gretchen, April gasped.

"I told you this would happen eventually," Nina said with a slightly smug tone, although her complexion was several shades lighter than usual.

One of Nina's predictions, usually far off the mark, had come true, and she wasn't about to miss the opportunity to promote it.

"Was he shot?" Gretchen asked Bonnie, remembering the specifics of Nina's premonition that someone would eventually shoot Ronny.

"No. Stabbed with some kind of knife," Bonnie continued. "One with pink nail polish all over the handle."

Gretchen's eyes slid to the floor, to her

open toolbox and the assortment of repair tools, all painted Poodle Skirt Pink.

Nina reached over with her foot and casually flipped the toolbox cover closed.

No one but Gretchen noticed.

Gretchen quickly gathered her unsold dolls and stored them under her table. The show had ended earlier than planned. The big attraction waited outdoors.

"Are you missing a knife?" Nina whispered, as they swung the puppies and purses onto their shoulders to join the throng of people moving outside. Tutu pranced lightly ahead, while Nina clutched her pink leash.

April, in spite of her bulk, had already outdistanced them in the race to the doors. The opportunity to view a murder was irresistible, and the hall was clearing out fast.

"Yes," Gretchen answered, remembering her search through the workshop. "But don't say anything yet. It can't possibly be mine."

"What kind of knife was it?"

"My hobby knife. I noticed it missing yesterday when I packed up. But it's just a razor blade in a holder. I don't think it could kill anyone. Cut them up pretty bad, but, as a murder weapon . . . ?" Gretchen shook her head. "Impossible."

Still, Gretchen had a sinking feeling that the knife was hers. How many other people paint their tools pink? She struggled to remember when she had last seen the knife. Did she paint the handle? Yes. She had painted it right before Nina left to have her hair done. Then Steve came in and ran his hands along the tools. He was the last person in the workshop aside from her. There was only one explanation. Steve must have taken it.

But why?

"It can't be mine," she said again, without confidence.

Nina harrumphed and continued moving forward.

Gretchen noticed an exit door off to the back of the hall. "Let's get out of the crowd," she said. "The police are never going to let all these people get close to the . . . scene." She couldn't bring herself to say *murder scene.* "And I have to see that knife. Come on."

Nimrod and Sophie sensed the excitement around them, and both rode high in their purses for a better view. Nimrod panted heavily, his tiny eyes alert. Sophie's topknot bounced.

Gretchen slammed through the exit door with Nina right behind her.

The Arizona sun temporarily blinded Gretchen. She quickly donned sunglasses and realized that they were standing at the rear of the parking lot. Even in early October, the heat struck her instantly. At least one hundred degrees. She moved to the side of the building and peeked around the corner.

A perfect view. Nina edged up next to her and shortened Tutu's leash to keep her close.

On the far side, about seventy yards away, police were trying to contain the swelling crowd. Ambulances and squad cars crept along, and Gretchen wondered how the authorities could preserve the crime scene and find potential witnesses with this mass of humanity.

A better question occurred to Gretchen. How did someone manage to murder Ronny in the middle of the afternoon in a full parking lot without being seen?

Uniformed police swarmed the lot. Several bent over something on the ground behind a car, but Gretchen couldn't make out a body. She felt weak around the knees and leaned heavily against the building for support.

Matt Albright rose from the huddle on the ground, looked over his shoulder, and spotted Gretchen. He did a double take, spoke briefly to another officer, and walked over.

"I think we can rule out premeditation," he said, the strain showing on his face. "This was definitely an expression of rage." He shook his head. "So much for a quiet day off. Why do I feel like I'm going to catch this case? Ronny wasn't on my list of favorite people, and I'm not particularly fond of dolls."

"Ronny could piss off the pope," Nina added. "Excuse my expression."

"You two should pack up for the day," Matt advised. "We're going to shut the show down until tomorrow. That's the only way to dispel the sightseers. We need to clear the parking lot. Our people can't even get their vehicles in."

"What happened?" Gretchen asked.

"Looks like the killer attacked as Ronny approached his car. He must have been waiting for Ronny."

"How awful," Nina said, eyeing Gretchen. "We heard he was stabbed. Glad that isn't true."

Matt frowned. "My mother was lurking around, soaking up as much information as she could pick up. That's classified information. We're withholding it for now, so you never heard it from me."

"It is true then?" Gretchen looked away from the activity, up at Camelback Mountain rising in the distance over the city. Red, barren clay. Like someone had tried to fashion a camel from potter's clay and failed.

"Sort of. Whoever killed Ronny also stuck an X-Acto knife in his back as a finishing touch." His frown deepened. "I don't get it, though. The blade wasn't long enough to do any real damage. It's the tire iron we found nearby that will turn out to be the murder weapon."

Nina stared at Gretchen, waiting for her response. Whatever she decided, she knew Nina would back her up. But Gretchen didn't know for certain whether Steve had taken the knife from the workshop, and she suddenly felt uncharacteristically protective of her former boyfriend. Gretchen couldn't share her suspicions with anyone, especially not with Matt, a cop. At least, not yet.

Gretchen met Nina's gaze silently.

"I better get back," Matt said.

He strode away.

11

Nina rammed through the Impala's gears. "I really don't know why you insist on getting involved in Daisy's life," she said. "She's perfectly happy where she is."

Gretchen didn't know how anyone could be content to roam the Phoenix streets without a place to sleep or a guaranteed meal.

"I'm not convinced of that," Gretchen said. "This is a good time to check on her, since we have a few extra hours. And maybe she knows something about Ronny that will be helpful. The street people seem to be connected to the city's pulse."

She gazed out the window. "Like Native American drum signals. I don't know how they do it."

Daisy, a homeless drama queen, and her alcoholic friend, Nacho, had entered Gretchen's life right after she'd arrived in Phoenix, and she felt a special fondness for them, even though their refusal to accept her offers of assistance frustrated her beyond words.

Traffic on Central Avenue edged slowly forward, the perpetual gridlock an inescapable fact of life in Phoenix. For once, Gretchen didn't mind. It gave her an opportunity to think about Ronny's death and Steve's connection to her knife.

"Why didn't you tell Matt that you think the knife belongs to you?" Nina asked from the driver's seat of her red Impala.

"I don't know. I'd like to wait a little longer. I just have a bad feeling about the whole thing."

"That's my girl. Your inherited psychic gifts are finally kicking in."

"Because I have a bad feeling about a murder, and my repair tool was used as a weapon?"

"Exactly." Nina punched the horn and slammed on the brakes when the car ahead of her stopped abruptly. "My nerves are shot," she said. "I think it's a combination of the heat and Ronny's murder."

"You should have let me drive."

"You're always lost. I'll take care of the driving. You pay attention to where we're going and start orienting yourself to Phoenix's streets. I've never known anyone with such a poor sense of direction."

"I haven't gotten lost for a long time."

"Right. Sure."

"There she is." Gretchen pointed. "Pull over."

Nina edged to the curb and idled in a no parking zone. "Make it quick," she said, adjusting the bows in her hair. "I don't want a ticket."

As soon as the car stopped, all three dogs began prancing in the backseat, running into each other and yipping. Gobs of canine goo streaked the back windows. Nimrod and Tutu recognized Daisy immediately, and their chorus resounded at a nerve-racking level.

Daisy sat alone on a wooden bench wearing a baggy purple dress and a red baseball cap, and weeping into a corner of the dress.

"What's wrong, Daisy?" Gretchen said, getting out of the car and sitting down beside her.

"Oh, hey." Daisy looked up and sniffed, trying to compose herself. "I'm okay."

"Your bedroom is still waiting for you, whenever you feel like stopping by."

"Thanks, Gretchen, but it's hard to get noticed by talent scouts way up there by the mountain. I need to be on the streets. Visible. Besides, I have everything I need right here with me."

She motioned to a shopping cart wedged between the bench and an electrical pole. It was packed with old clothes and other miscellaneous items Daisy had found in her wanderings.

"Any luck with the acting yet?" Gretchen slung her arms across the back of the bench. She saw Nina scowl at her from the car.

"Soon," Daisy said, sniffling. "I just need my first big break. Then it's Hollywood, here I come."

Gretchen wished she had paid more attention in her college psych classes. Daisy talked incessantly of her future as a movie star. There must be a clinical name for it. Not that a label mattered. The woman would never agree to psychological testing or medication.

"You know, I promised to look out for you," Gretchen said. After Daisy almost died in a car accident, Gretchen had made a vow to herself that she planned on fulfilling, with or without Daisy's cooperation.

"I know you did." Daisy's eyes were red and rimmed with tears.

"You're not making it easy."

"Don't worry about me. Worry about Nacho," Daisy said, beginning to sob again.

"What's going on?" Gretchen felt a tightness in her chest, and she sat up straighter.

"They did a sweep again. I can't find him."

"Oh, no."

Daisy shook her head sorrowfully. "They came in a van," she said, "and rounded us up as we came out of the soup kitchen. I ducked back inside, but Nacho wasn't quick enough."

Angry, Gretchen looked down the street as though she might spot the van. "How long ago?"

Daisy shrugged helplessly and looked off into the distance. "I don't know. Awhile."

Nina blew the horn.

"Come with us," Gretchen said, rising from the bench. "We'll help you look for him."

"I can't leave my stuff behind."

Gretchen eyed the mounded shopping cart. "It won't fit in the car," she said.

Daisy looked up and down the street, then she called out, and two women left a bench farther down and started over.

"We're neighbors," Daisy said. "They'll watch my things."

"Hey, doggies." Daisy slid into the back-seat, and the canines pounced on her with a volley of delighted squeals.

Gretchen saw Nina scrunch her nose at

the new odors permeating the Impala. Nina rolled down her window a few inches.

"Nacho's been relocated again," Gretchen informed Nina.

"Isn't that illegal?" Nina asked. "To take Nacho against his will and drop him off someplace else?"

"I suppose," Daisy said. "But what's he going to do about it? Sue?"

"They probably didn't take him far," Nina said. "Last time, wasn't he dumped in Mesa?"

"And he found his way back," Gretchen said to reassure Daisy. "He'll be back this time, too."

Nina nodded. "He could be anywhere, but he's resourceful."

She shot into traffic and wove expertly between lanes.

"You're right," Daisy said. "He'll come back. He wouldn't leave me by myself for long."

"You know," Gretchen said, changing the subject. "Ronny Beam was murdered a few hours ago."

"I heard," Daisy said.

"How did you find out already? It just happened."

"It's all over the street. Nobody liked Ronny much."

"That's an understatement if I ever heard one," Nina muttered.

"Last January he came to our campsite," Daisy said. "He said he wanted to see how we make it through the winter. Like Phoenix winters ever get that cold. He was really obnoxious. He had cheap wine in a paper bag and tried to panhandle from an undercover cop. Everybody was relieved when they arrested him and carted him away."

"Dumb as a brick," Nina said.

Daisy had all three dogs on her lap. Her newest fan, Sophie, rode in the crook of her arm. "Who killed him?" she asked.

Nina shrugged, her eyes on the road. "Could have been anyone who ever met the creep."

"Could be you," Daisy said. "You *really* didn't like him."

"Oh, my." Nina slowed down and glanced in the backseat at Daisy. "I had a fight with him yesterday in front of all kinds of witnesses."

"It was quite a fight," Gretchen said to Daisy. "She hit him with her pepper spray."

"What do you think, Gretchen? Am I a suspect?"

"No, of course not," Gretchen reassured her. "You were at your table the whole time, weren't you?"

112

Nina paused to think about it. Then she grinned widely. "Yup. I was."

"And you have all kinds of witnesses to that," Gretchen said. "You're off the hook."

Gretchen thought of Steve's altercation with Ronny, which had taken place in front of as many, if not more, witnesses.

She couldn't say the same for him.

Daisy showered and changed her clothes while Nina occupied her time with a training session for Sophie. This was Gretchen's chance to get some much-needed advice, and her aunt Gertie in Michigan was the perfect person to ask for it.

Gretchen could use a break from personal conflict, and the last thing she wanted was for Nina to know about this phone call. She closed the workshop door to ensure privacy.

Aunt Nina and Aunt Gertie didn't get along, mainly because they were both strong, opinionated alpha females. Gertie Johnson came from Gretchen's father's side of the family and was only related to Nina through marriage. Nina mentioned that fact every time Gertie's name came up in conversation.

When the familiar voice answered, Gretchen said, "How are things in the Upper Peninsula?"

"Still holding together," Aunt Gertie said. "The fall colors are at their peak. You should come for a visit."

"I'd like that. Still running your private investigation service?"

"Of course. Someone has to catch criminals. You don't expect my sheriff son to be doing much."

Blaze, Gretchen's cousin, ran the local law enforcement service like *The Andy Griffith Show*. Stonely, Michigan, had a lot in common with Mayberry. So did Blaze and Barney Fife. No wonder her aunt took the law into her own hands.

"And how are Star and Heather?" Her aunt had named all her kids for the horses she never had.

"They're fine. But you didn't call to chitchat," Aunt Gertie said. "I can hear it in your voice. Something's happened."

Gretchen related recent events, including her suspicions about Steve. "Maybe I should have told Matt the truth," she finished.

"You did the right thing. You don't even know what the truth is yet. If you had told him, Steve would be in jail right this minute, and the police would have considered the case closed."

"I'm aiding and abetting."

"Nothing of the sort. What if they had arrested you? If it *was* your knife, maybe you're being set up."

"I hadn't thought of that." In all the excitement, the ramification of the weapon in Ronny's back belonging to her hadn't sunk in. How could she explain how the knife got there?

"You don't really think Steve killed the reporter, do you?" Gertie asked.

"No." Gretchen wished her voice was firmer.

"Do you want to find the real killer?"

"Of course."

"Then figure it out."

That was Gertie. Making the impossible sound simple. In an emergency, Gertie Johnson was the person to be with. Totally self-sufficient. Maybe it came from living in the isolation of northern Michigan. Maybe it was just Gertie's resilient nature.

"Exactly what did Ronny say to you at the doll show?"

"He said that some story he was working on was about to blow sky high. He said something like this is better news than dolls murdering people."

"That's odd," Gertie said.

"The guy is . . . was odd. I'm sure the comment didn't mean anything."

Gertie's sigh was unmistakable. "This is

115

what I keep trying to tell Blaze. When murder's involved, everything is important. You need to find out what he meant by that."

"And how do I find out?"

"The guy was a reporter. He wrote stuff down, right?"

"Right." Gretchen remembered Ronny's recording unit.

"Start with a thorough search of his house. And Gretchen, watch your back."

The line went dead.

Gretchen's back was feeling extremely exposed and vulnerable.

"Ronny lived in the Palm Tree Trailer Park," Nina said. "Off of Twenty-fourth Street."

"Did Daisy tell you that?"

Nina nodded. "Daisy never stops talking."

"She knows everything. It's amazing."

"She just wants to stretch out on the couch and watch television all day. She's clutching the remote like it's a newborn baby."

Gretchen sat at the worktable. Pieces from a ball-jointed doll body lay before her. "Nineteen pieces," she said, holding up a lower leg. "And it's been taken completely apart. How am I going to figure this out? I hope I don't have this many dolls to repair again tomorrow, or I'll never get through them all. I've hardly started this bunch."

"First day is always the busiest. You'll have time tomorrow at the show to catch up."

Gretchen looked at the assortment of dolls requiring restringing and shook her head in dismay.

"Perk up," Nina said. "I have something special for you."

"What?" Gretchen spun her stool around. "A present? For me?"

"For you." Nina handed her a plastic bag with Beyond the Galaxy etched on the side. "Open it," she said, grinning.

Gretchen peeked into the bag, then looked at Nina, puzzled. She extracted a pair of glasses with cardboard frames and indigo-colored lenses. "Are they 3-D glasses?"

"No, no. These are aura glasses. They're going to help you see auras."

Gretchen stared at Nina. According to her aunt, colors emanated from all matter, including cacti, doll collections, and wee-wee pads. She could divine the future, she claimed, by studying the color surrounding a human body. Gretchen had no hard evidence to back up Nina's outrageous claim, nor was she expecting Nina to ever prove it conclusively.

"Put them on," Nina said, excited.

Feeling foolish, Gretchen slipped on the flimsy frames. "Now what?"

"Well? What do you see?"

Gretchen's gaze fell on Wobbles, her three-legged cat, who at the moment was occupied with a small, fuzzy ball. He batted it across the room and pounced, unaware that he had a physical handicap. "I don't know. I guess I see light around Wobbles."

Nina clapped her hands. "I knew you had the gift. Now, what color are you seeing?"

"I'm not seeing a color, just light." Gretchen pulled off the frames and looked at them. "The tint on the lenses must draw light."

"No, the tint has nothing to do with it," Nina said, indignant. "It's happening because of you. Keep working with them. With practice, you'll see colors, and then we'll talk about what the different colors represent. Eventually, you won't need the glasses. You'll be just like me."

Gretchen stifled a burst of laughter and turned it into a throat clearing. Just like her aunt? She didn't think so. No one on this planet was just like Nina.

"So you're telling me that you see different colors around everyone?"

"Almost everyone."

"Who's the exception?"

118

Nina squirmed.

"Come on, tell me." She was on to something.

"Men," Nina said, reluctantly. "I can't see male auras."

Gretchen chuckled.

"I can't figure men out either. I'm sure special glasses won't help."

"Do you like them?" Nina asked, meaning the glasses.

"Love them," Gretchen replied, meaning the men.

"You never know when they'll come in handy," Nina said. "Carry them in your purse."

"I will." Gretchen laid the glasses on the cluttered workbench. "I need to pack up more Ginny dolls for tomorrow. If the show had stayed open another few hours, I would have sold out."

She rummaged through her mother's sale stock and selected a safari Ginny, a graduation Ginny in a white robe, and a drum majorette Ginny in a red uniform. "These are so cute. I hate to sell them."

"You'll make your mother proud," Nina said, taking them from Gretchen and laying them on the worktable. She peered into the bag of dolls awaiting repair. "Look," she said. "Here's that package from our friendly

119

postal employee. You never opened it."

Gretchen sighed. "It's probably one more doll that needs repairing."

Nina ripped open the outer wrapping with one fluid, practiced motion and worked her fingernails around the edges of the package, loosening the tape. "It's wrapped well," she commented, removing a layer of bubble wrap and setting it aside.

Gretchen continued digging through boxes looking for more dolls her mother wanted to sell. "I can't find any more Ginnys. I guess I'll take Barbie dolls."

"Gretchen, look what was in the package." Nina held up a Blunderboo Kewpie doll.

Gretchen rose and took the Kewpie from Nina. She turned it over in her hand. The three-inch doll bore the O'Neill mark on its feet and the red heart on its belly. "It has the same markings as the one that broke yesterday. Only this one is real. And unbroken."

"Why send a perfectly fine doll to be repaired?" Nina asked. "That doesn't make sense."

Gretchen ran her finger over its naked, chubby body and almost dropped it in startled surprise.

Under her fingers, she felt a crack where the head and body had been reconnected.

"Nina, this one's been repaired, too."

"In the same place?"

"Yes."

Nina clamped a hand across her mouth theatrically, her eyes wide. Then she removed her hand to speak. "I have a bad feeling about this."

Gretchen stared at the doll. "It's a coincidence. A fluke."

"Then who sent it?"

Gretchen dug through the packaging but couldn't find a return address. "Was it wrapped in this?" Gretchen held up a brown paper bag.

Nina nodded.

Gretchen turned the bag over and saw Bert's Liquor printed on it. Then she looked at the rest of the packaging. "There's no note, but it looks like it was sent locally, from here in Phoenix."

"I have a premonition," Nina said, lowering her husky voice dramatically. "Someone sent this doll as a warning."

Gretchen placed the Kewpie in a stand and stood it upright on top of a bin filled with doll clothes. "We'll take it to the doll show tomorrow and see if anyone knows where it came from."

Like her aunt, Gretchen didn't believe in coincidence. But the reason why someone would send it escaped her. Nina thought it was a warning, but if so, where was the message?

The doll didn't need repair. That had already been done. And there was no return address.

What was going on?

12

When they headed for the Palm Tree Trailer Park, the sun burned orange as it moved over the horizon and twilight began to descend on the city. Gretchen checked her watch. Six o'clock.

"Okay, we're lost," Gretchen said from the driver's seat. She leaned forward to catch the next street sign.

"No, we're not," Nina said. "We're on Thirtieth. Keep going straight and slow down a little."

Gretchen eased off the accelerator.

"Okay, speed up and change lanes." Nina swung her head and looked back over her shoulder. "Quick."

Gretchen followed her aunt's direction. "What's going on?"

"We have a tail," Nina announced, her voice edging up an octave.

Gretchen glanced in her rearview mirror and studied the traffic behind them. "I don't see how that's possible," she said.

"I agree," Nina said. "You drive like you're trying to win the Grand Prix. Who could keep up?"

Look who's talking. Gretchen slowed for a changing light and eased to a stop. She checked her rearview mirror again.

"I noticed it a few miles back," Nina said. "I've been keeping my eye on the side mirror. Do a few more lane switches to make sure."

"Is it a Beemer?" Gretchen's first thought was that Steve hadn't been around the entire afternoon. He was bound to show up soon.

"No, it's kind of nondescript. Maybe a VW Jetta. It's black."

The traffic light changed, and Gretchen edged her bumper up to the next car. Nina reached over and blew the horn.

"Take it easy," Gretchen said, pushing her aunt's hand away.

Traffic cleared, and Gretchen cut into another lane without signaling. A car behind moved over, too.

"Let's try to find out who it is," Gretchen said. "It could be Steve."

"Now that you mention it, where has he been all day?"

"With any luck, he gave up and went back

to Boston."

Another lane opened, and Gretchen swerved into it. "The car's right behind us now," she said.

Gretchen peered into the rearview mirror, trying to see the driver of the car behind them. But the approaching dusk made the view murky. All she could see was a dark form.

The car sidled closer, its bumper threateningly near to Gretchen's car.

"If I was driving," Nina said, "I'd slam on the brakes. That would fix his wagon."

"Maybe we should pull over, Nina."

"Good idea. Then they can spill out of that car and gun us down without a fight. How many people are in there?" Nina answered her own question. "We don't know."

Gretchen pointed to a busy strip mall on the right. "Let's turn in and drive up to that Chinese restaurant. See what happens."

"I don't like this."

"We can't try to outrun them," Gretchen said. "We'll have an accident."

She turned right and slowly came to a stop in front of Yung Fu's China Buffet. The entrance to the restaurant was well lit.

The black car followed and pulled up along the driver's side of the Impala. Nina

squealed and ducked down, leaving Gretchen alone to face their pursuer. She lowered her window and watched the black
car's passenger window slide down halfway.

Gretchen strained to see the driver, but all
she could see was part of a woman's face
from the bridge of the nose and up. Large
black sunglasses concealed her features.

"You'll pay dearly for this," the woman
snarled, hatred in her voice.

Tires squealed as the driver gunned the
motor and disappeared.

"That was close," Nina said, practically
lying across Gretchen's lap.

"Thanks for the support," Gretchen said.
"If I ever need backup again, I'll be sure to
call you."

"What did she mean, 'You'll pay dearly
for this'?"

"I don't have a clue."

"What did she look like?"

Gretchen tapped Nina lightly on the top
of her cowering head. "Get off me, O Brave
One. I couldn't see her. She didn't roll the
window all the way down. Dark glasses,
dark hair. Could have been April or Bonnie,
and I wouldn't have known it."

"I need a drink." Nina rose to a sitting
position. "A mai tai sounds good."

"We might as well eat," Gretchen said.

"The police are probably at Ronny's trailer anyway."

"True, that's a point I hadn't considered," Nina admitted. "I don't know about you, but I have the creeps over this whole thing, and I'd rather not be in Ronnie's trailer in the dark. We can run over there another time."

They entered the Chinese restaurant, and after ordering mai tais, they sat in silence for a few minutes while sipping their drinks.

"I'm having Chinese broccoli in oyster sauce," Nina said, after perusing the menu.

Gretchen shook her head. "No oyster sauce for you. You're a vegan, remember?"

"What's wrong with oyster sauce? Is it really oysters?"

Gretchen sighed. "Why don't you give up? You'll never be a vegan. Do something realistic, like giving up red meat. Or refuse to eat mammals."

Nina clapped her hands. "That's a wonderful idea."

"Two Chinese broccolis in oyster sauce," Gretchen said to the waiter, relieved that Nina's vegan days were behind her.

"Maybe our tail was that floozy of a summer intern," Nina said. "You know, the one that —"

Gretchen cut her off. "I know which one

you mean. There's only one intern in my life. One too many. Steve said he broke it off with Courtney after I found out about them."

"Then she has a good motive to chase you down."

Steve's duplicity had been the reason Gretchen left Boston permanently, and a good enough reason to end their going-nowhere relationship. Had Courtney followed him to Phoenix?

"Breaking it off before you found out would have been better for him," Nina said. "He might have had a chance."

"No," Gretchen said. "Resisting completely would have been better. A college kid, can you believe it?"

Dinners came, and Gretchen poured tea for both of them.

After they had eaten, they broke open their fortune cookies.

Nina read hers first: " 'A person of words and not deeds is like a garden full of weeds.' Humph," she said. "I don't get it. Who makes up this stuff? What's yours?"

" 'Advice, when most needed, is least heeded.' "

Gretchen stuffed the bit of paper into her purse and said, "Tomorrow has to be a better day."

■ ■ ■ ■

Gretchen sat at the worktable and tried to forget the disturbing events of the last few days. Steve's reappearance in her life, the loss of her Ginnys and her money, Brett's accident, Ronny Beam's violent murder, her missing knife found in his back, the mysterious package containing the Kewpie, and a confrontation with the enraged woman.

Gretchen hated confrontation.

Steve had called while they were at the Chinese restaurant, and she had turned off her cell phone when she saw his number on the caller ID. She planned on leaving it off until sometime tomorrow.

She intentionally didn't check the kitchen answering machine either before retreating to the workshop, since she suspected he had called the house as well.

The house was so quiet. Daisy's bedroom door was closed, and she decided not to disturb her. Gretchen couldn't imagine having to find a place to sleep outdoors every night. Park benches couldn't be comfortable. No wonder Daisy always slept right through her visits to Gretchen.

Gretchen embraced the silence of the cozy room, welcomed it after the brouhaha that always surrounded larger-than-life Nina.

Nimrod dozed on his bed, and the nocturnal Wobbles sat on the table next to her, his eyes closed and a deep, throaty purr rumbling from inside of him.

She ran her hand through his silky black fur from head to tip of tail and thought about the hobby knife found protruding from Ronny's back. Her knife. Ronny was as abrasive as a Brillo pad, but who would have killed him? Even if Steve had taken her knife, he hadn't even met Ronny when it disappeared.

Steve was a tenacious trial attorney, used to stressful situations and able to remain calm in the face of just about any challenge. He handled the ugliest divorces and had been threatened often by vengeful spouses. He'd always prided himself on his ability to turn any situation to his advantage.

Steve couldn't have killed Ronny for one simple, telling fact: his ongoing bid for partnership in the law firm meant more to him than anything in the world. He would never act in a way that might harm his position.

But if Steve didn't kill Ronny, who did? Who had a motive?

Just about anyone in Phoenix who had crossed paths with the blundering, insensitive reporter.

The business phone rang beside her, and she waited impatiently for the answering machine's greeting to finish. Steve's voice, filled with barely concealed frustration, filled the room. "Gretchen, where are you? I've tried your cell and your main number. Pick up. I know you're there." A pause. "We need to discuss us. Stop hiding. I'll try back in an hour." He disconnected.

Spreading a towel on the worktable, she chose a doll from the repair bag and finished taking it apart — legs, arms, and head. She laid out the pieces, chose the right size elastic cording, and went to work on the doll's leg. She attached the cording through a hook in the leg, making sure it was snug, and ran it through the neck opening.

Wobbles yawned, stretched leisurely, and jumped down from the table. She heard Nimrod snoring softly and glanced down at him. His puppy tongue protruded from the side of his mouth.

As Gretchen worked, she kept stealing glances at the mysterious Kewpie doll. Her name hadn't been on the package. It had simply been addressed to the doll repairer and sent to the hall where the doll show was taking place.

Strange, although the entire thing was weird.

Someone wanted the doll repairer to receive the doll. But it was already repaired, so what was the point?

As much as she disliked admitting it, coincidence had to have played a part in the puzzle of the two Kewpies.

Who knew about the other Blunderboo?

Only the entire group of doll collectors milling around the Boston Kewpie Club's table. Were they connected in some way?

It didn't make sense.

Gretchen carefully lifted the Blunderboo Kewpie doll from the stand and again felt along its neck.

The repair work on the mystery doll was as good as her own work. Whoever had glued the pieces together knew how to do it. No unevenness in the joining.

She thought about the fortune cookie she had broken open at dinner. "Advice, when most needed, is least heeded."

What had Aunt Gertie said? When it comes to murder, everything is important.

I must be crazy, she told herself. *Don't do it.*

But I restore dolls, she argued back. *It can easily be fixed.*

Before she could change her mind, Gretchen took the doll to the kitchen, placed it in a pan of cold water, and brought the water to a boil. Ten minutes later, she returned to the workshop with the pan, lifted the Kewpie with serving tongs, and placed it on the towel.

Satisfied that the glue had sufficiently softened, Gretchen carefully pulled the head away from the body.

"You're crazy," she said again, this time out loud.

Certifiably insane, off your rocker.

She peered into the Blunderboo's body cavity.

Nothing.

She turned the head upside down and looked inside. Her heart thumped several irregular beats.

Something white. A piece of paper.

Gretchen extracted it with tweezers and studied the paper that had been folded multiple times into a tiny perfect square.

"What's up?" said a man's voice behind her.

Gretchen screamed.

The piece of paper fluttered to the floor as she reached for a repair hook and whirled. Nimrod, startled awake, stood and barked bravely at the intruder.

"A little testy," Detective Matt Albright

said from the doorway, eyeing the weapon in her hand, a small smile playing nervously on his lips.

"Doesn't anyone knock anymore?" Gretchen said.

"I did knock. And rang the bell. You didn't answer."

"So you just walk in?"

"I tried the door, and it was unlocked." He flashed his dazzling smile. "I didn't know if you were home. I wanted to make sure the house was secure and you were safe."

Gretchen threw the repair hook on the table and stooped to retrieve the paper she had found inside the Kewpie doll. She tucked it into her pocket, hoping Matt hadn't noticed.

She shouldn't have worried about that.

Matt's eyes followed the repair hook, and Gretchen suddenly realized her mistake.

It had pink nail polish on the end of it.

"We need to talk," he said.

"Sure. Come on in."

"I'd rather wait outside," he said, still eyeing the pink hook. "Two months ago, I couldn't even think about looking into this room." His eyes left the hook and met hers. "The doll thing, you know. Therapy's helping, but not that much. I'll be by the pool."

Gretchen picked up the hook, returned it to the toolbox, and slammed it shut. "I'll get us a beverage. Are you on duty or off? Wine or coffee?"

"It looks like it's going to be a long night. Coffee for me," he said.

"I can explain," Gretchen said, taking a sip of old-vine Zinfandel.

"Oh, please do. I can hardly wait."

"I discovered my knife missing the night before the doll show. The polish was hardly dry, and poof, it was gone."

Matt snapped his fingers. "Just like that? Into thin air?"

Gretchen nodded warily. "Don't you believe me?"

"You've never lied to me before."

Gretchen searched his face for signs of sarcasm, because she *had* lied to him in the past. At the time, she felt it was absolutely necessary. Had he known?

His face remained unreadable. He hadn't touched his coffee.

He leaned back in the lounge chair and laced his fingers behind his head. The pool glistened in the mild October night air. Spotlights placed strategically around cacti and shrubs highlighted the desert plants. Camelback Mountain rose against the skyscape, and the moon hung low beside it.

Gretchen ran a bare foot over the cool Mexican tile surrounding the swimming pool and took another sip of wine.

It could have been a perfect moment.

Matt had a compact, athletic body and a scrappy attitude. Completely the opposite of Steve, who had a good five inches on Gretchen's five eight. She could look directly into Matt's eyes without tilting her head. Steve was blond, fair-skinned, and slim. Matt had dark hair and a perpetual Valley of the Sun tan.

Gretchen took a larger gulp of wine and wondered why she was comparing the two men, since one was a cheat and the other was . . . well . . . married. Sure, he was in the middle of a divorce, but maybe they'd still work it out. And in any case, divorced men came with a lot of baggage, and Gretchen liked to travel light.

"And you have no idea who might have stolen your knife?"

Gretchen almost drained the glass and shook her head.

Was it a lie if she didn't actually say no out loud?

Matt flipped through a notebook and jotted something into it. Gretchen tried to read upside down but failed.

"We're running prints right now. I know it's your knife, but someone else's prints would help your testimony. I really hope yours aren't the only ones that show up."

Gretchen couldn't agree more.

"Since you're here, I'd like to report a theft," she said, relating the suspicious mix-up at the auction and the false address Duanne had given when registering.

When she finished, Matt said, "It sounds harmless to me, a simple mistake."

"I'm out three hundred dollars."

"I'll ask around. If I hear anything, I'll let you know." Matt leaned forward, resting his elbows on his knees.

He was *so* close. Gretchen took another big gulp of wine and wondered why she was so nervous.

"What's the story with Steve?" he asked.

"We broke it off before I moved to Phoenix."

"He doesn't seem to know that."

"Yes, well . . ." Gretchen finished the last sip of wine. Where was the bottle? Why was she feeling like a schoolgirl? "He's persistent."

"Men can be that way."

Why was he looking at her like that?

"What about you and your wife?" Gretchen asked.

"My mother must have told you we're divorcing. She wouldn't have passed up a chance to share that news."

"We never discussed it," Gretchen lied. "So, technically, you're a married man."

"Technically, yes."

Too bad, she almost said out loud.

They were both quiet for a minute. His body radiated major magnetism. She had to work to resist the pull.

Gretchen stood up.

Matt rose beside her.

"I'll let myself out," he said. "Stay out of trouble."

She watched him swing open the patio gate and disappear into the night.

What luck! He hadn't arrested her for withholding information. It certainly paid off to personally know the lead detective.

Gretchen thrust her hands into her pockets and suddenly remembered the paper. She pulled it out and unfolded it near a candle glowing on the patio table.

"Wag the Dog" was scribbled across the paper in large, loopy handwriting.

Gretchen slumped. What kind of message was that? She felt cheated.

There are all kinds of nuts in this world, she thought, blowing out the candle and closing up the house for the night.

After knocking and listening at the door, Gretchen entered the spare bedroom. Daisy must have checked out of the guest room while she and Nina were playing hide-and-seek with a black Jetta. An occasional meal, a shower, and a real bed for a short nap was all Daisy would partake of before quickly heading back to her life on the street. Gretchen couldn't see the attraction.

She turned off all the phones' ringers before turning on the alarm clock.

13

Gretchen slept fitfully and rose early Sunday morning, hoping a hike up Camelback Mountain would ease the turmoil in her mind.

By the time the sun came up at six thirty, she had already reached the footpath leading to the trailhead. Fifteen minutes later she paused to look at the valley below and experienced her usual wonder at the magnificent view of Phoenix. She followed a trail to the right called Bobby's Rock Trail, not nearly as long or as strenuous as Summit Trail, but she didn't have enough time before the doll show for the challenge of Summit.

Red clay dominated the landscape with a scattering of ocotillos, barrel cacti, and palo verdes. Gretchen used her binoculars to zoom in on the birdlife of the Sonoran Desert. She heard the high-pitched trill of a rock wren and searched for the elusive Gila woodpecker that builds its nest hole in saguaro cacti.

An hour later, Gretchen returned to the trailhead and spotted Matt on his way up. She watched him approach and observed the rigidness of his face, the tense jaw, and flashing eyes.

All business.

She gave him a tentative smile. "Hey," she said. "You're out early."

"Looking for you, as usual." He came to a stop. "You aren't on your way up, are you? I don't feel like climbing today."

"Nope. I'm going down."

"That's probably the best news I'll hear all day."

"What's up?"

Matt ran his fingers through dark, unruly hair, and Gretchen saw that he hadn't shaved this morning. "I should apply for a transfer to vice," he said. "It would be a cakewalk after this."

"Let's talk on the way back." Gretchen started down the path to the street. "I have to get ready for the doll —"

Ahead, she saw Steve walking at a fast pace up the street headed in her direction.

Great. Just great.

Steve looked up and spotted her. His pace increased.

Gretchen rolled her eyes and placed her hands on her hips in a confrontational stance. Steve might be king of the hill in a court of law, but he was approaching her mountain and her space. He'd picked the wrong hill this time. She had tried to block him out of her mind, but if he wanted to persist, she was as ready as she'd ever be.

Behind her Matt spoke quietly into a cell phone. "Send the closest unit," he said, and gave his position.

"Do you want to tell me what's going on?" Gretchen said without looking back at him, instead watching Steve stumble along on the rough path.

"Your boyfriend's fingerprints were all over the knife we found in Ronny Beam's back," Matt said. "I'm taking him in for questioning."

Gretchen couldn't believe what she said next. Of all the responses she could have given at that precise moment, of all the things she should have said in Steve's defense, considering their seven-year relationship and her deep conviction that he couldn't possibly have murdered Ronny, she blurted the first thing that popped into her head.

"He's not my boyfriend!"

"How's the doll show going?" Caroline asked. Her voice was light and airy. California agreed with her. Or maybe it was all the excitement of the book tour.

"Wonderful," Gretchen said. "I'm selling quite a lot of dolls."

Even though the show ended early because of Ronny Beam's murder.

Gretchen would tell her mother everything when she came home. Not now. She would only worry, or worse, abandon her tour.

"I knew you could do it," Caroline said. "Is Nina helping out?"

"Oh, yes. She's the highlight of the show."

Caroline laughed. "And Steve? Did you give him a big sendoff like you said you would?"

"A big sendoff? That's one way of putting it. I wish he hadn't come to Phoenix."

"I have to tell you, I thought you two might get back together. And I wasn't pleased at the prospect."

"I thought you liked Steve."

"I could see what initially attracted you to him, but he's changed. More self-absorbed, more easily angered, and less considerate of you. He's forgotten what's important in life."

"I think he'll find time soon to reflect on what's important," Gretchen said.

"I hope so. I wish him well."

"Me, too."

Nimrod and Sophie hammered it up for their expanding audience, easily drawing the biggest crowd of the show to Nina and April's table. Who needed dolls at a doll show to create a buzz when you had cute, miniature puppies?

Gretchen could hardly focus on the dolls she needed to repair. She even considered removing the sign that offered her restringing services. Customers pored over her remaining Ginny dolls and the new batch of Barbie dolls, yet all Gretchen wanted was privacy to sort through her emotions.

She had filled Nina in on the morning's events when she arrived at the hall, and they had agreed to keep Steve's situation a secret from the other doll dealers for the time being. And from her mother, who didn't need distractions from home to interfere with her tour.

Gretchen couldn't get the sound of the wailing sirens from this morning out of her head. She couldn't forget Steve's pale face peering out at her from the back of the squad car.

"That's him?" Steve had asked in disbelief right before being unceremoniously escorted into the squad car. "The guy who's replacing me? The Boy Scout from the doll show?"

This was *so* embarrassing. And awkward. "I never said I had a replacement for you. Nina did."

"I recognize the name. Matt Albright. This cop who's threatening me is the guy you're dating?"

"We aren't dating." Gretchen glanced at Matt in time to see a raised eyebrow and amusement playing at the corners of his lips.

"Can we discuss this later?" she said. "The police think you might have something to do with Ronny's murder."

"That's ridiculous." Steve turned to Matt. "I demand my rights."

Matt sighed. "I don't have to read you your rights," he said. "You aren't under arrest. Yet." He held up a pair of handcuffs. "I would use these if I was arresting you."

"I demand representation," Steve had said. "Gretchen, you need to follow us and post bail for me. Gretchen —"

"She doesn't have to post bail for you." Matt's voice held an edge of annoyance.

"You aren't under —"

"Gretchen. Wake up, Gretchen."

Gretchen blinked and found herself at the doll show. April hovered over her. "This woman wants to buy a doll," she said.

"Oh, sure." Gretchen fumbled through the exchange.

Afterward, she showed April and Nina the piece of paper she had found inside the Kewpie doll.

"Wag the Dog," Nina said. "The movie?"

"Dustin Hoffman starred in it," April said.

"And Robert De Niro," Nina added.

"Don't forget Anne Heche," April said.

Gretchen frowned at both of them. "Now that we've established the cast, can someone tell me what the movie was about?"

"What movie?" Bonnie appeared out of nowhere, followed by Milt Wood, clutching a shopping bag in his right hand.

"Wag the Dog," April said. "Gretchen found a message."

"What message?" Milt asked.

"It's about a scandal and the presidency," Bonnie explained, chattering right past Milt's question. "Robert De Niro is a spin doctor who creates a war to draw attention away from a scandal involving the president. It's a good movie."

"What does *Wag the Dog* mean?" Gret-

146

chen asked.

"What message?" Milt tried again.

Nina waved her arm wildly above her head. "I know. A dog should be smarter than its tail. If the tail is smarter, then the tail wags the dog."

Gretchen looked down at Tutu, Nina's frivolous schnoodle. Brain the size of a pinhead and she still managed to wag her tail. "I don't get it."

"What's going on?" Bonnie said. "What message did you get?"

Gretchen showed her the piece of paper. Bonnie's penciled eyebrows zigzagged. "There's a comma right here."

"Where?" Everyone leaned toward the paper.

"See that little mark right there?" Bonnie said, pointing.

"I thought that was a spot of dirt," Gretchen said.

Bonnie shook her red-wigged head. "That changes the message."

" 'Wag, the Dog' means something different than 'Wag the Dog'?" Gretchen asked.

"I'm the Kewpie expert around here, remember?" Bonnie said. "Chief Wag is the leader of the Kewpies. He has a flag with a capital *K* in his topknot." Bonnie stuck a hand on top of her head for effect, but Gretchen thought she was making an *L* rather than a *K*. Sign language for loser.

Gretchen stared at Bonnie. "Really?" she said. "Wag is the name of a Kewpie doll?"

"Really. So the dog must mean Kewpie-doodle Dog. He has wings, too, just like the other Kewpies." Bonnie beamed. "Got to go. If you need any more help, just call."

"I'm still searching for a special Kewpie to take home with me," Milt said. "Let me know if you see anything."

Gretchen watched them stride down the aisle. She was no closer to understanding the message inside the Blunderboo Kewpie than she had been when she first discovered it. Whether she read it as "Wag, the Dog" or "Wag the Dog" didn't matter.

Her cell phone rang. The number on the caller ID was unfamiliar. She answered.

"I haven't been charged with anything," Steve said. "But your boyfriend is holding me on suspicion."

"Can he do that?" Gretchen asked, ignoring the boyfriend reference.

"My fingerprints on the knife, and a public fight with Ronny right before he was killed aren't helping my case."

"I'll find you an attorney."

"Not yet." Steve sounded stressed but cautiously restrained. "I haven't told the

148

police everything, if you catch my meaning."

"You have to tell the truth, Steve. You're an attorney. You should know that."

"I'm committed to you, and I won't put you in a bad spot."

"You're the one who took the knife. You have to explain how it got in Ronny's back."

"If I tell him that I gave it back to you, you'll be the one sitting in jail instead of me. Unless going out with the detective assigned to the case exempts you from the suspect list."

Gretchen rubbed her weary eyes. "What are you talking about? You took my knife."

"I was sort of tinkering with it on your worktable and became distracted by our conversation, and later I found it in my pocket. But during the doll show I threw it down on your table. You know that."

"I know nothing of the sort." Gretchen thought about the clutter at the repair end of the table. Was he telling the truth?

"Don't worry, I'll protect you as long as I can."

"I don't need protection. I didn't do anything wrong."

"If you didn't kill Ronny, you better find out who did, because I know I didn't, and one of us is in serious trouble."

"Tell the truth, Steve. That's all I can recommend right now."

"Gotta go. Your boyfriend's back." Steve disconnected without hearing Gretchen's next comment.

"He isn't my boyfriend," she said into the dead phone.

14

Tulip Ray shades her eyes with the back of a tattooed hand. "I don't usually, like, get involved. Nothing personal. I like to, y'know, like, mind my own business."

"Just a few questions."

"Maybe someone else can, like, answer them. I have to get to work."

"It'll only take a minute."

Tulip sighs heavily for the dramatic effect. *All right,* she hopes the sigh implies, *but you're taking up my valuable time.*

"What?" she asks, tapping a foot against a privacy wall. *Hurry up,* the foot implies. *Make it quick.* She watches a lizard slink up the wall and duck behind a withered vine.

"You were standing on the curb?"

"Yeah, that's right."

"What did you see?"

"Not much. The deed was done when I looked out in the street."

"The deed?"

"That's an expression. I didn't, like, see a thing."

"How about the box? Did you see the box?"

"What kind of box?"

"Cardboard box."

"Maybe."

"What do you mean, maybe? Either you saw it or you didn't. Which is it?"

She narrows her eyes. "Yah, I saw a box. That guy who got killed had a box when he ran up."

"What happened to it?"

"You said this would only take a minute."

"We can continue our conversation downtown."

"Some other guy picked it up."

"What did he look like?"

"Like he's been sleeping on park benches for about a hunnert years. He had a bunch of blue clothes on, y'know? Smelled, too."

"Ever see him before?"

"Do I look like someone who'd know a bum?" She kicks aimlessly at the curb, then looks down at her black toenails.

Man, how she hates cops.

15

Everyone at the doll show was talking about Ronny Beam's murder in the parking lot yesterday. The vendors spoke quietly among themselves so their customers wouldn't overhear. *Nothing like murder to draw people together,* Gretchen thought, observing a renewed camaraderie among the competitors. People lined up for admission, many of them arriving out of curiosity. Thrill seekers.

Nina bought the Sunday newspaper, and they quickly scanned it together behind Gretchen's table. "Murder Among Dolls." Ronny, always in search of the story of a lifetime, had finally found it. Page one, front and center.

Many of the customers wanted to know the sordid details, hoping to hear more at the doll show than they'd learned from the local news. Gretchen kept her ears tuned to the rumor mill, hoping to learn something that might exonerate Steve.

If only he'd stayed in Boston.

At the first chance she had since arriving at her table, Gretchen keyed a number into her cell phone.

"Howie Howard, please," Gretchen said.

"Speaking," he said. "Who is this?"

"Gretchen Birch, remember me?"

"Any relation to Caroline Birch?"

"She's my mother." Gretchen thought again of the responsibility her mother had given her, and how she'd botched the task of acquiring the Ginnys.

"Wonderful woman." Howie's voice was rich and deep, perfect for an auctioneer.

A customer picked up a Barbie doll, lifted its dress, and peeked under. What was the fascination with Barbie's bottom? Nearly every potential buyer had to see what she had on underneath.

"You were at the auction at Chiggy's," he said. "I saw your name on the registration list."

"I'm sorry about Brett. I know how close you two were."

"I don't know what I'll do without him."

A customer approached with an armful of dolls, and Gretchen signaled Nina for help. Nina trotted over with Nimrod under her arm, and Gretchen turned away so she wouldn't be overheard.

"I wanted to confirm an address on the registration list," she said. "I must have written it down wrong. Brett gave me the wrong box of dolls, and I'd like to return it."

"You can give the box to me. I'll take care of it for you."

"It would be easier if I handled it myself so I can get my Ginny dolls back. I was hoping to sell them today at the show. Besides, you have more important things . . ." Gretchen let the sentence dangle awkwardly. More important things to do. Like planning a funeral and burying a friend.

"Suit yourself," Howie said. "What's the name of the guy you're looking for?"

"Duanne Wilson."

"Let me get the registration list." After a short pause, Howie came back on the phone and read off the address.

"That's exactly how I wrote it down," Gretchen said, disappointed. "The address doesn't exist."

"Then I can't help you," Howie said.

"Did he pay with a check? If he did, his address might be written on the check. I'm sure it was just copied down wrong."

Gretchen heard pages rustling on the other end of the line.

155

"You're fresh out of luck today. He paid cash."

Gretchen sighed heavily. She was at a dead end in her quest to recover the dolls.

"I have an idea," Howie said. "Maybe he lives on Forty-third Avenue, not Forty-third Street. Someone could have written down *street* instead of *avenue*."

"There's a difference?"

"You bet, little lady. A big one. Aren't you from around here?"

"I moved to Phoenix a few months ago. I'm still learning my way around," Gretchen said, perking up.

Howie chuckled. "We have numbered streets all the way down to Central Avenue, and then they turn into avenues. What you need to do is drive along Camelback Road and keep going. It's a long way."

"Thanks," Gretchen said. "You've saved my career."

She'd check it out after the show.

"Mailman," April called out. Gretchen looked up and saw Eric Huntington of the Boston Kewpie Club heading her way with a brown-wrapped package between both his beefy hands.

The package was small and square, exactly the size of the one delivered yesterday.

156

Eric stopped in front of Gretchen's table and smiled at Nina, who said, "I can already tell, you're much friendlier than yesterday's mailman."

"This package is a special Sunday delivery addressed to the doll repairer," he said.

Gretchen stared at the package. "Do I have to accept delivery?" she asked.

"Afraid so," Eric replied. "The label is very specific." He set the package down on the table and ran his finger along the address. "See. 'The Doll Repairer' in capital letters. That can only mean you, since you're the only one here."

"Mail doesn't run on Sunday," Nina pointed out, stuffing Sophie in her travel purse and slinging it across her shoulder. She plopped Nimrod down on Gretchen's lap.

"It *is* an enigma," Eric said. "Someone shoved the package under the club's table, of all places, then ran off. Rather scruffy character, probably earned a few coins to deliver it. I'm surprised someone didn't stop him at the entrance." His eyes followed Nina. "Where are you off to?"

"I need a cup of coffee," she said. "I've only had one jolt so far this morning, and I need another."

"I could use one myself," Eric said. "Mind

if I join you?"

Gretchen watched them walk away, Tutu in the lead, straining against her leash, and Sophie checking out the show's action from Nina's purse.

Nimrod settled into Gretchen's lap, and she bent down to rummage through her tools for the perfect doll hook to slice through the strong packaging tape.

She scanned the front for information. No return address. No postal stamp. Yet she recognized the same handwriting as the last package: large, loopy letters.

If this was someone's idea of a joke, the timing couldn't be worse.

"Aren't you going to open it?" April peered at her from the next table, her reading glasses perched on the end of her nose. A purple muumuu covered her enormous body like a pair of drapes.

"I don't know."

"Want me to do it?"

"No, I need some fresh air first. Can you watch my table?"

"Sure. Without Nina's dog act, business is light. I'll sit at your table. But don't stay out there too long. This heat will suck every bit of moisture out of your body."

Gretchen opened Nimrod's white poodle purse. His tiny tail beat madly in anticipation of a ride.

The tail thing.

If the dog isn't smart, the tail wags the dog.

Gretchen and Nimrod strolled through the hall, taking the show in for the first time. Yesterday's lunch break and a visit to the Boston Club's table had both followed the shortest, quickest routes.

Doll dealers nodded and greeted her, although most didn't know her well. Two months wasn't much time to establish contacts with the entire doll community. They accepted her because of her mother. Caroline was the center of everything related to dolls in Phoenix. She was an active member of the Dollers Club, a dealer in quality dolls, a successful author with the publication of *World of Dolls,* and she had a reputation as a gifted restoration artist.

"Where's your mother?"

"When's she coming back?"

"What about Ronny Beam? Wasn't that awful?"

"Come check out my Betty Ann dolls."

"Cute dog."

Gretchen made her way down each aisle, stopping to talk, offering up a willing Nimrod for infinite head pats. Finally she skirted the line of people coming into the hall and burst through a rear door used by the exhibitors, welcoming the late-morning sun reaching out to her. She closed her eyes and turned her face upward, enjoying the warmth permeating her skin after the chill of the air-conditioned hall.

Fresh air. She took it into her lungs and felt slightly better.

She found a few clumps of pampas grass at the back of the parking lot and released Nimrod for a short romp. He did the two-yard dash back and forth in front of her, ears flapping comically. Then he lay on his back waiting for a belly rub.

Gretchen shaded her eyes, crouched down to oblige him, and tried not to look toward the area where Ronny's body had been found. She didn't envy Matt. The list of suspects would be longer than the lines that kept forming to enter the doll show. She hoped he wouldn't overfocus on Steve and thereby stall the investigation.

In the distance, she spotted two forms moving toward the parking lot. The one wearing purple clothes and a red hat was pushing a shopping cart.

Gretchen grinned as she rose. She hoped Daisy's companion was the missing Nacho, and after another minute, she knew for sure.

Nimrod sat up on alert as they drew closer.

Daisy scooped him up, while Gretchen hugged Nacho. "Welcome back," she said, ignoring the ripe odor of stale alcohol and unwashed body.

"Quite a vacation I took," he said. "Ended up in Nogales."

"Trying to cross the border into Mexico?"

"I always liked foreign cultures."

Gretchen studied Daisy's friend. Scruffy beard, hair popping out in unlikely places on his cheeks, a strange growth on the side of his head that Nacho insisted was benign.

Gretchen should try to convince him to have it removed.

There you go again. Trying to change others to suit yourself. Worrying about your own comfort level, instead of accepting him for what he is.

"How's the little doggie?" Daisy had a special way with animals. Nimrod would have gladly abandoned Gretchen and followed Daisy's shopping cart forever.

"What brings you two to the doll show?" Gretchen asked.

"Looking for you," Daisy said. "I knew you'd be here. We have news you might be interested in."

"Street talk?"

Daisy nodded somberly.

The network among the homeless was a

far-reaching cache of information. The latest Internet technology had nothing on the street people's information highway.

Gretchen could only marvel at it.

"Tell me," she said.

"Word on the street is that Brett Wesley was murdered."

"Brett accidentally walked in front of a car," Gretchen said. "I was there."

Nacho shook his head. "He was pushed."

Pushed! The word from the napkin found in her purse at Garcia's.

"It was you," she said. "You put the napkin in my purse."

Nacho looked at her like she was crazy. "Didn't you hear what I said? He was pushed."

Gretchen blinked and shook her head hard. "I don't think so."

Daisy shrugged as if it didn't matter to her one way or another whether Gretchen believed them.

"Someone saw it happen," Nacho said. "We have a witness."

"Who?"

"I can't tell you that," he said. "You'll have to take my word for it and work with what I'm offering."

Nacho's word carried weight with Gretchen. He'd been right in the past. She trusted him. "Tell me more."

Nacho leaned against the shopping cart. "Brett Wesley was agitated, pacing, behind the truck. All of a sudden, he walks to the curb and looks down the street. Another guy, who's sitting in a parked truck, gets out and walks up behind him. They argue. Then the other guy practically picks Brett up and throws him into the moving traffic."

"Why didn't anyone else see this happen?" Gretchen pictured the scene, and the large crowd. A thin line of perspiration inched down the side of her face and she wiped it away. Heat? Or fear?

"Maybe the truck blocked the view," Nacho said. "Who knows?"

"What did the guy who pushed him look like?" Gretchen asked.

Daisy cooed to Nimrod, paying little attention to the conversation going on.

"Don't know. The person who saw it happen was sitting on the curb and couldn't see behind Brett. Also, he was a little . . . uh . . . incapacitated."

Great. Gretchen's "reliable" source of information was a lush.

"That doesn't help much," she said. "Could your witness remember anything significant?"

"The guy who pushed him got out of a

blue truck. That's all we have."

Gretchen looked up, thinking.

"Why are you telling me all this?" she said.

"You were at the auction."

"Along with a lot of other people. Shouldn't you go to the police?"

"Yeah right." Nacho snorted. "Very funny. I'm telling you as a friend. If you bring cops around, we'll deny it. And you'll lose my trust."

Gretchen's eyes narrowed. "Wait a minute. How do you know I was even there?"

A slight grin flickered across his face. "Talk on the street."

"Good to know I'm thought of among your friends. But . . ." She hesitated and looked at Nacho. "Something you said."

"I said talk on the street."

"No, not that. What color did you say the truck was?"

Gretchen had watched Howie Howard get into a truck after the accident.

"Blue," Nacho said. "The truck was blue."

"Yes," Gretchen said, feeling feverish. "It was, wasn't it?"

164

16

The Kewpie characters have delightful personalities, and all of them play an important part in their make-believe community. The cook, the carpenter, and the intellectual Kewpie make living in Kewpieville a wonderful experience, while the soldier with his rifle protects them from fears and tears. Other adorable collectibles include Always Wears Overshoes, Kuddle Kewpie, Blunderboo, a Kewpie dog, and Chief Wag, their fearless leader.
— From *World of Dolls* by Caroline Birch

"You can't be taking this seriously," Nina exclaimed from the next table. "They're homeless for a reason, Gretchen." She tapped a ringed hand against the side of her head.

"I thought you were working on compassion," Gretchen said. "And on accepting those who are different from you."

"Compassion I can do, not gullibility."

"I believe him." Gretchen scooped a doll from her to-do pile and began to restring it.

"You think Brett was pushed in front of a car and that Howie had something to do with it?"

Susie Hocker turned her head and stared at Nina from her Madame Alexander table across the aisle.

"Shhh," Gretchen said. "Keep your voice down. I don't know about Howie. He and Brett go way back. And what about the napkin? Someone had to have slipped it into my purse."

"Why would anyone do that?"

Gretchen looked up from the elastic in her hand. "I don't know."

"Next you'll be saying Ronny Beam's murder had something to do with Brett's death."

"The connect-the-dot lines are very short, Nina."

"They are, aren't they?" Nina moved over and sat down next to Gretchen with a thump. Sophie, the Yorkie, bounced on her lap.

"Two doll events back-to-back and a death at each of those events? Something's not right," Gretchen said.

"Was Ronny at the doll auction?"

166

"I didn't notice him there, but I hadn't met him in person yet and might not have recognized him. I didn't have that wonderful pleasure until the day after, when we went to Curves." Gretchen hooked a piece of elastic through the doll's neck. "Help me with this, Nina."

Her aunt put Sophie on the table and held the doll's head with both hands. Gretchen used the hook to work it through an elastic loop held by a stick.

"Thanks," Gretchen said, easing the head into place. "I was so nervous about bidding at my first auction that I didn't notice much going on around me. I suppose Ronny could have been there."

"Have you been practicing with your aura glasses?"

Gretchen threw Nina a quizzical look and searched quickly for a good excuse. "Have I had any time?" *Or desire?* she thought.

"Those glasses are important. They can help you solve crimes."

"I don't see how."

"You'd understand how if you were practicing."

"You have the gift without the glasses. Why don't you solve the murder — or, if Nacho is right, *murders?*"

Nina shifted uncomfortably. "I told you. I

167

can't see men's auras, and my sixth sense tells me that men are at the bottom of this. Now where are they?"

"Where are who?"

"The glasses."

Gretchen didn't want to tell Nina that the glasses were in her purse. If she did, she'd have to wear the cheap cardboard things right here at the show. "At home," she lied.

Before Nina could offer to drive over and get them, April finished an appraisal on an antique French doll and tottered over. "When are you going to open the package?"

"Never," Gretchen said. "I can't stand any more surprises. When I agreed to do this show, I thought my biggest problem would be sitting in the same spot for two days. Right now I could use a little more tedium."

April grinned widely. "The doll business is more exciting than you'd think."

That was an understatement.

Nina still had the repair hook in her hand and had begun to pick at the packaging tape with it. She worked her way through and pried open the small box. "This one is packed in newspaper," she said, removing a wad.

Some of the paper floated to the floor.

Gretchen, in spite of herself, leaned forward to peer into the box.

168

Nina removed an object wrapped in a brown paper bag and carefully opened it. "The bag's from Bert's Liquor again," she said, exposing the newest arrival, a chubby, smiling, four-inch Kewpie with a flag in his topknot standing on a small wooden platform.

"Chief Wag," Nina said, holding him up.

"Aw . . ." April said. "Isn't it cute? Butt naked except for the teeny red shoes."

"He doesn't have any markings," Gretchen said.

"Not all of the originals do. The platform is so he can stand up." April demonstrated by standing the Kewpie on the table.

"Well?" Nina picked up Sophie. "What's the verdict? Does it have a message inside?"

"Like *Message in a Bottle*," April said. "I loved that movie."

Gretchen reached out and ran her fingers over Chief Wag. She turned him over and searched every inch of his body. "No breaks," she said, surprised. "It's in perfect condition."

April noticed someone waiting at her table for an appraisal. "See you later. Let me know what happens." She lumbered away. Nimrod, napping in his poodle purse, woke when April brushed past, and he poked his head out.

Nina followed April to her table with both dogs, sliding a final glance at the Kewpie doll.

Gretchen stuffed the Kewpie back in its box, put it under the table, and turned to two new customers browsing her table. But part of her mind couldn't stop thinking about the newest arrival. Why was the package left at the Boston Kewpie Club table? Was Eric the anonymous sender?

She'd have to learn more about Eric Huntington and the Boston Kewpie Club.

Gretchen's eyes traveled to the box. The first delivery, the Blunderboo, had a message inside: "Wag, the Dog." Maybe it was preparing her for this doll's arrival.

And the note on the napkin. Was it from the same person who sent the packages? It wasn't clear whether it was the same handwriting.

Why go to all this trouble?

Gretchen could think of three possibilities:

One, the person who sent the dolls was playing some kind of strange joke on her. Considering the timing and the multiple deaths, Gretchen didn't appreciate the sender's warped sense of humor. She wasn't in the mood for a clever little scavenger hunt.

Two, both packages were sent by someone who wanted to share a secret but didn't want to reveal his or her identity.

Three, someone was trying to scare her. Her knife was found in Ronny's back; now she was receiving packages from an anonymous source.

None of these possibilities made Gretchen feel any better.

Gretchen glanced down the aisle. She felt exposed. And watched.

A few doll dealers caught her staring at them and waved. She quickly looked away.

Should she turn the dolls over to Matt? Let him figure it out?

That seemed like the most reasonable thing to do. She should also tell him about Nacho's visit and the napkin she found in her purse.

"I'm back," April announced behind her. Gretchen turned to see April's arms filled with wrapped hot dogs, a smudge of mustard on the corner of her mouth.

She handed one to Nina, and Gretchen watched her unwrap it and take an enormous, appreciative bite.

"Don't say a word, Gretchen," Nina warned, one cheek bulging like a chipmunk's loaded with nuts. "I can't stand one more minute without meat. I'm done eating grass."

"Thanks for treating," April said to Nina. "Isn't it good?"

"Better than lobster," Nina agreed.

April handed her two more hot dogs. Nina broke off pieces and fed some to the dogs. "Gretchen thinks someone's after her," she said, "because she found a napkin in her purse."

"I think someone's sending me messages, or warnings."

"Nina told me about your conversation with Nacho," April said. "Do you believe him?"

Gretchen nodded. "It substantiates the napkin. 'Pushed' didn't mean anything to me until today."

"Maybe Nacho put the napkin in your purse," April suggested.

"I don't think so," Gretchen said. "The bar area was crowded, but one of us would have seen him."

"That's true," Nina agreed.

April bent down and came up with the Kewpie. "These aren't the original shoes," she said.

"Really?" Gretchen said, taking the doll from April and examining the shoes. "You're right."

April pointed at Chief Wag's legs. "The shoes and the platform have been added."

"I wonder why? You're the doll appraiser. Why would someone change it?"

"No particular reason," April said. "People do weird things to their dolls all the time, and then wonder why their collections aren't worth anything."

Gretchen finished her hot dog and wiped her hands on a napkin. "Nina, you had coffee with Eric Huntington. Tell me about him."

"Eric doesn't know much about the doll business," Nina said. "He's here mainly to watch after his mother."

"Eric said he knew my mother," Gretchen said. "Did she ever mention him?"

Nina shrugged. "Caroline knows everyone."

Gretchen picked up Chief Wag. Not a chip or crack anywhere on his body. So why send him addressed to the doll repairer? She rummaged through her toolbox and picked out a solvent. She sprayed a tiny amount on the platform around the Kewpie's feet. Then she sprayed some along the top of his shoes.

"What are you doing?" April asked.

"An experiment."

"He asked me out," Nina said.

Gretchen glanced up quickly and saw Nina blush. She couldn't believe it. She'd never in her life seen Nina blush. "Eric did? He asked you out?"

Nina nodded. "Monday. I'm showing him around town."

"You go, girl," April said.

Gretchen worked more solvent into the glue and felt it soften slightly.

"What's that man over there doing?" Nina said.

Gretchen looked up and saw the photographer from the auction approaching her table. The Leica camera hung from his neck, and he looked paler and shabbier than last time she'd seen him, if that was even possible. Recalling his name, she greeted him. "Peter Finch."

"I remember you, too," Finch said, removing the lens cap from the camera. "You were at the auction. Mind if I take a few pictures?" He waved a hand at her dolls.

"You can't let him take pictures," April said, loud enough for him to hear. "I know this guy. He sells pictures of dolls on the Internet." She turned to the photographer. "Get your own dolls."

"Okay, okay. I don't want to make trouble." He looked over at Susie Hocker's Madame Alexanders.

"Don't think of going there either," April said.

Peter Finch slunk away.

"A few pictures wouldn't have hurt," Gretchen said, astonished at April's verbal attack on the photographer.

"He shouldn't be making his living from other people's dolls without offering them a percentage of the profits. There should be a law against what he does." April muttered under her breath to herself, but Gretchen caught the words, "Bottom feeder."

The platform holding the Kewpie in place came loose, and Gretchen eased it away from the doll. She tipped Chief Wag over. The bottoms of the red shoes were perfectly normal except for a little residual glue. She wiggled the Kewpie's bare legs and sprayed more glue around the shoe tops.

"What *are* you doing?" Nina said.

"Since the shoes and platform are modifications, I thought I'd see how they were applied."

"With glue," Nina said, exasperated. "Even I can tell that, and I don't know anything about doll repairing."

"I guess the real question is why someone changed the doll's appearance."

"Lowers the appraisal value, that's for sure," April said. "Any modification to the

175

original doll devalues it. Must have been owned by a beginner."

Gretchen slowly and gently removed the red shoes from the doll, exposing two chubby Kewpie feet. She laid the shoes on the table.

April picked them up, rolled them around in her plump fingers, and said, "Don't put these back on. The doll's worth a lot more without the shoes and goofy platform. I wonder why they were added in the first place."

"Because," Gretchen said, turning Chief Wag upside down, "the bottoms of his feet have been ground off."

17

Nina, drinking diet soda through a straw at that exact moment, coughed up some of it. "Down the wrong pipe," she sputtered.

April, the consummate doll appraiser, couldn't help saying, "It's not worth a nickel now."

"Please don't tell me something's hidden inside," Nina said. "This is too weird."

Gretchen, silently agreeing with her aunt, peered into the Kewpie's hollow legs. "I do see something." She drew tweezers from the toolbox and poked inside the doll.

April saw a customer approaching her table and called out, "You'll have to come back in five minutes. I'm working on something else at the moment." She leaned forward. "This is so exciting."

Gretchen extracted a small square of paper, neatly folded in quarters.

"Keep going," April said. "Don't stop now."

Gretchen unfolded the paper. "It's a name," she said. "Percy O'Connor."

"Let me see that." Nina plucked it from her fingers. "You're right. That's all it says."

"Maybe this Chief Wag belonged to Percy O'Connor," April suggested.

"It's possible." Gretchen was hesitant. "If that's so, he went to a lot of trouble to put his name inside of it."

"I've never heard of collectors defacing their own dolls to put their names inside," April said. "It isn't done."

"Like cattle branding," Nina said.

"But he destroyed the doll's value," April insisted.

"Has anyone heard of Percy O'Connor?" Gretchen asked.

Nina and April shook their heads.

"What's going on over there?" Susie Hocker called from across the aisle.

"We're wondering if you know anyone by the name of Percy O'Connor?" April called back.

"Never heard of him. Is he giving a presentation or something?"

"Something like that," April said to her, heading back to her table. "I better get back to work. If you find out who he is, holler over."

"Find out who who is?" Eric Huntington

178

said, leaning over the table and startling Gretchen and Nina.

"Percy O'Connor," Nina said.

Gretchen shoved the red shoes back onto the Kewpie's chunky legs, hoping Eric hadn't noticed the missing feet at the very bottom of the doll.

"He was a Boston doll collector," Eric said.

"Was?" Gretchen asked.

"He's dead."

"This must have been his doll." Nina held up the Kewpie. "His name was inside."

It was too late to give her aunt a warning signal. Nina's cosmic antenna had malfunctioned. Again.

Eric frowned. "It's possible that the doll belonged to him. He collected Kewpie dolls. But what do you mean, his name was inside?"

Gretchen watched Eric's face. If he had packaged the doll and sent it to her, he was an impressive actor. No sign of recognition flickered in his eyes.

Nina held up the piece of paper with Percy's name scrawled across it.

Eric stared at it. "A Kewpie doll belonging to Percy O'Connor was inside the package I handed to you?" He was either genuinely surprised or an accomplished fraud.

179

"What makes you think this doll was in the package you delivered?" Gretchen asked. "We didn't tell you that."

Eric pointed to the floor. "Brown bag, newspaper, and the same packaging. I simply surmised that you had recently opened it. The Kewpie would have fit conveniently inside the box. Quite a sleuth, I must admit."

"Very astute of you, Sherlock," Nina said, a silly smile on her face. "Do tell us about Mr. O'Connor."

"Percy O'Connor pretended he was of the Old Guard from the wealthiest end of Boston. Old, old blood, he said, but of course, the actual blue bloods of Boston knew he wasn't, and he never quite fit in. His father came into some money during the war, I believe, an inheritance or something."

"Nouveau riche," Nina said.

"Exactly." Eric nodded solemnly. "Aside from quite an impressive collection of dolls, he was also an avid historian. Fascinated with World War Two. Talked about it ad nauseam."

"I assume," Gretchen said, "he was a member of the Kewpie Club?"

"Yes, but not an active member. He rarely attended meetings."

"When did he pass away?" Gretchen took the piece of paper from Nina and glanced at the name.

"Just three weeks ago. But he didn't exactly pass on. Percy was well into his seventies, yet he had boundless energy, worked out at the men's club, swam, jogged. Incredible form really, for his age. Remarkably healthy, we all said down at the club."

Eric's weak chin and flabby jowls contradicted his own claim to physical fitness.

"So what happened to him?" Nina asked, a starry look on her face.

Gretchen knew what Eric was about to say. Nina would attribute this knowledge to Gretchen's alleged psychic abilities. But it was deduction, really. No one from the doll community seemed to be dying of natural causes lately. Why start now?

"The poor boy was shot dead. Right in his home, in the library."

Nina, the supposed psychic, hadn't seen it coming. She gasped and covered her mouth with a jeweled hand. "How awful."

"Two shots to the head, it was," Eric said, immersed in the drama and savoring Nina's reaction. He held up his forefinger and thumb in the classic pistol pose and said, "Bang, bang."

Nina gave a theatric squeal, setting off the

dogs. All three started barking madly, emitting piercing, shrill yaps. The story of Percy O'Connor's untimely demise was temporarily interrupted while Nina quieted the dogs.

"Doggie cookies," Nina shouted over the yipping, rapidly distributing a round of biscuits. "I have to take them outside for a little walk," Nina said. "Would you like to join me, Eric?"

"My pleasure," he said.

"Wait a minute." Gretchen put up both hands to stop them. "What happened? What's the rest of the story? Did they catch the killer?"

"Alas," Eric said. "The police had very little to go on. Nothing was stolen, so they ruled out robbery. No one seemed to have a personal vendetta against Percy. Nothing that the police could sink their teeth into, so to speak. All very strange."

Nina had already thrown a purse over each shoulder, each containing an energetic ball of fur, and Tutu, the self-absorbed schnoodle, pulled impatiently on her pink leash. "Ready," Nina said to Eric.

"The only thing out of place," Eric continued, "I mean when the police arrived, was . . . well, besides the poor boy slumped over his rosewood desk . . . was a Kewpie doll shattered on the floor."

"Really?" Gretchen felt queasy. "What kind of Kewpie?"

"If I recall correctly, it was a Blunderboo," Eric said, taking Tutu's leash from Nina and guiding her down the aisle.

"What's with all the Blunderboos?" April said, after Gretchen filled her in. Business was light at the moment, allowing the dealers time to visit with each other.

"I think someone's trying to scare me by sending Kewpies to me." Gretchen nervously rearranged the dolls on the table to fill gaps where some had been selected for purchase. "What if I'm next?"

"Next?" April exclaimed, frowning over the top of her reading glasses. "Next to what? Die? Ridiculous. You aren't next."

"Three deaths, April. Count them." Gretchen held up her hands and ticked off the fingers on her left hand. "Brett, Ronny, and this Percy O'Connor."

"Yeah, so?"

"I accidentally inherit a box of Kewpie reproductions. Never mind that they are awful copies. Focus on the fact that there's a Blunderboo in the box. Then Ronny's killed, and a Blunderboo is delivered to me with a message inside."

"The Blunderboo could have come before Ronny was murdered."

Gretchen nodded. "Next, we learn that this doll collector in Boston was murdered, and what's found at the scene?" Gretchen clapped her hands together. "A Blunderboo Kewpie doll."

"A coincidence?" April said weakly. Even she was no longer convinced.

"Afraid not."

"But why you?"

"I keep asking myself the same question."

"Maybe you saw something at the auction, but you don't know that you saw it, but the murderer knows you know and has to silence you before you realize that you know what you know and expose the killer." April stopped for breath.

Gretchen decided not to ask April to repeat her theory. "Why grind off the bottom of Chief Wag's feet?" she said.

"You're being tested? To see how smart you are?"

"Whoever sent it knew I wouldn't be fooled," Gretchen said. "I think I'm being watched. It's a spooky feeling."

April opened a large bag of potato chips and crunched on one. Stress seemed to increase the woman's hunger. "I'll bet it is. Where's Nina?"

"She's walking the dogs with Eric."

Walking the dogs reminded Gretchen of the "Wag, the Dog" note hidden inside the Blunderboo. "Maybe the first message had two meanings."

"You sure do switch topics quickly," April said. "I can hardly keep up. What message?"

"Wag, the Dog."

"Two meanings? Like a double entendre?"

Gretchen thought about it. "Sort of. The sender wanted to alert me to Chief Wag's appearance so I would discover the piece of paper."

"How could the sender know you would crack open the doll head?"

Gretchen shrugged. "If someone sends a doll for repair, I usually check it over very closely. I guess it's possible that I would have opened it regardless and attempted a better repair."

"That's a stretch," April said.

"But 'Wag, the Dog' still could have meaning. Like in the movie. Maybe I have to stay smarter than my tail." A thought occurred to Gretchen. "I had a tail yesterday."

"Very funny," April said. "Ha, ha. Was it long and hairy or short and bushy?"

Gretchen smoothed a Ginny doll's dress. "I mean someone followed me. A woman in a black Jetta. When I stopped, she pulled up next to me and told me that I would pay, then she sped off."

April stopped munching. "That's scary. Maybe you should tell Matt and have him assign a bodyguard. Maybe, if you're lucky, he'll volunteer to personally protect you. That is, if he isn't too busy guarding Steve."

"I wonder how Steve's doing." Gretchen had forgotten all about him.

"Maybe he and Matt are bonding."

"This isn't funny, April."

"Have to laugh," she said. "Or you'd cry."

Gretchen watched her return to her table. A steady stream of people continued to stop and look at Gretchen's Ginny dolls and Barbies, but business had been better the day before. Not many were buying today.

Gretchen's cell phone rang. The caller ID displayed her mother's mobile number.

"Hey," Gretchen said.

"Hey, yourself. How's business?"

"Great," Gretchen said, forcing a light tone that she didn't feel. She wasn't about to alarm her mother with disturbing news. "I'm almost sold out of Ginnys, and the repair basket is full. I can't seem to work through it."

Caroline laughed. "Take them home, and I'll help you when I get back. Things are going well here, too. This was a whirlwind tour. I'm taking the day off from working to visit friends. Is Daisy still staying at the house?"

"She came around but vanished like she always does."

"Daisy's good for Nina. My sister needs to be reminded of social issues occasionally. It keeps her grounded on earth."

"When are you coming back?"

"I'd like to stay a few extra days. I want to drive along the coast and visit bookstores."

"No problem," Gretchen said. "By the way, the Boston Kewpie Doll Club is in town."

"Stuffed shirts, aren't they?"

"Eric Huntington likes Nina."

"Who's he?"

"The president of the club's son. Helen's son. Remember him?"

There was a pause on the other end of the line. "Can't say as I do."

"He says he met you."

"Maybe he did. My mind is going in my old age. Say hi to Nina. She could use some male attention for a change."

Gretchen closed the phone and glanced down the aisle, her eyes scanning the crowd. She had that feeling of being watched again but didn't see anything, or anyone, out of place.

18

It isn't a fair fight from the very first punch, but Albert Thoreau learned long ago that life isn't fair. He has no false illusions, therefore he isn't prone to indulge in emotions such as disappointment or recrimination.

This he firmly believes.

He has no illusions.

What he *does* have are delusions.

Drinking helps him escape the worst of reality. But, as another blow lands on the side of his face, he wishes he had waited until a little later in the evening before imbibing.

Or possibly he should have started earlier and passed out someplace safe.

As he goes down, knees all rubbery and head spinning, he notices specks of blood on his shirt.

The blood is the same color as the sky, he notes, staring upward, flat on his back. The entire world has lost its vivid colors.

Monochromatic. Just like life.

"Tell me where it is, and I'll stop." His attacker's breath is warm and smells like sour milk.

Once, long ago, Albert had done a little boxing, the old two-step in the ring.

Lightweight.

"Tell me."

Albert thinks about taking a swing. No point. His assailant has an arsenal of lethal weapons.

He'll take his chances surviving a pair of fists rather than a heavy metal flashlight or police baton.

Maybe Nacho will happen along and rescue him. Then he remembers he is supposed to join Nacho at their usual meeting place.

No help coming from that quarter.

"All any of you miserable derelicts understand is pain. Have a little more."

The man leans down and delivers another blow, and Albert feels his eye swelling shut. There is only one chance to escape.

A last look up at the colorless sky, a roll to his side.

Then Albert goes limp and plays dead.

19

Gretchen had learned quite a bit from her first doll show. For one thing, she learned never to turn away without keeping a watchful eye over one shoulder.

She learned this the hard way when she turned back to the table after talking to her mother to find muscular, solid Milt Wood holding Chief Wag in his hand.

"What do you want for it?" he asked, beaming with delight.

Gretchen sighed. "Mr. Wood, you have the misfortune of admiring dolls I can't sell to you. This one also belongs to a client."

"Tell me who, and I'll approach the owner personally with an offer."

"I can't tell you at the moment."

"You are remarkably obstinate, Ms. Birch, for a woman who hopes to make it in the doll business." Milt wore a smile, but his eyes were steely.

Gretchen picked up the packaging she'd

discarded on the floor and showed him the label. "No return address," she said. "I don't know who sent it."

Milt turned the Kewpie over. "It looks like it's in perfect condition."

Gretchen took the doll from his hands and returned it to the box before he thought of removing the red shoes.

"Once I find out who it belongs to, I'll pass along your name."

"I won't take no for an answer."

Gretchen looked at him sharply. Something about the man left a bad taste in her mouth. The slightly raised tilt to his head gave her the impression he was looking down on her.

Am I psychic? Or a good judge of people?

Gretchen snorted self-derisively. *A good judge of character? Come on, I'm the one who spent seven years on Steve.*

If Steve was an example of her stellar judgment, she should give up on men while she had a little self-respect left.

She glanced at Milt, hoping he hadn't heard her snort, but he was bent over the box, still coveting the doll.

Gretchen pushed Steve from her mind with one final thought. Let him stay in jail for awhile. Serves him right.

"Did you know Percy O'Connor?" she

191

asked Milt, pulling the doll box away and closing the cover. Of course he would know the man if Percy had belonged to the same club.

Milt nodded. "What happened to him was horrible. And to that reporter yesterday. What is the world coming to? I don't envy that detective."

"Detective Albright? Have you seen him here?"

Gretchen had been keenly aware of his absence from the show today.

"Oh yes," Milt said. "Hasn't he been by your table? He's been questioning exhibitors most of the day. Haven't you seen him?"

"Why, no."

Maybe Matt was simply trying to gather more evidence against Steve. In any case, Gretchen was glad that he was being thorough. Strange though, that he hadn't stopped by.

"Have you seen Matt?" she called over to April.

"He asked me a few questions earlier," she called back.

"What kind of questions?"

"Oh, I don't know."

"You don't know what he asked you?"

A pink flush spread across April's face. "I didn't want to tell you. You've been under enough pressure."

"What? Tell me."

"He wanted me to vouch for you and Nina, to make sure you were accounted for around the time that Ronny was killed."

"And?"

"And I knew that Nina was right here with the dogs the whole time."

"I was here, too. Did you tell him that?"

April squirmed like a giant nightcrawler on the end of a fishing hook. "I couldn't, because you weren't. That was right around the time that Bonnie offered to watch your table so you could go see the Boston Kewpie Club's table. Remember? I had to be honest with him."

Gretchen turned to Milt. "I was at your table when Margaret explained the different kinds of Kewpie dolls to customers. Maybe you can tell that to Detective Albright."

"He asked me about you," Milt said. "I remember seeing you and told him that. But I think it happened after Margaret's demonstration."

Uh-oh. This isn't good.

"There you are," Nina said, as though Gretchen and the entire table had shifted to a new area and Nina had been looking everywhere for her. "Take Tutu and wrap the end of her leash around the chair leg for me, would you?"

"Good day, ladies," Milt said, moving along. "Let me know about the doll, Ms. Birch."

Gretchen made a mental note to quiz Milt later about Percy O'Connor.

Nina had Sophie and Nimrod on tiny leashes, and they ran wildly around each other until they were hopelessly tangled. Gretchen secured Tutu and went to work untangling the puppies.

"There you go," Gretchen said, handing them back to Nina.

"I ran into Bonnie on the way in," Nina said. "She said to remind you that cocktails start at five at her house. We'll finish up here at four o'clock, pack up, and head right over."

Nina hung the empty traveling purses on each side of Gretchen's chair and scooped the puppies onto her table. "I've signed up enough clients to keep me busy for two months," she announced. "This show has been great for my business."

April leaned against Gretchen's table. The entire table shifted. "It's wrecked my business," she grumbled. "I've never had so many customers, yet so little business, at the same time." April lowered her voice while Nina fussed with the dogs. "Next show I'm going back to a solo enterprise. Either that or . . ." she glanced at the dogs, "I'm changing careers."

"Nina, can you watch my table for a few minutes?" Gretchen asked, already making her way down the aisle.

"Sure," she heard Nina say.

She found Matt on the far side of the hall near the main door, leaning against Shelley Mack's doll table and writing in a notebook. He was dressed in shorts and T-shirt, sunglasses on top of his dark hair, the faint smell of Chrome cologne hanging in the air.

Gretchen took a deep breath of the scent. "You're asking people about me?" she said, trying but failing to keep the concern out of her voice.

"Routine," he replied, looking at her with those deep, piercing eyes. "Didn't your mother teach you any manners? It's polite to greet me warmly to throw me off guard before any type of verbal assault. It's a rule. Care to start over?"

"Keep my mother out of this." Gretchen crossed her arms defiantly, then thought better of the defensive pose and swung her hands to her hips. Being around Matt always threw her timing off. "You're going about the entire investigation all wrong," she said.

"Ah, so you came over to tell me how to do my job." He tucked the notebook in a back pocket and pushed off from the table.

Shelley Mack leaned across her doll table, squeezing her arms together to expose as much cleavage as possible. "Anything else I can do to help, Detective Albright?" She was obviously even more affected by the cologne than Gretchen. Shelley batted goo-enhanced eyelashes.

"Thanks, Shelley. That pretty much wraps it up. You've been a big help."

"I'll be right here if you need me."

Matt stepped away from the doll table, and Gretchen followed.

"Let's go outside," he said. "I can't breathe in here."

"Don't you want to hear my alibi?" she said when they found a slice of shade under a palm tree.

"Do you feel you need one?"

"I think I do, since you've been asking everyone else about it."

"Shoot."

"Shoot?"

"Tell me where you were when Ronny Beam was killed."

Gretchen told him about Bonnie's offer to watch her table and about the Boston group discussing Blunderboos. "Milt remembered that I was there, and your mother can tell you that she wanted me to see the club's Kewpies."

"I still see a gap in time where you aren't accounted for," Matt said. "But I don't think it matters. I think we have our man."

"Steve? You don't still think he did it?"

"He argued with the deceased shortly before the murder. His fingerprints are on the knife, and several witnesses saw him out in the parking lot before Ronny was killed. How much more evidence would you like?"

"But what about the real murder weapon?"

"The tire iron didn't have any prints on it."

"Steve isn't capable of murder."

"Everyone has the potential."

Brett, Percy O'Connor, and Ronny Beam were connected through a trail of Kewpie dolls. So was she, for that matter. The messages inside the Kewpies made her fear she was involved more deeply than she wanted to be.

Should she tell him everything she knew?

If she told him about the deliveries, he might think she was making a clumsy effort to shift suspicion away from Steve. Would he look more closely at her?

Matt Albright was too full of himself to

see the truth. Arrogant, self-absorbed, stub-born . . . She searched for more adjectives to describe him. Why did she even think for one moment that she could confide in him?

The detective standing in front of her with the ridiculous smirk would probably scoff at her concerns and dismiss them out of hand as sheer fantasy.

"Has Steve requested legal representation yet?" Gretchen asked instead.

"I offered, he refuses. Says he's waiting for you. That's one of the reasons I circled your name in big bold red pen. Any idea what he's talking about?"

"None," Gretchen said. Was Steve trying to protect her? How chivalrous of him to come through for her. Finally. But too late. "Can I see him?"

"No. He's still in a holding cell. Until he's charged, he can't have any visitors."

"How long can you hold him without charging him?"

"Not much longer."

His eyes locked onto hers. Gretchen squirmed under his gaze. What was it about this man? He induced too many conflicting emotions.

"I wouldn't have pegged him as your type," Matt said. "I thought you'd go for someone . . . I don't know . . . more sensitive, more artistic."

"Really?"

"Anyway, I'm sorry it happened to you. Your boyfriend's in a heap of trouble."

"I don't know how many times I have to say this . . ." Gretchen didn't finish the sentence. Why bother?

She stomped back to her table, plopped into her chair, and selected a five-piece toddler doll from the repair pile.

Before Gretchen could immerse herself in repair work and temporarily forget all the peripheral intrigue going on, Nina, canines in tow, walked the few steps from April's table. "I kept an eye on your table, but nobody wanted to buy anything. The place is starting to clear out. What's wrong? You're so pale."

"Steve's still in jail. I guess witnesses saw him in the parking lot." She leaned back in the chair. "Matt must think I know what happened or that I'm an accomplice of some sort."

"Your knife and Steve's fingerprints? It doesn't look good." Nina bent down to stroke the three dogs on the floor around her feet. Tutu put her jealous little muzzle under Nina's hand every time Nina gave Nimrod or Sophie attention. "I bet that's exactly what he thinks."

Nina straightened, and her face turned the color of Elmer's glue. At first Gretchen thought it was because of what she'd just said, but Nina was staring at Gretchen's arm. "Don't move," Nina said, jerking her hand out in front of her like a cop stopping traffic. "I don't want to panic you, but sit very, very still."

April, coming up behind her, looked at Gretchen and screamed.

"Quiet," Nina commanded.

Gretchen did what Nina asked. "What?" she said, barely breathing.

April had her hand at her mouth.

Nina grabbed a Barbie doll. "An insect crawled out of Nimrod's purse. It's on your arm. Maybe I can flick it off."

"That's not an insect," April squealed. "It's a scorpion."

"Oh, no." Gretchen stopped breathing. She felt something on her bare left shoulder.

Nina rounded on the poisonous insect. It was apparent that she planned to attack from the back.

Ready to faint, Gretchen reviewed the symptoms of a scorpion sting: excruciating pain, severe swelling. She could live through pain and swelling. *Don't panic,* she warned herself.

Also possible: frothing at the mouth, difficulty breathing, convulsions. Though death from a scorpion sting was rare, she wasn't fond of the convulsion thing. Or of gasping desperately for air.

She knew all the trivial details associated with the insect world because the most terrifying thing that could ever cross her path was any sort of bug. Centipedes, ticks, spiders, crickets, the list was infinite. "I hate bugs," she whispered without moving her lips, working to stay in control. "Get it off."

"Hold still," Nina warned. "They have sense organs on their undersides. Once it senses you, you're a goner."

"That must make her feel real good," April said, talking through the fingers spread across her mouth. "I can't watch." She turned away. "Let me know when it's over."

Gretchen felt it crawl down her arm, and she risked a peek, which didn't help her mental state.

The yellowish insect stared at her through its buggy, blinkless eyes. Lobster-type pinchers and a hooked tail curled across the top of its inch-long body. It was so close she could see the venomous stinger on the tip of its raised tail.

"Help," she croaked.

"As long as the tail is curved on its back like that, you're okay," Nina said from behind her.

"What are you waiting for?" April said. "Get it off her."

"I . . . I . . ."

"You can't do it, can you?" April turned to the main aisle and screamed, "Someone help!"

Gretchen felt dangerously light-headed.

"Detective Albright," she heard Nina say. "Quick. Shoot it with your gun."

Gretchen felt a gentle breeze across her arm. She blinked, and the insect was gone.

She saw a sandaled, male foot descend on the invader. The foot zoomed in, the floor rose, and she felt herself falling sideways.

The world went blissfully black.

20

"What a hunk," April exclaimed, wrapping her dimpled arms across her chest. "I'd plant a scorpion on myself if I thought Detective Albright would save me."

"It was a nightmare," Gretchen said from her chair, her voice still shaky. "I can't believe I fainted."

Thanks to April's screams, the Phoenix Dollers show drew to a dramatic close, the grand finale taking place at Gretchen's table with most of the remaining shoppers and dealers looking on.

For the first time in two days, Nina and her traveling dog circus hadn't held center stage.

Gretchen would have gladly given back that dubious honor.

"You would have clunked your head on the floor if Matt's reflexes hadn't been sharp," Nina said.

"Where were you when I passed out?"

"I was paralyzed," Nina said. "Every muscle in my body stopped functioning. I don't understand it. I started out intent on saving you, then when I got close enough to stare the beady thing in the eye, I froze. I'm so sorry." Nina bent down and gave her a heartfelt hug. "It was a good thing Matt heard April screaming."

"I sure did bring the house down," April added.

Once Gretchen felt strong enough, April and Nina helped her pack up the remaining Ginny and Barbie dolls and carry them to her Toyota Echo. Gretchen opened the trunk and noticed that the parking lot was almost empty.

"Someone must have put it in Nimrod's purse," Gretchen said. "First the napkin, now a scorpion."

"You already said that, repeatedly." Nina leaned against the car. "Matt Albright didn't agree with you. He said you needed time to recover, that the shock must have affected your reasoning."

"My question is, was the scorpion meant for me or for Nimrod?" Gretchen hugged the tiny puppy. She would have survived the sting, but what effect would the venom have on a three-pound poodle?

What kind of monster would harm Nimrod?

"We can't be sure the scorpion didn't crawl in on its own," Nina said.

"You had the purse when you and Eric went outside. Did you place it on the ground?"

"No. I let both puppies run around in the back parking lot, then I used their leashes. I had both purses on my shoulder the whole time."

"Nimrod and Sophie weren't in their purses at all?" Gretchen asked.

Nina shook her head.

"Then how did it get inside? Scorpions don't fly."

"There has to be another explanation," April said. "People don't carry scorpions around with them."

Gretchen ignored April's protests. "Could someone have put the scorpion inside without your noticing?"

"I suppose so," Nina said. "There was quite a crowd hanging out around the entrance. I didn't pay much attention."

Gretchen didn't ask whether Eric might have had the opportunity. The look on Nina's face suggested she had feelings for him, and Gretchen didn't want to burst that romantic bubble unless she had to. Besides, she knew the answer. Of course he had the opportunity. More opportunity than anyone else.

"If what you think is true," April said, "and someone did this intentionally, then the scorpion wasn't meant for you, Gretchen. Whoever put it in the purse couldn't know that Nina wouldn't put Nimrod back in the purse. It was lucky for him that Nina led him back on his leash. Otherwise, he would have been stung."

Gretchen shuddered at the thought. "Then the scorpion *was* intended as a murder weapon," she said. "Someone tried to kill Nimrod."

The stakes had been raised. Someone wanted to harm Gretchen's dog, and that demanded her immediate attention. The tiny poodle and her three-legged cat were dependent on her for their care and support, and she didn't intend to let them down.

Gretchen felt Nimrod cuddle closer against her. He rested his chin on her folded arm.

"Nobody," she said to Nina and April, "messes with my dog."

"What's this?" Nina gestured at the box of

worthless Kewpies stowed in Gretchen's trunk.

"That's the box I've been trying to exchange with Duanne Wilson. I have to assume that the winning bidder of these copies has the Ginny dolls that I bought at the auction."

Gretchen opened the back door, and Nimrod wiggled out of her arms and into the car. She shut the door and returned to the trunk, pulling the box toward her and opening the top flaps. "The dogs broke one of the reproductions, and I glued it back together, but I didn't have time to go through the box thoroughly. Now I think we need to take a better look at these, since Kewpie dolls keep popping up in unlikely places."

April peeked in. "I can give you a free appraisal on the spot. It's all garbage. Junk, junk, junk. Chiggy was *really* bad at making dolls." She shook her head in disgust while she pawed through the dolls.

"Ah, look here," she said. "The real thing. But still worthless."

April held up a Blunderboo Kewpie.

Gretchen noted a crack along the side of its face and a wedge of bisque missing. "Why so many Blunderboos?"

April peered through the hole in the

bisque to the interior of the doll. "Nothing there," she said. "Hollow. See." She handed it to Gretchen.

"You're right." Gretchen wasn't disappointed yet. She still had hopes that the box of dolls would reveal something important.

"Rats," Nina said. "I was hoping to find jewelry. Wouldn't that be something, if we stumbled on a smuggling ring?"

"With our luck, it would be a drug ring," Gretchen said.

"Why did she have one real Kewpie with the ones she made?" Nina asked.

"Probably used it as a guide for her reproductions," April said.

"Like a pattern? I get it."

"I'm cracking the dolls open," Gretchen announced.

"All of them?" Nina said.

"What's a little more damage?" April agreed, breaking into a smile. "I have a hammer in my car." She lumbered off, although having a mission seemed to add a noticable bounce to the lumber. April watched demolition derbies on television. This would be right up her speedway lane.

"What about this Duanne person?" Nina asked. "Won't he be mad if you break his dolls?"

"I made every effort to return them to

him," Gretchen said, holding up a Kewpie reproduction with a grimace at the poor workmanship. "It's not my fault that he didn't leave his correct address."

Bonnie's car pulled up, and the window on the driver's side slid down. "My house," she said. "Don't forget. One hour." The glowing sun cast its light across her red wig, making it appear harsh and brassy.

"We'll be there," Nina called.

"Okeydokey. Tootles." Bonnie drove away as April returned with a hammer and a folded newspaper.

"Let me," April said, picking up a doll and laying it on the asphalt on top of a sheet of the newspaper. Gretchen transferred the box to the ground, and she and Nina crouched beside April.

"Not that one," Gretchen said, pointing to the doll in April's hand. "That's the one I fixed at home after the animals knocked it from the bookcase. I know there's nothing inside it."

April laid it aside and began cracking open one Kewpie doll after another. Gretchen and Nina sorted through the broken pieces, looking for clues. Soon the box was empty. Broken shards of clay covered the newspaper.

"Nada," Nina said.

April picked up the doll that Gretchen had repaired and with one solid stroke, broke it open.

"Zilch," Nina, the commentator, said.

"I told you it wasn't necessary to break it," Gretchen said to April. "I fixed that one myself."

"Leaving no earth unturned," April said. "Get it? Earth and clay?"

"That's stone, April," Gretchen said. "No stone unturned."

Gretchen unlocked the front door of her mother's house with Nimrod swinging from her shoulder and one hand full of mail. She dropped the mail on the kitchen table, released the poodle from his traveling bag, and looked around for Wobbles. The episode with the scorpion had her on edge. To her relief, the cat stalked into the room. Nimrod spotted him and ran in circles around the totally indifferent feline.

She flipped through the mail. The last piece was addressed to her. An invitation to a private memorial service for Brett Wesley, Tuesday night at eight.

Gretchen opened cans of food and played referee while her pets ate. Nimrod, true to form, bolted his dinner then tried to take Wobbles's share. Gretchen distracted the puppy with a small rubber ball in a game of catch.

She considered carrying in the boxes from the trunk, but it really could wait until morning. She'd done enough work for the day.

Through the workshop window facing Camelback Mountain, Gretchen saw dusk approaching. The orange glow of the setting sun glistened in ribbons over the red clay, highlighting the desert shrubs and solitary cacti. Climbers still traversed the mountain, but most were making their way down. From this distance they looked like industrious ants.

Nimrod curled up on his bed in the corner and closed his eyes. Gretchen didn't want to break the news to him yet, but he wasn't through for the day. He had a cocktail reception to attend.

No way was she going to let him out of her sight again.

And what about Wobbles? Would the same evil-minded person try to harm him?

Gretchen grinned. Wobbles was a street fighter. He'd left his signature scratches on many overconfident canines. Anyone who messed with Wobbles ended up looking like shredded paper.

Besides, no one would actually break into

her home, let alone harm Wobbles, right?

No one had any reason to.

Tomorrow, she would throw out the box of crushed Kewpie dolls.

If she ever managed to track Duanne Wilson down, she'd have to pay him for the broken dolls. That is, assuming he returned her box of Ginny dolls. Gretchen really didn't think she'd ever see them again.

But she couldn't help making another attempt to find Duanne, even though she knew she'd be noticeably late to Bonnie's party.

On her way out again, Gretchen bought a city map at the first gas station she passed and tried to make sense of it. After studying it for several minutes without finding Forty-third Avenue or her present location, she attempted to fold it. Giving up, she threw it in the backseat.

Nimrod watched from the passenger seat with tilted head while she dug through her purse for the original slip of paper she'd used to write down Duanne's address.

The inside of the purse was a disaster. She'd have to clean it out or she'd have to carry two purses — one for her and one for Nimrod.

Finding the address, she set out with Howie's directions fresh in her mind.

When she turned onto Camelback Road, Gretchen thought she spotted her tail again. So she veered down a side street at the last second without using her turn signal, and looking in her rearview mirror she saw the black car turn down the same street behind her, almost clipping another car. Horns blared and brakes squealed, and Gretchen took a hard right at the next crossing and sped away into the darkening night.

The drive seemed to take forever. She watched through her rearview mirror for the other car. The street numbers descended until she crossed Central Avenue, then the numbers began to ascend again as avenues.

This wasn't so hard. And she didn't even need the map.

She turned onto Forty-third Avenue and parked along the street to get her bearings. She found an address on a carpet store across the street. Her address was in the next block up. She drove a little farther, parked, and stuffed Nimrod into her already crammed purse.

Walking along, Gretchen noted that the block was mostly commercial buildings. In fact, they all were.

Not one single family residence. No apartment buildings. No condos.

But this time, at least the address she had

written down existed.

Gretchen entered a tattoo shop, pretty sure she wouldn't find Duanne Wilson inside.

Her developing psychic intuition was correct.

They'd never heard of him.

21

The party was picking up speed when Gretchen arrived with Nimrod in tow. He joined his own party of miniature dogs in the back entryway. A baby gate kept the canine revelers from joining the human throng.

People from all aspects of the doll business jammed the open, rounded rooms of Bonnie's modest Arizona-style home.

The club president's dolls had their very own separate display room off the entryway — in consideration of her son's severe phobia, Gretchen assumed. Pine curio cabinets housed Bonnie's collection of fragile and expensive Kewpie dolls. Cloth and hard plastic Kewpies adorned the chairs and tables, and Kewpie plates and cups lined ledges along the walls.

Nina met Gretchen at the doggie gate with Sophie, her current Yorkie trainee. "Sophie's family wants her socialized, so I'm keeping her a few extra days. This certainly is the place to acclimate her to her own kind."

"Are all these dogs past clients of yours?"

Nina, decked out in a vibrant orange pant-suit, nodded proudly, sipping a martini from a large glass hand-painted with colorful swirls. "Business has been good. Doll collectors love purse dogs. Who knew? I only started the training program last year, and I can hardly keep up with the demand." She pointed. "There's Rosebud; you remember her."

Gretchen grinned at the little Maltese.

"And Enrico." Nina pointed at a Chihuahua.

"I can't believe it," Gretchen said, remembering him as a pint-sized Tasmanian devil. "Enrico's behaving himself."

"He comes to visit me frequently for a refresher course in social skills."

Nina led the way to a cocktail bar in the corner of the crowded living room. Gretchen chose red wine and then scanned the room. She recognized most of the people in the room from the doll show. Eric Huntington waved, and Nina scurried off his way.

"So sorry to hear about your Steve," Bonnie said over her left shoulder.

"I thought that was confidential," Gretchen said.

Bonnie swept her hands across the room.

Gretchen followed her hand and saw Matt chatting with Howie Howard. "I overhead Matty talking on the phone. It's awful."

Just great. If Bonnie knew, the entire Valley of the Sun knew. Bonnie was like an old-fashioned bullhorn, trumpeting news more effectively than the late Ronny Beam's *Phoenix Exposed.* And about as accurate.

"I wonder how long he'll get for killing Ronny?" Bonnie said.

"He hasn't been charged, as far as I know."

"It's only a matter of time."

"*If* that happens, he'll have a trial, Bonnie. A jury has to prove him guilty."

"He did it. Matty's good at his job. He wouldn't arrest the wrong person."

Whatever happened to innocent until proven guilty? Once suspicion fell on someone, people automatically assumed the worst.

Guilty until proven innocent seemed the new American philosophy.

Gretchen felt compelled to help Steve.

Her aunt Gertie's advice resonated: *"Search Ronnie's house, and watch your back."* She should have followed her aunt's direction.

Tomorrow, at the first light of day, she would start her quest for the real killer. Now that the doll show was over, she could put all her effort into it.

She made her way across the room to join Howie and Matt. The auctioneer wore a ten-gallon cowboy hat that took up most of the alcove where the two men stood. It would have been easier navigating around an open umbrella.

"This is the perdy lady in person," Howie said after Matt introduced her. "Find your Ginny dolls yet?"

"Still looking."

"They'll turn up," Matt said.

"Unless you have information I don't, they're gone."

Matt grinned at her. "I'll see what I can do. You never know."

"You just keep busy trying to find Ronny's real killer," Gretchen said icily.

"That was one little jerk of a guy," Howie said. "He had me so mad, I almost hog-tied him inside my truck."

Gretchen looked at him sharply. "Was Ronny at the auction on Thursday?"

"Didn't see him on Thursday, which was lucky for him, but he showed for the estate sale on Wednesday."

"I didn't know anything about an estate sale," Gretchen said.

"We auctioned off the household goods, furniture, dishes, appliances, that sort of thing. Brett caught the little weasel inside the house going through some of Chiggy's personal things and escorted him off the property. If he'da showed up Thursday, I really *would* have tied him up and left him to squeal." Howie stopped to take a drink from the bottle of beer in his hand. "Ronny Beam had a snake tongue that a rattler would have been jealous of."

"I'm sorry to hear about Brett," Matt said. "Tough break. He seemed like a nice guy."

"The best," Howie agreed.

"Any evidence of foul play?" Gretchen threw it out there to see what developed.

"Foul play?" Howie said. "Whatever gave you an idea like that?"

Both men stared at her.

Gretchen concentrated on running her finger around the rim of the wineglass. "Speculating, is all."

"Do you really think that little lady driver planned to run over Brett?" Howie said. "I've known him for years, all the ins and outs of his life, all the people he knew, and I never saw her before the accident."

"Maybe someone pushed him," Gretchen suggested. She wanted to mention the blue truck to gauge Howie's reaction but decided against it.

Howie tipped the brim of his Stetson hat.

"No disrespect intended, but they grow large imaginations in your family. I know your mother, and you're the spittin' image."

Gretchen chose to take that as a compliment. She noted that Matt watched her closely, amusement playing on his lips.

"Detective Albright," Gretchen said, "what do you think?"

"I'm glad you asked. I want to know how someone who talks as slow and relaxed as Howie Howard can become an auctioneer."

Howie chuckled. "You have to learn to chant in rhythm and practice tongue twisters. Here's one for you. A skunk sat on a stump and thunk the stump stunk, but the stump thunk the skunk stunk. Go ahead and try it."

Gretchen knew that Matt had intentionally redirected the conversation, and she appreciated his consideration. But what kind of detective would rather thunk skunks than solve crimes? She gave Matt a withering glance, which he didn't notice, and walked away.

She smiled with satisfaction when she realized that something really important had occurred: she had connected the two dead men. On Wednesday, one day before Brett died and two days before Ronny was killed, they had been together in Chiggy Kent's house.

"That was quite a bombshell you dropped on Howie," Matt said to her when their paths crossed shortly after in the kitchen. "He's grieving for Brett and doesn't need that kind of speculation right now."

"You changed the subject to protect Howie's feelings?"

"Least I could do."

"I have information that Brett was pushed in front of that car," Gretchen said.

"Tell me about your source. According to the responding officer's report, not a single eyewitness came forward. Everyone's attention was riveted on the auction."

Gretchen felt her face flush and tried to stop it from deepening. "I'd rather not."

"Are you withholding important information in an ongoing investigation?"

"Ongoing? Did you say ongoing?"

"Police business. My mouth is sealed. Now tell me who your source is."

"I promised I wouldn't tell."

Matt rolled his eyes good-naturedly. "Oh, please. How about if I promise not to tell anyone else? Would that help?"

"Only if you cross your heart."

"You believe that Brett was a murder victim." He folded his arms across his chest.

"Here's your chance to prove it."

"Even though you're going to laugh, somehow I'm involved in all this," she said. "I didn't imagine the scorpion at the doll show, and I didn't imagine the black Jetta. They were real."

"What black Jetta?"

"The one that's been following me. The first time it pulled up next to my car and a woman threatened me. She said I would pay."

"Did you get a good look at her?"

Gretchen shook her head. "It was dark, and she had privacy windows."

"You said 'the first time.' What happened the second time?"

"The same car followed me tonight."

"Are you sure?"

"Pretty sure."

For a moment Matt looked thoughtful. Then his professional mask descended, and he gave her an inscrutable look. "Tell me the rest."

So she tried. She told him what Daisy and Nacho had told her. About the man who shoved Brett into the street's traffic, about the blue truck, and about Howie leaving the auction in a blue truck.

"You know how rumors start and spread," Matt said. "Still . . ." He looked thoughtful.

222

"I need the name of the witness who allegedly saw Brett being pushed."

"I don't exactly have a name."

"What do you have exactly?"

"A description."

"Okay, let's start with that."

"The man who saw Brett pushed into the street was sitting on the curb."

"What was he doing on the curb?"

Gretchen paused. "You aren't going to think he's credible."

"Try me."

"He's homeless."

Matt smacked his head with an open palm. "Jeez, Gretchen, that isn't what I wanted to hear. You know indigents are the worst possible witnesses? First of all, he probably won't even talk to a cop. If he does talk to me, he'll change his story. And a jury . . . well, I'm sorry if you don't want to hear this, but they won't believe him. Next I suppose you're going to tell me he was drunk. Gretchen, wait, where are you going?"

Gretchen marched off and joined a group of collectors standing by the makeshift bar. She saw several women encircle the handsome detective as he tried to follow her.

Matt Albright was infuriating. Bullheaded, self-absorbed, cynical, narrow-minded.

223

She had almost shared the cryptic Kewpie doll messages with him. Imagine his response if he'd heard about "Wag, the Dog."

From now on, she'd manage just fine without his help.

22

Daisy pushes her shopping cart filled with all her earthly possessions and turns toward the viaduct where Nacho usually sleeps. It's dark now, and so she hurries.

Another fruitless day on the hot streets waiting for a talent scout to pick her out of the crowd. Even her new getup, purple flowered sundress and feathered wide-brimmed red hat, like those Red Hat Society ladies wear, hasn't attracted any Hollywood-style attention.

And the cart! She doesn't need any more weight to push around, what with her back about to break, but tell that to a man. Work, work, work, while they sit around drinking cheap whiskey and telling outrageous lies to each other, leaving her alone to guard the treasures in her cart.

She struggles along, the beams of light from the overhead streetlights casting a false sense of safety. But she isn't fooled. More than ever before, she needs Nacho's protection through the long, moonless night ahead.

Poor Albert Thoreau had been beaten up pretty badly, she's heard. Both eyes swollen and punched black, nose flat and repositioned to the left of center, lips puffed, he laid motionless in the alleyway surrounded by fellow outcasts. Only the sound of irregular and ragged breathing proved that he had not departed for hobo heaven.

"Lucky he isn't dead," they say.

And if he has told, she will be next.

Has he?

"Cops! Don't trust them," someone in the group had said, disgust apparent in the wad of spit aimed at the ground. "Here's your proof. What did Thoreau ever do to anybody?"

Daisy has her suspicions about Thoreau's current condition. She hasn't lasted this long on the wild streets of Phoenix without her innate sense of imminent danger.

The darkness of the viaduct's underbelly looms before her. Cars roar overhead even at this late hour. The shopping cart's wheels squeal as they jerk forward, and Daisy makes a mental note to find a little oil tomorrow and lubricate them.

She squints into the gloom as a form

materializes from behind one of the viaduct's steel girders, striding toward her,
arms swinging lazily, an unlit flashlight
clutched in a muscular hand.

"Good evening," Daisy says, fighting the
fear. "What brings you all the way down
here?"

23

Gretchen rose before dawn, fed Nimrod and Wobbles, donned hiking attire, and headed briskly toward Camelback Mountain. Early morning was the only time of day to climb the mountain in relative peace.

Gretchen prided herself on her ability to tackle the most strenuous trails, so she struck out boldly for the extreme tip of Summit Trail. A quarter mile in, she passed a steep northeast-facing cliff and spotted creosote and brittle bushes clinging to the side. Only a few flowers came into bloom in October, but she did see scattered desert lavenders and yellow blossoms on a sweet bush.

A Harris antelope squirrel scurried across the trail, its tail long and bushy, a white stripe along its flank. It stopped at a safe distance and scolded Gretchen as she marched upward.

Monday morning. Back to work for millions of Phoenix residents. Soon, downtown traffic would be in gridlock, and sidewalks would crowd with bustling workers clutching coffee cups and newspapers.

Except for Brett and Ronny. Ronny had written his last inflammatory news article, and Brett had worked his final auction. What secret did they stumble upon?

The groomed trail ended abruptly, and the only way up now was over rough rock. Gretchen dug into the red rocks with hands and feet, her mind on the two men. The place to start would be where their paths had converged.

How did their deaths link to a murder in Boston? Percy O'Connor's unsolved murder must be connected in some way. She thought of the resplendent group of Kewpie doll collectors visiting from Boston. Helen Huntington and her son, Eric. Margaret Turner and Milt Wood.

And Steve. Hapless pursuer of unrequited love? Or impulsive killer?

Gretchen stopped abruptly as she was about to grab a handhold on a large rock ahead of her. She heard the ominous rattle before she saw the snake. A rattlesnake. She froze and eyed the tiny newborn, its single rattle threatening her from two feet away. Gretchen knew better than to underestimate it because of its small size.

In autumn, rattlesnakes congregated in crevices. She had read about them when she first arrived in Phoenix, educating herself about all the poisonous critters in the American Southwest. Gila monsters, tarantulas, black widows, scorpions, and rattlers. She'd hoped never to encounter any of them.

The snake must be migrating along scent trails left by its mother and would winter with hundreds of others coiled for warmth in snake dens.

Find the nearest hospital within two hours if bitten, the literature read. She'd also read that most people were bitten because they tried to run away.

She slowly pulled her hand back, shut her eyes, and willed herself to remain motionless.

When she opened her eyes again, the snake had resumed its journey, slithering steadily through the rocks.

Gretchen shivered, although the October dawn was already radiating increasing heat into the Valley of the Sun. Today the temperature was expected to again pass the one hundred degree mark.

She stood tall and watched the snake vanish. What course would she choose now? To continue her trek, risking another encounter until she reached the apex, or retreat in fear and admit defeat?

Yesterday, she might have scrambled back down the mountain, vowing to hug the more civilized paths in the future.

Today, with Steve still in jail and herself inexplicably drawn into the bloody puzzle, she set her sights on the tip of the mountain and continued her ascent.

She'd passed the point of no return.

Gretchen headed for the Palm Tree Trailer Park with a fresh cup of coffee but no plan on how to break into Ronny's trailer. She brought her doll repair toolbox just in case she needed mechanical assistance, and she brought Nimrod for . . . what? Company? Certainly not for protection.

She glanced in the passenger seat at the happy, bouncing puppy. She'd asked Wobbles to join them as they prepared to leave, but he'd answered with a loud, sharp-incisored meow and narrowed eyes, signs of an unequivocal no.

Her increasing conversations with her pets was a sure sign she was losing her mind.

What if Ronny's trailer didn't produce anything helpful? What if she was arrested for breaking and entering? She didn't even have bail money now that she'd lost three hundred bucks and the profits she would have made from the dolls.

Once she decided to join the dark side, she did it up big. Breaking into Ronny's trailer today, withholding evidence in a murder investigation yesterday. She thought about the messages in the Kewpie dolls. Was that evidence? She didn't know yet.

Matt Albright could eat bat guano for all she cared. The man popped into her mind when she least expected him to. *Quit thinking about him.* The very last thing she wanted to do was get involved with a married cop.

She whizzed down Twenty-fourth Street, watching for unwelcome company in her rearview mirror. The encounter with the rattlesnake had frightened her. *Live large,* she thought. *Life could end sooner than you think.*

The sign facing the street read The Palm Tree Mobile Home Community and announced several homes for sale in the "Exclusive Community That Draws a Rich Tapestry of Backgrounds."

Whatever that meant.

Gretchen pulled in, proud of herself for finding the address without having to ask for directions. She passed by several mobile homes and found the address she had looked up in the Phoenix telephone directory the night before. No private, unlisted number for a man who welcomed gossipy snitches and colorful fabricators into his singular life.

She parked next to his carport and got out. "Nimrod, stay," she said. No sense incriminating both of them.

Would a credit card inserted next to the door lock work? She'd seen that on television. She should have updated her sleuth skills to include the latest technological advances. Oh well, something from her doll repair kit would have to do.

A man in a sleeveless undershirt opened the door of the mobile home next door. In the distant past, the undershirt had been white, although it had probably never quite fit him. An enormous potbelly spilled out from the bottom of it. "What you doin' over there?" he shouted.

This wasn't the best time to flash her toolbox and master her lock-picking skills. Rule number one for future reference: attempt break-ins only after dark.

"You deaf or sometin?" His screen door slammed behind him. "I said, what you doing?"

Rule number two. Learn to lie well.

"I'm . . . uh . . . Ronny's girlfriend. I want

to pick up some of my things."

"Like what?" By now he'd shot off his one-step porch and aimed his belly toward her with the precision of a steamroller. His personal appearance didn't improve up close and personal. Were those his boxer shorts?

"Uh . . . personal effects," she stammered. "I can come back later if this isn't a good time."

He studied her openly with bloodshot eyes. "You know Ronny kicked the can?"

Gretchen nodded and managed to tear up. "I heard."

"Didn't know Ronny had a girlfriend. How about that. Keepin' you under wraps so the rest of us can't get a chance." He stroked his exposed midsection. "How about that?"

Was it something in the trailer park's drinking water that produced the Neanderthal effect in its male residents?

"I'll come back later." Gretchen stepped backward toward the Echo, keeping a sharp eye on him in case he tried to grab her hair and drag her off.

He waved a hand. "No, no, help yourself. Nothing left to steal, I suspect. The cops woulda taken anything worth sometin'. You got a key?"

Gretchen shook her head. "He never gave me one."

The beady red eyes drilled into Gretchen's cleavage, then drifted up to meet her eyes. He grinned. "Must be your lucky day, cuz I got one." He held up a key chain brimming with keys. "I'm manager of this exclusive community."

That worked well, Gretchen thought while he fiddled with the door.

The hardest part of her charade was convincing him that she didn't need his help.

"Take your time," he said, eventually giving up. "I'm sure you must be all broke up about losing your boyfriend. If you need a shoulder to cry on, I'm available."

"You'll be the first one I think of," Gretchen said. How lucky could she get? Meeting one of Phoenix's most eligible bachelors.

The inside of Ronny's trailer smelled like a mélange of dirty socks and rotting garbage. Considering that only forty-eight hours had elapsed since Ronny's death, Gretchen had to assume that the offensive odors weren't the consequence of his absence but native to his habitat.

Feature articles from *Phoenix Exposed* had been ripped from the newspaper and taped on kitchen cabinets and the refrigerator, like displays of children's artwork. The infamous article denouncing Nina as the leader of the alien dog world hung from a cabinet door directly in front of Gretchen.

She ripped it down, crumpled it into a ball, and tossed it into a heap of folded paper bags in the corner. Ronny could have opened his own grocery store with the number of bags he collected.

The bathroom seemed the simplest place to start and the least likely to produce any worthwhile information. Hemorrhoid treatment, hair pomade, and a messy assortment of uncapped toothpastes and shampoo bottles.

As Nina would say, "Zilch."

Gretchen had started on the living room when her cell phone rang.

"Hey," Nina said on the other end. "What's your plan for today?"

Gretchen picked up a pile of porno magazines from a marred coffee table and dropped them on the floor in disgust. "You're up early."

"I have coffee in my hand and the world at my fingertips. I wanted to catch you before you started working away in your little beehive. Want to have lunch and discuss today's plans?"

"I don't know. I'm pretty busy right now,"

Gretchen said, looking at unidentifiable goo on Ronny's coffee table and wishing she'd brought latex gloves. Rule number three: wear gloves, for a variety of reasons. Gloves protect against the mismanagement of fingerprints as well as against diseases.

"What are you doing today? Restringing all those dolls from the show?"

"That, and a few other things."

"Well, call me if you break free."

Gretchen wished to break free all right, from this sorry excuse for human existence. The stench alone made her want to burst from the trailer and fill her lungs with fresh air. Instead, she methodically finished searching the living room and tiny kitchen.

Next, the bedroom.

Gretchen was beginning to doubt Aunt Gertie's ability to make sound investigative decisions. This was fast becoming a really bad idea. Cavemen lurking outside and germ warfare inside.

The bedroom was indescribably dirty and the source of most of the odor. Ronny, it appeared, liked to eat in bed and use the floor as his landfill for leftovers.

She tiptoed through the unidentifiable waste to the closet and flipped the light switch next to it.

Aha. Ronny's office. File boxes were

stacked on the floor, three deep. Papers were strewn across the tops of the boxes, and Gretchen stared at the mess with dismay. No way could she wade through that much paper in the time she had.

What would her aunt Gertie do?

She keyed in Gertie's home number and crossed her fingers. *Please be home.*

Gertie answered on the third ring.

"Good job," Gertie said when she heard about the closet. "Keep this up, and there's a job waiting for you here in the beautiful Upper Peninsula. I could use a smart investigator like you."

Snow nine months of the year, summer bugs the size of radishes, and wild bears in the backyard. No thanks. That was one job Gretchen didn't intend on applying for.

"You should come and visit me sometime," Gretchen said, remembering her manners.

"Not in this lifetime, Honey. Too hot and too many weird critters. Scorpions, black widows." Aunt Gertie clicked her tongue. "Don't think so."

"Back to my problem," Gretchen said, encouraged to refocus when she looked out the grimy bedroom window and saw the friendly neighbor walk past, not two feet from the side of Ronny's trailer.

"Yes, well, you're looking at his filing system. That's where stuff goes when he's through working on it. Find his current files."

"But where? This place is a dump."

"You just have no experience with men, especially eccentric, single men."

"You got that right. But what does that have to do with finding files?"

"His current files are in one of three places. Either under the bed . . ."

Gretchen grimaced. Anything and everything could be under Ronny's bed.

". . . on top of the refrigerator, or in the bathroom."

"I already checked the bathroom."

"Most men like something to read while they're going about their morning business. The bathroom would have been my best guess. Since you started there, you and I must be nuts right off the same tree."

Aunt Gertie probably had that nut thing right.

Gretchen thanked her and hung up as the community manager walked back again the way he'd come, his eyes riveted on Ronny's trailer.

She quickly crouched beside the bed.

That's where she found his working papers, just as Aunt Gertie predicted.

And the top manila folder had Percy O'Connor's name scribbled across it in large, red letters.

24

"I can't believe you went on a spy mission without me," Nina whined from a stool at her kitchen counter while popping liver treats to the dogs. "Someone must have put you up to it." Her eyes narrowed in dawning comprehension. "Gertie! You've been asking that Gertie Johnson for advice. She's nothing but trouble, and you know it."

"She's also my aunt, and she has her own investigation business. Why wouldn't I consult her?"

"I know all about Gertie's so-called 'business.' Your mother talked me into going with her to Michigan once. Gertie has a ratty old pickup truck with Trouble Busters handwritten on the side of it, and she lives in a town with a total of twelve residents."

"That's an exaggeration," Gretchen said. She helped herself to a cup of coffee and a chocolate croissant. She bit into the pastry. Pure heaven. "Besides, if I remember cor-

241

rectly, you liked the idea a few days ago."

"That was when I thought I was included in the mission." Nina's jealousy settled into a pout.

"I didn't want you along with me this morning. What if I had been caught? I'd need someone on the outside to bail me out of jail."

"I hadn't thought of that."

Tutu, Nimrod, and Sophie skidded by in a whirl of flying playfulness. Toenails clicked across the tiled floor. Nina jumped up and let them out into the gated backyard. When she came back, she eyed the folder on the counter.

"Have you looked inside yet?" she asked.

"Nope. I was waiting for you." Gretchen licked chocolate from her fingers. "Let's get started." She opened the folder and found scraps of paper with scribbled notes tossed in haphazardly. She picked up the top sheet.

"It looks like an early draft for one of his stupid articles," Nina observed. "You can't trust anything that goof wrote."

"Shhh, I'm reading." Gretchen skimmed over numerous misspellings and red-lined markings. The article was in the early stages of development and didn't flow in a coherent manner. Not that much about Ronny had been coherent anyway.

She handed the paper to Nina and scanned another.

"Tell me, tell me," Nina said, not bothering to look at it.

"Read it yourself." Gretchen slid the second sheet toward her.

"The pages are all marked up, and parts are crossed out. Just tell me."

"Okay, according to Ronny's notes — and we'll reserve judgment based on the source — Percy O'Connor's father, William, was a profiteer during World War Two."

Nina frowned. "A profiteer, like Rhett Butler?"

"You're thinking of the Civil War, Nina. But I suppose the fictional Rhett Butler *was* a profiteer, since he was a blockade runner and his motives weren't always honorable. But William O'Connor was a black marketeer during the Second World War. Remember your history? Remember rationing? People couldn't get basic supplies like gasoline and sugar."

"Right." Nina nodded studiously. "My mother, your grandmother, lived through it."

"According to Ronny, William O'Connor dealt in food — steaks and other meats that were impossible to buy in America at the time. He made a fortune in the 1940s, but he had to hide the money from the tax collectors, so he converted the cash to diamonds."

Nina slapped her hands together. "I told you we were onto something big like smuggling, didn't I?"

"You did."

"Imagine making a fortune selling steaks." Nina sipped her coffee with a dreamy look on her face.

"Anyway, local gossip — that's Boston gossip, because that's where this is supposed to have taken place — believed he had hidden the diamonds in dolls. Kewpie dolls, to be specific."

Nina's eyes grew wider. "Eric said a Blunderboo Kewpie was found smashed on the floor when the body was discovered. Percy O'Connor was killed for his diamonds!"

"And it accounts for his family's rapid rise into a high social economic class."

"But you can't trust anything penned by Ronny Beam."

"Nina, I can't believe I'm saying this," Gretchen said. "But I think Ronny's allegations might be correct. It explains why Percy was murdered. It even goes a long way in establishing a motive for killing Ronny. He was planning to expose Percy's family his-

244

tory, and someone didn't want that to happen."

"But what about Brett? How would his death tie in to the diamond theory?"

Gretchen thought about the auction and the mixed-up boxes. Again she saw Brett selecting dolls and boxes and handing them to Howie Howard, his longtime business associate and best friend.

"Either the killer didn't find the diamonds in Percy's home, or too many people knew about it." She spoke slowly, thoughts churning in her head. "Somehow, someway, Brett crossed the wrong person's path or got himself mixed up in the diamond theft, and for whatever reason, was eliminated."

"Lots of whatevers and somehows in our theory," Nina said. "Maybe the killer didn't want to share the loot and offed Brett."

"You're starting to sound like a gangsta," Gretchen said.

"It's all coming together in a circle." For dramatic effect, Nina drew a large circle in the air with her arms. "What did Ronny Beam, Brett Wesley, and Percy O'Connor all have in common?" Nina didn't wait for an answer. "Dolls, that's what. Maybe Ronny didn't collect dolls —"

"I can vouch for that," Gretchen said, remembering his trailer's collectibles were of the kind most people disposed of.

"But he was murdered at a doll show, and that's significant."

Gretchen went back to the open folder and spread out two more sheets of paper.

One was a copy of an article torn from the *Boston Globe.*

"He copied most of his material verbatim," Nina said after reading the piece. "What a louse."

"Quit speaking ill of the dead, Nina."

"I spoke ill of him while he was alive. Why do I have to clam up just because he's dead?"

Gretchen tuned Nina out and focused on the file. The *Boston Globe* had printed the story on August 6 of the previous year. She vaguely remembered seeing it when she lived there. "This article doesn't name names," Gretchen said. "It's a piece on the effects of the black market during the war. William O'Connor's name doesn't appear. It's a very general outline of profiteering activities. Ronny must have discovered additional information."

"Or made it up," Nina said.

Gretchen set the copy of the article aside and picked up the last item in the folder. "A letter," she announced to Nina, holding it up.

" 'Dearest Florence'," Gretchen read aloud. " 'Your willingness to assist me in my quest for my well-deserved and long-awaited fortune tugs at my heartstrings. Family must always stick together. Just don't plan on double-crossing me, or you'll go the way of all other flightless birds. Another meal for a hungry predator. Keep casting molds. Eventually you'll get it right'." Gretchen looked up at Nina. "No signature."

"Give me that," Nina tugged it out of Gretchen's hands and read it herself. "Jeez," she said.

"Who's Florence?"

"Florence," Nina said with a flourish, "is Chiggy Kent's real name."

Howie Howard's comment the night before at Bonnie's party popped into Gretchen's head: *Brett caught the little weasel inside the house going through some of Chiggy's personal things and escorted him off the property.* Ronny must have taken the letter and the *Boston Globe* article from Chiggy's house on Wednesday.

So far, she could attribute several deaths to the hunt for hidden treasure, starting with Percy O'Connor's in Boston. Then a cross-continental trek to Arizona and two more murders: a doll auctioneer's assistant and a second-rate reporter trying to legitimize his work with a real story instead of his usual trashy tales.

Gretchen had wandered into the middle of the mystery because of a mistaken box of Kewpie dolls. But how *did* that box fit in? She and Nina and April had searched every Kewpie in the box without finding a single clue to the dolls' significance.

Better get rid of Chiggy's broken Kewpies as fast as possible.

"You have enough to go to the police," Nina said.

"No, I don't," Gretchen argued.

"This is too scary."

Gretchen's cell phone rang. She didn't recognize the number showing on caller ID. When she answered, she heard Steve's voice.

"Well, I can kiss that sweet partnership deal goodbye," he said curtly. "I'm sure I'll be charged with first-degree murder anytime now."

"Where are you?"

"Tucked away where they can watch every move I make."

"I'll help you find a criminal attorney," she offered. "You'll beat this."

"What makes you so sure?" he said petulantly. "Everyone else thinks I murdered

Ronny."

Gretchen could have told him the truth, since she knew him better than anyone else did. Steve didn't have much capacity for anger in spite of his silly, macho confrontation with Ronny. That was the only time she'd seen him even slightly ruffled. Most of the time, he remained remarkably indifferent to everything and everyone around him.

Steve couldn't have killed Ronny because he didn't have any passion inside him.

Instead she said, "I trust you. If you say you didn't do it, you didn't do it."

"Well, I can't say the same for you. That's why I've made my own arrangements for representation. And Gretchen, I'm going to tell the truth, even if it implicates you."

"I've told you all along to be truthful. Nothing you can say will hurt me."

Steve humpfed.

"What's that supposed to mean?"

"I was in a cell for one very long day, in the company of the worst degenerates you're ever likely to meet."

Gretchen heard a hairline crack in his asphalt composure.

"The universal opinion in the bullpen," he said, "is that you set me up with your cop boyfriend."

"That's preposterous," Gretchen said when she'd recovered from the outrageousness of his comment. This from the man she had almost married.

She thought about defending herself against his charges, but she'd played defense for the entire length of their relationship. Always apologizing for being herself instead of the woman he thought she should be, always making amends for perceived missteps. The list of faux pas grew steadily over the years. The attorney in Steve couldn't leave the drama in the courtroom and carried his litigation over into their relationship.

Without another word, she hung up.

Turning to Nina she said, "Silly Steve swims surely south seizing sticks. There's a tongue twister for Howie Howard."

"Was I supposed to follow that?" Nina asked.

"Steve's grasping at straws. You're never going to guess what his latest theory is." She summarized the conversation. "We better figure out who really did it very soon. He's cracking."

Gretchen began gathering up her belongings. Traveling with a purse dog entailed almost as much strategic planning as traveling with a baby. "I think I'll find our homeless friends and see if they've heard anything new."

"I have to spend a few hours training Sophie," Nina said, her eyes shifting from side to side. Gretchen recognized the signs. Her aunt was looking for a way out. "Why don't you leave Nimrod here, and I'll put him through a refresher course. How's he been doing?"

"Great. Except when I tell him to hide, he ducks into his purse and falls asleep at the bottom."

"You call that a problem?" Nina scooped the tiny teacup poodle into her arms. "Let's try a new trick today, buddy," she said to him.

"I'll see you later." Gretchen headed determinedly for the door.

"Lunch?" Nina called out behind her.

"Not today," she said without turning. "I have to figure out some way to help clear an old boyfriend, and I'm not sure how to accomplish it."

"Clueless?"

Gretchen put on her sunglasses as she stepped into the late-morning sunshine. Clueless was right.

25

After fighting gridlock traffic, Gretchen found Daisy sitting on a park bench on Central Avenue, her trusty shopping cart containing her life story at her side. Nacho, looking grim and menacing as usual, sat beside her. When he saw Gretchen pull over to the curb and jump from the car, he rose without acknowledging her presence, handed something to Daisy, and strode rapidly away.

"What's with him?" Gretchen said, plopping down beside Daisy. Heat rose in waves from the concrete, and she looked around for a more shaded spot to sit.

She missed shade trees more than she missed anything else from back home in Boston. Oaks and red maples and towering elms. She'd traded them for lanky, transplanted palm trees and spindly desert shrubs. Phoenix's desert landscape offered no relief from the sun's hot rays.

"He's mad at you," Daisy said, her arms crossed in front of her, same red hat pulled down close to her eyes, same purple dress. "You snitched."

Gretchen watched Nacho's back disappear among the lunchtime crowd. The man was like a chameleon. "Snitched about what? I never snitched."

Daisy held out the object Nacho had given to her before hurrying off.

Gretchen took the photograph from her and winced. "The poor man. What happened to him?" A battered face stared at the camera through a swollen slit in one eye. The other eye was completely closed. His face looked like ground hamburger.

"His name is Albert Thoreau. I thought you might know him," Daisy said stiffly. Gretchen knew Daisy was studying her reaction with a steady, judging gaze. She shook her head. At least she thought he was a stranger to her. With his face swollen into an unrecognizable mass, she couldn't be sure.

Gretchen looked away from the picture in her hand. Life on the street was decidedly hard. "Should I know him? Is he okay?"

"He's alive, and that's all I can say for him."

"What happened?" Gretchen asked again.

253

"You told the cops that Thoreau saw that guy get pushed into the street."

"No, I didn't." Gretchen argued in her defense. "I never saw the man in this picture before." With wild accusations slung by Steve and now Daisy, she should have been the one studying litigation techniques and defensive strategies. "Daisy, you were in the parking lot when Nacho told me someone had seen Brett pushed, but he refused to tell me who it was. Don't you remember?"

"Well, you must have told somebody, because a cop came after him."

Gretchen looked at the picture again. "A cop did this?"

Daisy nodded.

Gretchen blanched, remembering that she *had* told a cop. Matt Albright. She hadn't gotten a name from Nacho, but she did tell Matt about the witness's account of what had taken place on the curb in front of Chiggy Kent's house. How hard would it have been for Matt to find him? Simple. Hit the streets and start asking questions.

She forced herself to look at Albert's battered face again.

Could Matt Albright have done this to Albert Thoreau? "What makes you think Albert's beating had anything to do with what he saw at the auction?" she asked.

Daisy's eyes shifted away. "I just know, is all," she said in a small voice. "Albert's sister is famous, you know, and he used to be, too."

Gretchen gave her a hard look. Fame played too much of a role in Daisy's life.

"I need a place to lay low for a little while," Daisy said, drawing Gretchen away from a jumble of disturbing thoughts. "Can I go home with you?"

Gretchen, startled by the request, felt hopeful that Daisy was moving in the right direction, away from her destitute life. It was the first time she had ever reached out for help. "Sure," she said. "Do you want to tell me about it?"

Daisy shook her head. "There's something ugly happening on the street right now. This could have been me," she said, taking back the picture and waving it at Gretchen. "I've been advised to find a safe house for the time being. But I have to bring my shopping cart."

Gretchen looked at the cart, then at the trunk of the Echo. "I can get your things inside, but the cart itself is too big." Then she realized she hadn't emptied the trunk last night after the doll show. Daisy's so-called treasures would have to fit in the backseat.

"I can't leave my cart. I'll find someplace else to stay."

Daisy stood up and smoothed her dress, defiance in her stance and in the sharp glint in her eyes.

"Wait," Gretchen said. "I have an idea."

Digging her cell phone out of her pocket, she called Nina. "I have a favor to ask."

"Okay," Nina said. "I don't mean okay, I'll do it. I mean, okay, tell me."

"Daisy needs a place to stay and insists on bringing her shopping cart along. It won't fit in my car."

"I'm taking back every single okay that I've ever uttered. I know what's coming next."

"So . . ."

"I hate sentences that start with so."

"I thought you could run down here and pick her up."

"How thoughtful." Nina let out a noisy sigh. "This is going to cost you big time."

"Anything."

"All right, I'll bring her back home with me. Karen Phelps wants me to start training her pup, and I've been putting her off because I haven't had time. Ask Daisy if she's willing to help."

Gretchen relayed the request, and Daisy broke into a wide grin.

256

"I guess that's a yes," Gretchen said, giving Nina directions and sealing the deal.

As Gretchen drove away, she saw Daisy give her a shy five-finger wave and sit back down.

She also saw the black Jetta pull out right behind her.

At first, Gretchen didn't think anything of it. Traffic along Central tended to be tight and congested, and even here in this valley of incredibly intense sun, black cars weren't an exception, and Volkswagen Jettas were the car of the moment.

What drew Gretchen's attention to the tail was the proximity of the other car. Any closer, and they'd be sharing the same rearview mirror.

Now what? Should Gretchen call the police or try to lose the car? Maybe she should drive to the police station, but her pursuer might drive past, and Gretchen wouldn't be any closer to identifying her.

At that moment the driver must have realized that she had breached the imaginary line between a comfortable following distance and extreme road rage, because the Jetta blended back into the obscurity of traffic.

What a dope Gretchen was. She should get the Jetta's license plate for starters. Gretchen checked her mirror, but the car had allowed some distance to separate them.

Paper and pen within reach, Gretchen slowed, waiting for the other car to creep forward. Still, it was too hard to get a license number while looking through a mirror with one eye and scoping out the flow of traffic ahead with the other. Not to mention the license number appeared backward in the mirror, making it that much harder to read. And the traffic was as thick as a flock of migrating geese.

Ahead, a light turned red, and she eased to a stop. The Jetta was once again right behind her, now too close to read the number.

Impulsively, Gretchen set the brake, jumped out, and ran to the back of her car. She read the license number with no time to spare for glancing at the other driver, and jumped back into her own car as the light changed. As she drove, she wrote down the number.

The Jetta stayed right behind her. She switched lanes. So did the Jetta.

Maybe jumping out at the light hadn't been the smartest move she'd ever made. What if the driver had shot her? Or tromped on the accelerator and crushed Gretchen against her own car?

What did the woman hope to accomplish by following her? Gretchen wanted to pull over, stomp back to the other car, and demand answers to a growing number of questions.

Did the Jetta driver want the box of Kewpie dolls? It just happened to be in her car's trunk at this very moment. If she gave it up, the scare tactics might stop. The lethal scorpions and mysterious packages with creepy messages inside might go away. It made sense to get out of the middle, wherever that was. Let them know she wasn't a threat any longer and didn't want anything to do with the Kewpies.

Aha! She had a plan.

At the next intersection, Gretchen stopped abruptly when the light turned to red, and she trotted to the back of the Echo with her hands up in classic surrender position.

The Jetta driver's mouth dropped open at the same time that Gretchen popped the trunk and removed the box of broken Kewpie dolls. She placed it on the hood of the Jetta, directly in front of the driver's window. Relieved to note that she wasn't facing the barrel of a pistol, she managed a weak wave and ran back to her car just before the light turned green.

As she turned onto Lincoln Drive, she

watched the woman leap from her car and grab the box. Horns blared behind the Jetta as the light changed again, and the traffic hadn't moved.

Gretchen dug in her purse for her cell phone.

"I'd like to report an incident of road rage," she said when the Phoenix Police Department's dispatcher answered. She filed the report, giving all details including the numbers of the Jetta's license plate and her own cell phone. "I'd like to know who that car is registered to."

"We'll send a car. We have one close by," the dispatcher said.

"I just want the name of the driver."

"That's not up to me. I'm a police dispatcher, not your personal information clerk."

Whatever happened to the courteous, helpful public servant of the past?

"Go about your business," the dispatcher advised. "We'll be in touch."

"Sure," Gretchen said, with no idea why she'd bothered calling the police. All she wanted was the name of her pursuer, and she couldn't even get that. Once her complaint passed through enough red tape to produce the information she needed, she would have died of natural causes.

Or unnatural causes.

Ten minutes later, she was driving home with an alert eye out for the Jetta and a bag of green chile burgers from a fast-food drive-through in the passenger seat. Her cell phone rang.

"I hear you had a close encounter," Matt said.

"Of the third kind," Gretchen responded cautiously, the photograph of Albert vivid in her mind. "News travels fast. I didn't know you hung around dispatch centers."

"I don't. This one requires special attention, so they notified me."

"I should be flattered." For the first time, Gretchen realized the power of his position. Was he having her watched? As a detective in the Phoenix Police Department, his authority extended further than that of an ordinary patrol cop. He had access to everything and every one. Frightening, once Gretchen really thought about it.

"Just tell me what happened," he said, sounding concerned.

"This car has been following me in a very aggressive way. It almost hit me. Whoever it is, is trying to scare me. It's working."

Matt asked her to repeat the license number.

There was a long pause on the other end.

Then Matt told her the name of the person registered to the black Jetta.

Her turn for a long pause. He must have thought she hung up, because he said, "Hello? Are you still there?"

She groaned audibly.

"This is extremely embarrassing for me," he said.

"Great. Just great. I'll leave you to handle it. If it happens again, I'm filing harassment charges."

Gretchen hung up.

She had just given her box of dolls, the one she hoped to use in negotiations; to Matt's crazy, estranged wife.

"Well," Nina said from the other end of the line. "Bonnie told us she was a psych case. Now we know for sure."

Gretchen swung into her carport just as her ear, pressed against the receiver, was beginning to hurt. She made a mental note to add more minutes to her cell phone plan and buy a headset. "Why me? She doesn't have any reason to follow me."

"She must have caught on."

"Caught on?" Gretchen turned off the ignition.

"It's obvious to everyone but you that Matt's hot on your heels, and it isn't because he wants to give you a speeding ticket."

"That can't be true."

"It is. You both have foolish smiles on your faces whenever you run into each other. Stop fighting against it and go with the flow."

"Do you think Bonnie told his wife about me?"

"It isn't a long shot. I bet that's exactly what happened. Blabby Bonnie's been trying to set you two up for a while now." Gretchen imagined Nina grinning widely. "You and Matt want to go out with Eric and me tonight?"

"Give it up, Nina. I'm not dating Matt. He hasn't even asked me out."

"This is the twenty-first century. You don't have to wait for him to ask you. Turn the tables. Get aggressive."

"Butt out, Nina. I'm still trying to extricate myself from one man."

"I'll put a bug in Matt's ear."

"Don't you dare." Gretchen knew her aunt certainly would dare. The idea might have appealed to Gretchen yesterday. Today, after seeing the photo of Albert Thoreau, she had too many doubts about Matt.

She decided not to tell Nina about Albert's beating until she had concrete information to back up her fear that Matt had attacked the homeless man. She hoped it wasn't true.

It seemed so out of character for him.

Of course, she had badly misjudged Steve. She had believed in him, too.

"Did you pick up Daisy?" Gretchen asked.

"She's working with Karen's dog right now."

"What should I do about the box of Kewpies? I can't believe I gave it to the wrong person."

"Forget about it," Nina said. "You'd have to ask the queen bee for it back, and you know what the queen does if she spots a new queen emerging?"

"I don't want to know."

"She kills the new queen."

On that positive note, Gretchen signed off and grabbed the bag of green chile burgers. They smelled wonderful. One for now, and two for snacks later. She had to find time to cook a healthy meal one of these days, instead of existing on junk food. Like two days of hot dogs at the doll show and these cholesterol-soaked burgers.

She rounded the corner of the carport and dug for her house keys, wishing again that her purse was more organized. Everything she needed always seemed to rest at the very bottom.

When she stepped onto the porch, she saw it.

A package propped up against the door, positioned so she couldn't miss it.

Postal stamp — Phoenix, Arizona.

Handwriting — the same.

Gretchen thought about ignoring it. Maybe if she didn't acknowledge its existence, it would vanish.

She looked up and down the street, a tiny sliver of fear traversing her spine.

She made another phone call, gave the package wide berth when she entered the house, and sat down to wait for April to arrive.

26

This hundred-year-old baby is a collector's dream. In addition to the Kewpie doll, you can find Kewpie paper dolls, stickers, plates, postcards, salt and pepper shakers, and mini babies. They're affordable and fun. Most popular are Kewpies in action poses, those holding unusual items, and Kewpies with animals. Add one to your collection, and you'll be hooked for life.

— From *World of Dolls* by Caroline Birch

"Why me?" April said, her voice expressing flattered pleasure. She wore her salt-and-pepper hair tied back in a big scrunchy and another tent-sized muumuu, royal blue this time and patterned with hummingbirds.

"That's what I've been saying to myself ever since these packages started arriving," Gretchen replied. "Why me? The answer continues to elude me."

"I mean, why did you call me instead of Nina? You two are usually tight as a pair of jeans on a teenager."

"I called you first because you've been in the doll business your whole life, and I need an experienced, critical eye."

"You also want me to open this package, and you know that Nina would have wimped out, leaving you to do it yourself. One more hidden message, and she'll fall apart."

"Will you just open it, April?"

"What if it's a mail bomb?"

"None of the others were." Gretchen began to regret her decision to ask April for help, but she couldn't have faced the task by herself.

Both of them eyed the package. The first two Kewpies had been delivered to the doll show. This one had her name on the label and, worse, her home address. No escaping the fact that this one was meant exclusively and irrefutably for her. No generic "current resident" feel to it like the ones at the show.

"Sent on Saturday. The day you got the first one." April ripped brown paper away to reveal a square, dirty-looking box. "Don't worry, this is the last one you're going to get."

"How do you know that?" Gretchen's eyes were riveted to the box.

"Everything comes in threes."

"You've been hanging around with my aunt again."

"I always believed in the rule of three." April ran her fingernail under a piece of tape holding the top of the box closed, opened the cover, and peeked inside. "For example," she said, removing an object wrapped in a brown paper bag. "You've received three packages, so this is the last one, and there have been three deaths, Ronny, Brett, and this Percy fellow. Three murders, so we're all done with those."

"That's reassuring."

"Unless another set of threes begins." April didn't attempt to open the paper bag. "And you could be the first in the new trio."

"April, you're a breath of fresh air," Gretchen said with only a mild hint of sarcasm. "Now, open it before I explode."

"That's why my parents named me April. I was born in April on a fine spring day." She tried to hand the wrapped object to Gretchen. "You finish opening it. I've done my fair share." When Gretchen refused to take it, she set it on the table between them.

April said, "You're approaching this from a very negative angle, like you think something evil is lurking inside. I think the exact opposite; someone is trying to help you find

268

the truth."

"Then that person could just speak up. Ring me on my cell phone and lay it all out. That would be the way I'd handle it."

April put her hands on her hips. "Well, everybody isn't like you. Maybe this person is scared of retribution or retaliation."

"Retribution is the same as retaliation."

"Are you going to open it or not?"

Gretchen gingerly picked at the bag, lowered her head to the edge of the table, and looked inside.

"It's Doodle Dog, isn't it," April said knowingly, impressed with her own analytical skills.

Gretchen pulled out a Kewpie dog, a replica of the one that Rosie O'Neill had sketched for the first time almost one hundred years ago. Doodling rough drawings of her beloved Boston terrier the Kewpie dog had materialized under her guiding hand.

White with large black spots, one big spot on the top of his head. Happiness radiated from his glowing little face. A happiness Gretchen was finding it hard to share.

"Well," she said, shoving the dog at April. "Is it worth anything?"

April grabbed the reading glasses that hung from a chain around her neck, placed

269

them on the tip of her nose, and tilted her head. "Interesting." She took the dog and turned it over. "It's not bisque, so it isn't one of the original pieces. This one's made of porcelain, rather than hard plastic. Hmm . . ."

She removed her glasses. "Wasn't worth much even before someone snapped off the back leg. See right there?" She ran her hand along the dog's haunches. "Glued back on."

Gretchen groaned and covered her eyes, elbows spread wide on the table.

"Are those green chile burgers I smell?" April said, sniffing the air, returning Doodle Dog to the table, and zeroing in on the bag lying on the kitchen counter.

"Help yourself," Gretchen said, splaying her fingers helplessly and studying the Kewpie dog.

"You want one?" April asked, cramming the burger in as if she hadn't eaten for a week.

Gretchen waved her over, and they sat and ate and stared at the Kewpie dog.

"Kind of cold," April observed, taking another big bite.

"I forgot I had them once I found the package."

"It's okay. Kewpies are fascinating," April said, one cheek bulging. "In the early 1900s, women would pluck their eyebrows to imitate Kewpie brows. Kind of like surprised dots. That's how popular the dolls were."

Gretchen chewed but couldn't taste the burger. All she could think about was what they would find inside the doll.

"You look white as a ghost," April said.

"I don't want to open the dog. I don't want anything to do with this series of murders and packages. It gives me the creeps to think that someone is watching me."

"You have to face your fears."

"Easy for you to say. You aren't the target."

"I still have that hammer in the car," April said. "Want me to get it?"

"No, we can use my tools in the workshop."

"Are you going to eat that other one?" April seized the last green chile burger in one hand and the Doodle Dog in the other and followed Gretchen into the workshop.

Wobbles appeared from nowhere, as usual, stretched himself long and lean, then rubbed against Gretchen's legs. She stopped to give him just enough love and attention to hear his satisfied, deep-throated purr.

She missed Nimrod and wondered when Nina would return with him. A few months ago she would never have believed that she could adapt to a dog in the house. She wasn't exactly canine friendly, preferring the solitary company of Wobbles to any yappy, attention-seeking dog. But there was something about the little guy . . .

"Are we going to do this, or are you going to play with your cat?" April dug through the toolbox, and before Gretchen could intervene, the woman had smashed the Kewpie dog wide open on the worktable. Bits of porcelain fell to the floor.

"April, I wanted to preserve as much of it as I could."

"Wasn't worth anything," April insisted.

"Maybe we shouldn't have touched it. The police could have dusted it for prints."

April held up her hands in surrender. "We can stop right now and call Detective Albright." Then she grinned. "He might have to perform a body search in case we're withholding more evidence. That would be sweet."

"Continue on, Miss Marple," Gretchen said, wanting no part of Matt Albright. "We really don't need the police."

April extracted a piece of paper from inside the Kewpie dog and turned pale as she read it. She handed it to Gretchen.

" 'History repeats itself. You're next unless you start thinking outside the same old box.' "

Gretchen thought she might faint. The piece of paper floated to the floor, and April bent and picked it up. "Do you still think someone's trying to help me?" she asked April. "This . . ." she motioned at April's clutched hand. ". . . couldn't be more threatening."

The series of cryptic notes that had been delivered specifically for her carried a frightening message. A message she had to figure out. The first one, "Wag, the Dog"; then a name, "Percy O'Connor." The napkin with the bold, startling word, "Pushed!" Now this, the most menacing of all: "History repeats itself. You're next unless you start thinking outside the same old box."

"What box is the note referring to?" April asked.

"I'm dead," Gretchen said. "I gave away the box."

"I'm really confused." April sat down on a stool slowly, as though testing it in case it couldn't hold her weight.

Gretchen filled in the missing events for April, describing the street chase and her decision to surrender the box, only to find out that the pursuer was Matt's soon-to-be ex-wife.

"I'll never get it back now," she moaned. "The woman probably threw it out when she found out it was only a box of broken doll pieces."

"It's gone for sure. She must think you're the nutcase." April reread the note. "But this says to start thinking outside the same old box."

"That's the only box," Gretchen pointed out.

"What about the other box, the one with the Ginny dolls?"

"Gone."

"Maybe that's the one you should be looking for."

Gretchen heard the front door open and the familiar tapping of dog paws running down the hall. "Hey," Nina called out. "Daisy and I are moving her things into Caroline's spare bedroom, if that's okay?"

"Great," Gretchen called back. "Join us in the workshop when you're finished." Nimrod rounded the corner and literally jumped into her arms. "Welcome back, bud."

A few minutes later, Nina appeared. "Why does everyone look so glum?"

"Tell her," April said.

Nina's eyes grew wider when she spotted the smashed Kewpie dog. April handed her the message. Gretchen took a deep breath and related the parts Nina had missed.

The only thing Gretchen left out of her accounts was Daisy's story about the homeless man's savage beating by a cop. She didn't know why she was keeping this to herself. Maybe she was protecting Matt's reputation until there was more proof. Once certain members of the Phoenix Dollers heard, the news would travel like light rays in space. Besides, he was the club president's son, and Bonnie deserved advance warning.

"I still think you should take what you know to the police," Nina said. "Someone's threatening your life."

"Not necessarily," April said, and repeated her theory that someone was trying to help solve the crimes. "One of the messages had Percy's name inside. Right?"

"Right." Gretchen was beginning to catch up with April's reasoning now that the shock of the third package had subsided. "Why would the killer give me a clue like that? It doesn't make sense." She banged her open hand on the worktable. "April's right. Someone's trying to help."

"Must be a mental case," Nina said. "An escapee from the loony bin."

Gretchen managed to shake a playful finger at her aunt. "Another socially unacceptable comment. Remember your pledge to be more sensitive."

"I don't remember making any such pledge." Nina stooped and caught Nimrod as he ran past. "Want to see what he learned? This is amazing. He's so smart for a puppy."

Without waiting for a reply, she held him up and looked into his eyes. "Nimrod, parade." She put him down and he bolted for the door leading to the pool, pushing through the tiny pet door. Gretchen could hear him barking. He continued to bark until he slid back through the opening and tried to climb up Gretchen's ankles.

"What was he doing?"

"Parading around the backyard strutting his stuff," Nina said. "Isn't it cute?"

"My neighbor is going to have a fit," Gretchen said. "She complains about me every chance she gets. And I don't see the point."

"Lighten up, niece, it's for fun."

April stood up. "Let's go to Curves and catch up on gossip. Maybe we'll learn something new."

"And let's bring Daisy along," Gretchen said, confident that Daisy would eventually share more information. Gretchen had only to wait long enough and keep her close by.

"She can be my guest," April said. "I need

the points."

"She has to join before you earn them," Nina pointed out. "Based on her current income, do you really think she might sign up?"

"I'm taking my own car," Gretchen said. "I have errands afterward."

"She's ditching me again," Nina said to April. "I just know it." She looked at Gretchen. "Daisy can ride over with you. Until she takes a shower and washes her clothes, I'm keeping my distance. Even the dogs noticed. We had to ride over here with the windows open."

"She's showering right now," April said. "Can't you hear the water running?"

"We'll wait for her." Gretchen opened the patio doors leading to the swimming pool and cabana. "I have something that will fit her until she washes a load of laundry."

As the women gathered their purses, dogs, and other paraphernalia, Gretchen waited in the workshop doorway, staring at the remnants of the porcelain dog that Rosie O'Neill had hoped would bring happiness to all who encountered it.

27

Lilly Beth Straddler stands in her front yard watering the miniature roses she has just planted. *That landscape specialist really knows his stuff.* Heavenly Days, that's what he called this particular type of rose. Loves heat and sun and never goes dormant, he promised her.

She wipes a thin line of perspiration from her forehead. *Must be a hundred and twenty outside, and here we are in October.*

Lucky for her she decided to water them right away before they wilted, or she might have missed the whole thing. What with all the privacy walls surrounding the homes, it is almost impossible to keep up with what goes on in the neighborhood.

Hard to know what the neighbors even look like, no one being especially friendly. Walls everywhere. Not too conducive to chitchat from one yard to another.

Of course, she notices the truck parked

on the street, and right away she knows it doesn't belong to a repeat customer, although with that doll business they have going over there, anything is possible.

Why, she herself has personally filed a complaint over them operating out of the house like that. This subdivision isn't zoned for retail, and that's exactly what she said to the commissioner. Let them take their business where it belongs, she'd said. Dragging down property values, she'd argued. Setting a precedent. If it wasn't stopped, pretty soon you'd have all kinds of business signs sprouting up on the lawns, and that would be the end of the neighborhood. Not that they had a doll sign out front, but who knew what they'd come up with next?

But it all fell on deaf ears. Probably bought off the judge.

She has finished soaking the roses when the police officer walks toward her from the other side of the house next door. Lilly Beth drops the hose, a wild jet of spray jumping back at her. She sidesteps and scurries over. What could it possibly be? A break-in? In this neighborhood? Lord help us.

"They just left," she says, "that Birch girl and a bunch of other women. People traipsing in and out of that house at all hours, it's a wonder they made it this long without trouble."

She hears barking on the other side of the Birches' door. Several different pitches of barks, which means a houseful of dogs. The noise from those animals! Lilly Beth wonders what the local rules are regarding pets. How many are legal? One? Two? Tomorrow she'll follow up.

She taps her head with the palm of her hand. What is she thinking? She can follow up right this minute, since the proper authority is standing right before her.

"I think they own too many dogs. Do you know how many are . . . what's the word . . . legal?" she feels disappointed when he shakes his head. "Never mind, I'll call down to the local station. Are you from the local station?"

The police officer strides forward, arms swinging loose and with authoritarian hands, she thinks, wide and powerful.

"Oh, hello, Lilly Beth," someone calls from the sidewalk.

Drats, now all the other nosy neighbors are spilling out of their homes like ants following a crumb line. Janice Schmidt waves a greeting, glances at the police officer, and continues to move past, an extra-wide stroller rolling ahead of her with two sleeping toddlers inside.

Lilly Beth notices the police officer stop abruptly when he sees Janice, like the fizz went out of him or like he'd been bent on a task and then changed his mind.

"You need to go back in your house, ma'am," he says, flashing a badge just like in the movies. "This is a homeland security issue, highly classified. Talk about it to anyone, and you risk prosecution."

"Oh, my. Well, yes, of course, Officer." He guides her along, pushing on her back, a little too hard, she thinks. "Anything I can do to help, you just call me. I'm a patriotic American, not like some I could mention." She gives a meaningful glance back at the Birch house.

She opens her door. What a pushy officer. "I'll keep close tabs on them for you," she says. "Don't you worry."

He continues to stare at her house even after she backs away from the window. Then he gets into the truck and drives away, probably to return later with reinforcements. Strange that he didn't drive a squad car, but maybe that was too obvious for homeland security. He wouldn't want all the neighbors wondering why a police car was parked out front.

She hopes she hasn't interfered. She does tend to rush in impulsively without thinking things through. If she had stayed on her own side, maybe he would have crashed down the door with one powerful, bionic-like leg and seized evidence that would implicate her neighbor in some kind of international spy operation.

She vows to stay close to her window in case things heat up.

28

On the way to Curves, Gretchen tried to steer the conversation back to Albert and his brutal beating, but Daisy's single-track mind was zeroed in on her future acting career and her chances of success. As hard as Gretchen tried, there was no rechanneling the woman's focus.

April and Nina led in their own cars, forming a caravan through the Phoenix streets. Even though Gretchen thought she knew the way, she gunned her Echo through a questionable light rather than risk abandonment by the other two.

She followed them into the parking lot. Mondays were always high-usage days at Curves for Women, after all those extra pounds added in the pursuit of weekend pleasures.

"It's the holidays coming up," April commented. "Everyone's trying to get in shape for Thanksgiving so they can go at it again."

Bonnie, Rita, and several other doll club members had already begun their workouts. Gretchen and her group jumped in wherever there was room and called out to each other as they exercised around the circle of machines.

April stayed close to Daisy so she could show her the equipment.

"You're new here," Bonnie said to Daisy. "Where do you live?"

"Close by me," Nina said quickly. "Right down the block."

"Hear you have a big date tonight," Rita called to Nina.

"That's right. Eric's taking me out to dinner at the Phoenician, where the Boston Kewpie Club is staying."

"Wow," April said.

"The resort has eleven restaurants," Nina said.

"I've eaten there," homeless Daisy said, her legs pumping up and down on the stepper.

Nina threw her a warning glance.

Gretchen thought Daisy handled the equipment and the workout better than most of the longtime members and once again wondered about her background.

"Steve's out of jail," Bonnie said, a sly look on her face. Her eyes slid to Gretchen. "But of course you knew that."

Gretchen continued running on a platform.

"Really."

"Tell her the rest," Rita urged. "Everyone else knows."

"Steve can't talk to you anymore. He met with his lawyer, and he said Steve's to have no contact with you."

"Why on earth . . ." Nina began, frowning.

"Only thing I can think of," Bonnie said, all innocence, "is that his defense is going to be that you did it. Remember, it was your knife."

"The knife didn't kill him," Gretchen said.

"Bonnie, you know better," Nina scolded. "Gretchen had nothing to do with Ronny Beam's death."

"That's the truth," Daisy said with conviction.

Gretchen whirled to look at her, but Daisy seemed oblivious, preoccupied with shoulder presses.

"Change stations now."

Nina bumped into Gretchen, who hadn't moved. "Pay attention. You're supposed to move."

Gretchen saw all eyes on her, all waiting for a response to the news about Steve.

What could she say?

To change the subject, Gretchen said, "Anyone else going to Brett Wesley's memorial service?"

"When is it?" April asked.

"Tomorrow night."

"Haven't heard a thing about it."

"Me, either."

"I wasn't invited," Rita said.

"Maybe," Nina said, "the service is for those who were at the auction that day?"

April nodded agreement. "Someone put the invites together from the registration list."

Gretchen sincerely hoped that all the bidders were invited. Maybe the memorial organizers had Duanne Wilson's correct address. Maybe he would show up. She had a few questions for him. For that matter, she had a few questions for Howie Howard. She crossed him off her mental to-do list for today. Tomorrow night at the memorial would be soon enough.

Peter Finch, the photographer, lived in South Phoenix, according to the address on the business card he'd given her at the auction. With South Mountain as a backdrop, Gretchen drove down Fifty-first Street and turned onto Southern Avenue. She gazed at the dilapidated apartment building on her left, slowed, and pulled to the curb.

She made her way along the sidewalk leading to the building, stepping over and around an assortment of toddler trikes. A drape in the closest apartment moved slightly, and Gretchen saw fingers in the shadows grasping the heavy material.

Where was Nina when she really needed her? Probably having her hair done again, or her nails repaired, or Tutu's nails polished.

Her niece's life might be in jeopardy, and Nina was off primping.

What had she been thinking to call the number on Peter Finch's card and agree to meet at his apartment? He could be Jack the Ripper incarnate for all she knew. Gun toting was legal in Phoenix as long as the weapon wasn't concealed.

Instead of a gun she had Nimrod, although that didn't make her feel any safer.

Gretchen rang one of six buzzers on the outside of the building, the one labeled P.F. She saw Peter's bony, unshaved face peek out at her from a door pane. Then he unlocked the door and ushered her into his apartment.

Gretchen sized up the room. Sagging couch, weathered wood breakfast table, small refrigerator, no stove, hot plate on the counter. No obvious sign of weaponry, no piano wire coiled on the table. Aside from the ratty furniture, he owned a sleek forty-two-inch flat-screen television and one of the fanciest computer and printer combinations Gretchen had ever seen.

What his space lacked in basic luxuries, he made up for in electronic gadgetry.

A bachelor, for sure.

Gretchen looked around for signs of a woman's touch. Not a thing.

"Over here," Peter said, leading her to the computer. "I shoot digital all the time. It's so easy. I'll show them to you on the monitor, if that's okay."

"Sure." Gretchen moved closer.

Nimrod's tiny face poked out of his poodle purse, and he seemed inquisitive rather than threatened. Possibly a good sign.

"Is that a real dog?"

Nimrod's ears perked up as though he knew he was the center of attention.

"Never saw a dog in a purse before."

"I hadn't either until my aunt started training them."

"What did you have in mind? Just dolls from that auction?"

Because Peter Finch had snapped pictures of dolls lying on the flatbed truck, she had used that fact to set up this appointment. A ruse.

She wasn't interested in doll pictures, unless . . .

"Did you take any pictures of Ginny dolls?"

"Refresh my memory," he said. "What does one look like?"

Gretchen described the doll and the box the best she could.

"I didn't shoot anything already packed in boxes." He started up the computer, and Gretchen heard the motor kicking in. His fingers flew on the keyboard, and photographs began popping up on the screen. "Grab a seat," he said, motioning to a chair next to him.

She sat down next to him with Nimrod still in her shoulder bag, and for the first time wished he was larger and more intimidating. A German shepherd or pit bull would be good.

"To be honest," she said, "I'm not really interested in the doll pictures."

Peter pushed back in the chair. "Well, what then? All I take is pictures of dolls."

"Yes, well, I was hoping you took a few pictures later when Brett was struck by the car. People pictures, maybe of the accident scene. You said on the phone that you were still at the auction when it happened."

"Awful, what happened. Unbelievable."

"Don't you have some pictures of the accident?" Gretchen asked again. "Any at all would help."

"I know what you're thinking. I'm supposed to be a professional, and a professional would have taken pictures. But, frankly, I was so stunned I completely forgot. Brett was a friend. I still keep seeing it happening all over again in my head."

"I understand," Gretchen said softly. The image of Brett crumpled in the street like one of her broken dolls flicked through her thoughts often, too.

"As far as the boxed dolls, I didn't take pictures because Chiggy was firm about that."

"So you were there on Wednesday, too, the day before the auction?"

"I was. She said no pictures of the stuff in the boxes in the corner of her bedroom. The boxes were supposed to be taken out to the retirement community when she moved. That's why I was surprised to see one of them on the auction block."

Gretchen sat up straighter. "Are you sure?"

"Sure, I'm sure. She told me not to touch them, and I saw her boxing up those Ginnys you're talking about. Brett must not have been paying attention, because I heard somebody behind the flatbed the day of the auction giving him a hard time about it. Sounded like someone might of slapped him, and I heard a man say, 'You better get it back right now.' "

Peter shook his head. "Brett must have been so shook up, he ran right out in the street without looking."

"Did you tell the police that?"

"Oh, yes, an officer came by after the accident, and I told him just what I told you."

The photographer clicked on an icon, and one of Chiggy's dolls appeared on the screen. Gretchen wasn't past the wincing stage every time she saw one of Chiggy's poorly made copies.

"See all the stuff in the background," Peter said. "I haven't had time to play with the photographs, fading out all that extra stuff. These aren't scheduled to hit the Internet for a few more weeks. I like to play with light and color for a while first."

Gretchen studied the photographs as Peter scrolled through them. Not the best quality, she thought. And he hadn't been careful with his backdrops. Gretchen could see other dolls from the flatbed behind the posed doll. He continued clicking until pictures of the crowd appeared.

"I thought you said you didn't take pictures of the accident," Gretchen said, recognizing other bidders from that day's auction.

"I didn't."

"What are these then?" Gretchen pointed at the screen.

"You asked if I took pictures of the accident. I didn't. These are from afterward. See that one? That's the back of the ambulance as it drove off. Finally got my wits about me by then and started shooting."

"Could I have copies of these?" Gretchen asked, keeping any sign of eagerness out of her voice.

"I shoot quick and often. There must be a couple hundred shots. Do you want to go through them first?"

"No, I'd like to buy them all."

Peter looked surprised. "Tell you what, you have a computer at home, right?"

Gretchen nodded.

"I'll download all the pictures, and you can look at them on your own computer. I won't charge you much."

Gretchen nodded. "Great."

Peter efficiently zipped through the files.

"When did Chiggy tell you to stay out of the boxes in her room?" Gretchen asked while she watched him work.

"Wednesday night. She was bossing the mover around, and she gave everyone strict orders to stay out of her bedroom, because the only things in there were her personal belongings."

"Who else did she tell this to?"

"Howie was at the house, but he spent most of the time out by the truck getting organized. But I thought Brett heard her for sure. That's why I can't understand how he could have mixed up her personal boxes like that. He must have picked that box up before the mover got to it, and hauled it out to the truck. Like I said, he must not have listened. And me, I was there, of course. I called Chiggy up as soon as I saw the ad in the paper and asked permission to take pictures of the dolls."

"Anyone else?"

"That newspaper reporter, Ronny Beam, who wanted to write a story about the dolls." Peter tapped more keys, and the screen went blank. "Oh, yes, and that guy from Boston."

Gretchen, rising from a seat next to the computer, froze. "What guy from Boston?" she managed to ask.

"Tall, blond, about your age, maybe a little older. Can't remember his name." Peter rubbed his rough face. "Steve something, I think it was."

29

It took Gretchen three tries before she punched Nina's phone number in correctly, only to learn that Nina had turned off her cell. Where could she be? Gretchen checked her watch. Six o'clock. Ah, yes, the big date with Eric Huntington at one of the Phoenician's exclusive restaurants. Cocktails beforehand in his suite. No wonder she found herself connected directly to Nina's voice mail.

She walked down Southern Avenue so Nimrod could sniff and go about his business. She tried to organize the events of the last six days, starting with Wednesday, the day before the doll auction and Brett's death, and the subsequent chain of unexplained occurrences.

The news that Steve had been in Phoenix a day earlier than she thought, and that he had been at Chiggy's house, disturbed her greatly. Her confidence in his innocence dissipated like the daylight now leaving the city. What had he been doing there?

Now that Gretchen had discovered that Steve had been at Chiggy's home along with Brett, it seemed that Steve had possible connections to all of the murdered men, even Percy O'Connor, since both of them lived in Boston. As for Steve's connection to Ronny Beam . . . well, he had shoved the reporter around in front of a hall full of shoppers.

Maybe the police *had* arrested the right man.

She shuddered at the thought. How little we know the people closest to us.

Nimrod spotted a woman ahead of them walking a great dane. The mighty hunter wagged his tail and gave two sharp yips. Gretchen quickly turned around and headed toward the car to avoid the enormous dog and its owner.

Who else could it have been? Howie Howard, by his own admission, had a dispute with Ronny over Chiggy's personal belongings and had thrown him out. He also was present when Brett died. And Albert, the homeless eyewitness, saw the killer get out of a blue truck, and later Gretchen observed Howie getting into a blue truck and driving away after the ambulance left.

As far as murdering Ronny, Howie easily could have waited for him in the parking lot. But so far, he, like Steve, had no real connection to Percy that she knew of. Yet.

Gretchen loaded Nimrod into the Echo and pulled away from Peter Finch's home.

Of the small group who had assembled at Chiggy Kent's house to prepare for the auction, two were dead and two were at the head of her suspect list. Only the photographer and Chiggy, aka Florence, remained beyond scrutiny — for the time being.

But what about the incriminating note that Gretchen found in Ronny's file? It was addressed to Chiggy from a family member eager for what he saw as his inheritance. Despite its implication that Chiggy was involved in a fraudulent scheme, the old woman suffered too many debilitating medical problems to kill two strong men like Brett and Ronny. From what other members of the Phoenix Dollers said, Chiggy and her oxygen tank could hardly make it across the room.

Tomorrow Gretchen would visit the woman at the nursing home.

Who else should be on her list of suspects?

What about the members of the Boston Kewpie Doll Club?

Eric Huntington had delivered the second

package to her. He'd known Percy and was also a lifelong Bostonian, like Steve. For Nina's sake, Gretchen hoped Eric wasn't involved.

Then there was Milt Wood. Something about him gave Gretchen the creeps.

She shook her head, chiding herself, as she drove in circles trying to find her way to Camelback Road.

She couldn't add Milt Wood to the suspect list just because of a feeling. That was too Nina-like. She'd leave auras and energy fields to her aunt and proceed with hard facts.

Fact one, regarding Milt Wood. He tried to buy two Kewpie dolls from her, becoming increasingly offensive and pushy when he didn't get his way. He remained persistent even when told that one of the dolls had been extensively repaired and wasn't worth purchasing. Fact two, Milt had easy access to Percy, just as Steve and Eric had.

Who else? Detective Matt Albright. Not that he was on the suspect list. He certainly had an air of arrogant self-confidence about him, but last she heard, that wasn't a qualifier for murderous intent. Although the promise of treasure might trip a latent trigger. Who knew what went on inside a killer's mind?

And Albert had been beaten by a cop. That cop could have been Matt.

Her opinion of the detective was sinking as rapidly as a rock thrown from the summit of Camelback Mountain. He was probably gathering evidence to make his case and earn himself a big promotion, and he had chosen a brutal, cruel avenue to the top. Assaulting helpless indigents was as low as anyone could stoop.

So much for the men in Gretchen's life. Once this situation was firmly behind her, she vowed to distance herself from the entire male population and focus on her career. Men had already taken up too much of her time and energy, and the only thing she was getting for her efforts was disappointment.

Shouldn't she be home right this minute, answering business calls and repairing dolls? Piles of unfinished broken dolls didn't put food on the table, or give her the income necessary to get her own place.

You're still living with your mother, she reminded herself. *Time to grow up and move out.*

Gretchen entered the Biltmore Fashion Park with Nimrod riding in her purse and walked briskly through the exclusive mall until she found what she was looking for.

Ricardo's Fine Jewelry.

Young, fashionably bejeweled women helped customers from behind resplendent display cases.

"Nimrod, hide," she commanded as she entered the store. Nimrod ducked down.

She strode past the glistening cases and toothy sales staff to the back of the store, where an elderly man with coke-bottle eyeglasses sat stooped over a cluttered worktable. "Can I help you?" he said, reluctantly glancing up from a Rolex watch he was repairing.

"I have a hypothetical question," Gretchen said, wondering how best to approach the subject. The truth would take too long to explain, and besides, he would write her off as a kook. *She* almost didn't believe what she was thinking. Okay, so a small fib was the best tactic. "A bet I have going with a friend."

He looked at her questioningly.

"If a little doll, a hollow doll, about this big," said Gretchen, holding her forefinger and thumb apart to approximate three inches, "was filled with diamonds, would it be heavy enough to alert anyone who handled it that something was inside?"

The jeweler frowned. At first, Gretchen

thought he might dismiss her as crazy or — worse — a potential thief. Maybe he had an alarm button under the table like a bank teller and was alerting the police at this very moment.

After a long pause to size her up, the jeweler said, "Not necessarily. It would be relatively light, hard to detect by a casual observer. Even one who might hold it. That is, as long as the diamonds were secured so they weren't rattling around inside." He rose from the table. "Not a likely scenario though."

"Why not?" She felt Nimrod stirring in the bottom of the purse. He liked the game of hide, but he was easily distracted. Gretchen dug a liver snap out of one of her pockets and casually dropped it into the purse.

The jeweler looked through his magnification glasses at the purse, then over the top of them at her.

"Why isn't it likely?" she asked again.

"A doll filled with diamonds would be worth an immense fortune. Who would own that many diamonds?"

"How many diamonds could a doll that size hold? Hypothetically."

"Ten or twelve fine diamonds could fit easily into a doll that size and could be worth a million dollars or more, depending on their size, brilliancy, and clarity."

"So a doll filled with diamonds could be worth multimillions."

"Correct. Hypothetically, as you say."

"Thank you, you've been a big help."

Gretchen smiled at him broadly to express her gratitude.

"Well?" he said.

"Well, what?"

"Who won?"

For a moment, Gretchen didn't understand his question. Then she remembered the imaginary bet.

"I did," she said. "I won."

A million dollars or more. A fine, sparkling jewel of a motive. A million plausible reasons for murder.

Like winning the lottery.

Gretchen thought back on all the things that had happened to her in the last few days: the scorpion, the killer's use of her hobby knife, the messages that continued to arrive addressed to her. She sincerely hoped she would win. It was apparent that the killer thought she was close to either the diamonds or the truth — or both — and he was taking steps to stop her.

She had to win. Or at the very least, come out of this unharmed.

As she stepped out into the warm desert night, Gretchen opened the poodle-embroidered purse and praised Nimrod for remaining out of sight. His furry body bounced to the top of the purse, and Gretchen fed him another treat.

All she wanted to do was walk away. But how? She hadn't asked for any part of this, but she was into it up to her neck, like quicksand, and she was sinking fast.

The truth, and that alone, would save her.

"I don't know what you're doing here," Nina said through clenched teeth. "Can't you see this is a private dining room? And look at the way you're dressed."

"I'm not staying long," Gretchen said, extremely conscious of her wrinkled shorts and inappropriate footwear. Flip-flops were acceptable nearly everywhere these days, but as Gretchen looked around her at the opulence of the Praying Monk, the Phoenician's finest private dining room, she could think of one exception. She sat down and buried her feet under the table, sliding the tapestry-covered chair Eric provided closer to the table.

Nina gasped when she noticed Gretchen's purse. "Please don't tell me Nimrod's in there." She clutched her heart.

"All right, Nina, I won't. You look lovely."

Nina shot her a look. "You could have left him at home with Daisy."

The entrée dishes had been quickly removed, and coffee and crème brûlée arrived with an extra spoon for Gretchen. Eric pointed up at the barrel-vaulted ceiling. "Wonderful design, isn't it?" he said.

"I don't mean to interrupt your evening," Gretchen said, after agreeing with him, "but I hope you don't mind answering a few questions."

Nina snorted. "Couldn't you wait until tomorrow?"

"I don't mind." Eric patted Nina's hand comfortingly.

"Tell me about Percy's history," Gretchen said. "Where did his family's fortune come from?"

"Ah, you've heard the rumors."

Gretchen nodded.

"The story goes that his father made his fortune as a profiteer during the war. That part of the O'Connor past has been confirmed by local historians, an indisputable fact, and was the main reason why Percy could never be accepted in certain Boston social circles. Black marketeering was an unsavory profession, at best, when the country was working together to ration

304

scarce supplies. Whether his father really converted his wealth into diamonds is strictly hearsay, and a bit unrealistic, I imagine."

"One report suggested that the O'Connors hid diamonds inside of Kewpie dolls." Gretchen dipped into the crème brûlée that Eric offered her, recalling that she hadn't eaten anything for hours.

Eric laughed. "Nonsense. What report was that?"

"She doesn't remember offhand," Nina said. "Do you, Gretchen?"

Gretchen felt a sharp heel grinding into the top of her foot, warning her that Nina had reached the end of her patience. Gretchen felt a stab of shame that she was about to bring Nina's evening to an abrupt closure.

"Pretty quiet in that purse," Nina observed. "If he wakes up and causes a ruckus, I'll never live down the embarrassment."

"You could never embarrass me," Eric said to her with a warm smile. "You are the epitome of grace and charm."

Gretchen took a sip of coffee.

"You know," Eric said, rubbing his plump chin in thought, "I recall hearing once of documents hidden in dolls. A United States citizen spying for the Japanese sent damaging information regarding our ships at Pearl Harbor via messages inside of dolls. The FBI finally caught on, and she was arrested."

"How does Percy fit into that?" Nina said.

"He doesn't." Eric sipped his coffee. "I'm simply saying it's been done, and there's a certain fascination among the general populace regarding that whole subject of dolls and hidden secrets. Your suggestion might not be as far-fetched as I originally thought." His eyes widened. "Oh. I see where this is going. A smashed Kewpie doll was found in the study along with Percy's body. Do you suppose the doll contained diamonds? The police didn't find anything missing. Perhaps that was the motive."

"That's my best guess," Gretchen said. "Only the killer didn't actually find any diamonds."

"What makes you think that?" Eric rearranged his chair and crossed his legs.

"Because I think he's in Phoenix, which can only mean that he's still looking for the treasure. Why else would he risk exposing himself? If he had the diamonds, he'd be long gone."

"Or she," Nina said, drawn into the intrigue in spite of herself. "You can't automatically assume the killer is a man. I'm a woman's libber from way back." She grinned broadly at Eric. "I believe in total equality."

They gazed into each other's eyes for a while, and Gretchen used the time to check on Nimrod, lying next to her feet, still curled in the bottom of the purse, sound asleep.

Finally Gretchen said, "He — or she — arrived just in time for Chiggy's auction and the doll show. Don't you see?"

"I'm afraid I don't." Eric's voice turned icy, and he uncrossed his legs and leaned toward her. "You aren't implying that one of my club members is responsible for the demise of that abrasive reporter and the poor auctioneer's assistant, are you? Our group was established years ago. Every single member is like family to me."

"That's quite a leap in logic, Eric. You're implying that Brett and Ronny were killed by the same person who murdered Percy O'Connor. Interesting." Gretchen firmly met his eyes and didn't waver. "I didn't think of that. You arrived at that conclusion seconds after hearing the facts, whereas I . . . well . . . it wasn't obvious to me until you said it now." Gretchen smiled sweetly.

"I . . . I . . ." Eric blustered, thrown off guard. "I merely stated the obvious."

"Still, it's simply speculation, and I'm sure the police will think of every angle." She didn't believe that for a minute. "You're very good at analysis."

"I read extensively." Eric's face was unfathomable. "Law enforcement and the criminal mind have always fascinated me. But I don't appreciate your implications. You may pretend you aren't suggesting a Bostonian mass murderer in our midst all you want, but I know you are. I suggest, Ms. Birch, that you allow the police to handle murder cases. Stick to doll repair."

"Let's go, Nina," Gretchen said, her eyes still locked on Eric.

"Wha . . . Why?"

"I stopped by to check on Tutu earlier, and she must have eaten something that disagreed with her. She's lying on her little bed, moaning horribly, and she can't get up."

"Why didn't you say something sooner?" Nina almost tipped over the chair when she rose.

Gretchen hadn't crashed Nina's party just to quiz Eric on Percy's history, although the information she gleaned had been worth the trip. The real reason stood in front of her, impatiently waiting for Gretchen to gather up Nimrod and race home.

If diamonds were the killer's motive, the stakes were higher than Gretchen ever imagined.

Until the murderer was exposed, she couldn't leave her aunt alone with anyone, even her new friend, Eric Huntington.

The only way to safely and quietly remove her from his company was by duping Nina into believing that something was wrong with her beloved dog. Nina would be incredibly angry in a few minutes when she found out the truth.

Most likely Eric had nothing to do with the recent deaths. There certainly were enough other suspects running around loose, including her own ex-boyfriend, who seemed to have more than a few secrets. Perhaps Gretchen had ruined Nina's first real date in years over unfounded fears.

But Gretchen would rather have an angry aunt than a dead one.

From now on, they were sticking close together.

30

Tuesday morning Gretchen sipped coffee and watched the sunrise from a window in the doll repair shop. On a regular day not marred by recent dead and disturbing occurrences, dawn brought a vibrant energy to the start of her day. This morning she'd risen earlier than usual after a fitful night's sleep interrupted by murky dreams. Murky because the dreams hovered on a fragile line close to horrifying blackness. They weren't certifiable nightmares, but close enough to force Gretchen out of bed before daylight rather than risk having another one if she dozed off again.

Dark and foreboding thoughts continued to run through her head as she sat at the window.

Why had Steve followed her to Arizona in the first place? It was out of character for him to seek reconciliation. He had always left that to her. Steve, staunchly cautious and emotionless when dealing with their conflicts, had paid a heavy price for finally allowing real human emotions to surface.

But he was too late. Gretchen had seen other relationships crumble because one of the partners refused to acknowledge the other's discontent. It seemed as though change was usually offered after the door to reconciliation had already closed. If only Steve had been a little more attentive to her and a little less so to other women, she probably would have stayed with him forever.

He'd reacted too late to save their relationship, way too late. But Gretchen couldn't bear to see him destroyed. He'd lost his chance for partnership at the law firm in Boston as well as her. She hoped, for his sake, he'd manage to prove his innocence, keep his freedom, and move on with his life.

Like she was trying to do.

After seven years of couplehood, she was struggling through a vast and complex desert of singleness, and today, another perpetually sunny Arizona day, Gretchen felt totally alone in the world. But aloneness, as she was finding out, wasn't synonymous with loneliness.

In fact, it felt good, sort of renewing.

Gretchen selected a doll from a repair bin.

She applied a line of glue around the edge of a kid leather patch she had made before the doll show, worked the glue around with her fingers, and placed the patch over a hole in a French fashion doll's leather body. She used a doll hook to secure it against the doll's body.

Nina had been furious when she learned that Tutu was fine and that Gretchen had used the dog as an excuse to wrench her away from that intriguing man. "Jealous," Nina had snarled, "jealous that I might find a shred of happiness."

Nina, the drama queen, had made it very clear that Gretchen should stay out of her path until she cooled down.

Whenever that might be.

The phone rang, and her mother's cell number appeared on the caller ID.

"What's new?" Caroline asked.

What's new? Why did her mother have to ask that every time she called? Gretchen wasn't about to spoil her trip, but her cover-ups were quickly becoming full-blown lies.

"New? Not much. I'm working on the dolls from the show."

"Is Steve still in Phoenix?"

Oh, yes, he is. "Unfortunately."

"He has a lot of pride. It'll take him some time to come to grips with your decision."

"I have a few repair questions for you," Gretchen said, steering the conversation to safer topics.

They spent a few minutes talking about some of Gretchen's more complex doll repair problems before disconnecting.

Dolls. Her eyes swept the shop's wide assortment of dolls and doll parts. How could something created with such loving hands, that invoked memories of warmth and comfort in adults as well as children, become a tool of greed and destruction?

Gretchen laid the doll aside, rose from the worktable, and wandered to the kitchen.

She found the note from Daisy right after she poured a cup of coffee. "Gone to an audition. Be back later. Don't let anyone go into my room." Gretchen wondered how the woman managed to disappear without a trace. Did she have an invisible cloak? Gretchen grinned. An audition. Daisy, always waiting for her star.

Still smiling, Gretchen went to the cabana next to the pool, which she had taken over when she moved in. Her mother had remodeled the bathhouse, and now it served as a guesthouse for visitors. More of a casita than a cabana.

Staying there made her feel as though she had a place of her own.

Gretchen tapped a few keys on her computer, and the screen lit up. Last night she had quickly scanned through Peter Finch's pictures, but weariness and her argument with Nina had prevented her from a thorough study of them.

What did she hope to see? A grinning murderer mugging from one of the pictures?

That would be a good start.

Scrolling rapidly through the photographs of dolls, she stopped when she came to the series of pictures taken at the scene of Brett's death, after the ambulance pulled away. Gretchen recognized some of the people milling around on the curb.

A woman who'd bid on a couple of Chiggy's worst reproductions.

The driver whose SUV had struck Brett, a Phoenix Police Department investigator at her side, her hands clasping a face that registered anguish.

Half of Howie caught in another photo, his left side. Gretchen saw raw grief etched along the portion of his jawline that showed. Real pain, or contrived emotion for the camera? From everything Gretchen had heard, Howie and Brett had had a long and close friendship in addition to a business relationship, synchronized like the gears inside the wristwatch repaired by the jeweler.

Pictures popped onto the computer screen, and Gretchen continued to click slowly through them. Uniformed police officers caught in the camera frame, frozen in varying positions among groups of stunned onlookers.

Gretchen searched for the face of the homeless man who had claimed to have witnessed a murder, although by the time these photos were taken, he might have moved away from the accident. The homeless community and the local police force, Gretchen knew, barely tolerated each other. Street people like Nacho, Daisy, and Albert didn't trust cops. Maybe for good reason, considering what happened to Albert. Paranoia would have driven him away at the first sign of trouble.

How long had the spectators stayed along the street after Brett was struck and killed? It had seemed to Gretchen that time stood still, but in fact, at least one agonizing hour had elapsed between the first squeal of tires and the time when she had wandered up to the registration desk to get the Kewpie doll owner's address. By then, the police had already interrogated those closest to the accident and had encouraged the rest to move on.

She thought about the sequence of events. A call for an ambulance, the wait for it to respond, the paramedics' efforts to revive Brett before transporting their unresponsive patient, the police and their search for eyewitnesses. The ambulance pulling away, and everyone remaining in Chiggy's yard, in shock, moving aimlessly around the flat-bed truck.

Gretchen leaned heavily on her elbows and squeezed the bridge of her nose as she continued to search the pictures. Oh, the glory of modern technology. Digital cameras, no longer constrained by antiquated film and the costs of processing, allowed a photographer to shoot continuously, almost like movie frames, catching the action in a series of fluid movements. Photo after photo.

Viewing Finch's pictures brought back memories that would haunt her for a long time. She relived the horror of that moment when she first realized what the squeal of tires meant. When she saw Brett lying in the street.

Her own father had died next to her. Again she heard the squealing tires and the impact of the other car slamming into the driver's side of her father's car.

Old memories that wouldn't fade.

She wasn't looking forward to the memorial service tonight.

"I'm an old friend of hers," Gretchen said to the administrator on the phone, after looking up the number for Grace Senior Care.

"I don't see a Chiggy Kent listed here," the voice replied, sounding young and hesitant.

"I'm sorry. I forgot. Her real name is Florence. Florence Kent."

"Just a minute."

Gretchen heard papers rustling.

"Yes, I've found her."

"Good. I'd like to drive over and visit her."

"I'm sorry . . . Ms. . . . what did you say your name was?"

"Um . . . Mary Smith." It was time to go undercover for her own extended good health.

"I'm sorry, Ms. Smith, but Ms. Kent has been moved from assisted living, and she isn't accepting visitors."

"Moved from assisted living?"

"Yes, she now requires an elevated level of care."

That translated to nursing home care.

Gretchen remembered talk among the other club members of the ever-present oxygen tank.

"But she only arrived last week. Surely her health hasn't declined that rapidly." According to Peter Finch, Chiggy had been well enough a week ago to supervise the disposition of her household furnishings and arrange to auction off her collection of handmade dolls. "I was under the impression that she had some sort of apartment arrangement."

"I really can't tell you any more than that. The federal privacy act doesn't allow me to elaborate on her condition without her written consent. Would you like to speak to my supervisor?"

"I don't understand why I can't visit with her. Chiggy . . . I mean, Florence was an active member of the Phoenix Dollers Club, and I'm representing the members when I say we are all concerned about her well-being. You can't just shut her away and refuse to allow us to visit."

"It was her wish to discourage visitors. She isn't being held against her will. Can I get my supervisor?"

"How about family? Can family visit?"

"She was very clear. Absolutely no visitors. I'm getting a supervisor." The woman sounded impatient but continued to hold her ground.

"That won't be necessary," Gretchen said, glad that she had blocked her call before dialing the senior care center. She'd assumed that they would have caller ID, and she didn't want her real identity known.

"I think I'll drive over and make the request in person."

"This is a gated senior center."

It figures, Gretchen thought. The old woman had been permanently locked away.

Gretchen inched along the sidewalk while tiny Nimrod scurried along beside her. He stopped often to sniff the ground and mark his territory.

"Hello there," someone said.

Gretchen turned to see a woman around her age walking rapidly toward her, pushing two toddlers in a double stroller.

"You must be Caroline Birch's daughter," she said. "I've seen you coming and going but haven't had a chance to introduce myself. I'm Janice Schmidt, and these are my twins, Troy and Tim. They're almost two."

Gretchen smiled at the twins and wiggled her fingers next to her face in a silly wave. "Hi, kids. This is Nimrod. We're going for his daily walk."

Not the most disciplined walking-on-a-leash trainee, Nimrod proceeded to wrap the leash around Gretchen's feet in a frantic burst of energy. She stepped out of the center before becoming completely ensnarled. The twins spotted the miniature puppy and leaned out of the stroller, giggling in unison.

"I hope everything is okay at your house," Janice said. "Did someone break in, or try to?"

"I'm sorry?" Gretchen said, confused. "A break-in?"

"Yes, well, I saw Lilly Beth speaking to a police officer in your front yard, and I assumed . . ." She let the sentence fade away, a pink flush rising from her neck. "Judging from your reaction, you don't know anything about it, do you?"

Gretchen glanced at Lilly Beth's house and thought she saw someone step back from the window. Her mother had warned her about the nosy, gossipy neighbor as soon as Gretchen moved in. "Don't speak to her," she'd said. Lilly Beth will turn your words against you no matter how innocently spoken. Nina had agreed that the woman was poison.

"Tell me," she said to Janice.

"I don't know anything else. They spoke for a little while, and the officer left. I assumed he was responding to a break-in at your house or perhaps a tripped alarm."

Lilly Beth had been nothing but trouble for the Birch family, attempting to shut down the doll repair business her mother had started and going so far as to call the police several times over vividly imagined and nonexistent infractions.

What had she called the police about this time?

"When did this happen?" she asked Janice.

"Yesterday afternoon."

What had they done wrong this time? Closed the door too loudly when they left? Allowed a scrap of blown litter to linger a moment or two in the front, where it had drastically reduced Lilly Beth's property value? A facial expression that Lilly Beth had interpreted as hostile? One more citizen complaint, and Gretchen would begin to fight back.

"Look, I've had my own share of trouble with her," Janice said. "But she's just a lonely, bitter woman who needs someone to extend a hand in friendship. You're thinking she called the police, planning to make trouble for you, and you're probably right. I shouldn't have said anything. It only creates more problems, and I'm sorry I was part of it."

"It's okay." Gretchen picked up Nimrod and let the twins feel his soft fur. "She can't do anything to cause real harm. I'll let it go."

Janice let out a sigh of relief. "I can't imagine what it could have been about," she said, her forehead creasing as she spoke. "I did find one thing a little odd, however."

"What's that?" Gretchen asked.

"The police officer wasn't in a squad car. I didn't see him pull up to your house, but he drove away in a truck. Isn't that a bit unusual?"

Gretchen felt prickles of fear on the skin of her exposed arms. The sun, comfortably warm a moment ago, felt unbearably chilly. "What kind of truck?" she asked in a whisper, pretending to be engrossed in puppy play with the children.

"A pickup truck. I don't think I've ever seen that kind of vehicle used by the police department. Well, maybe he was on his way home from work, off-duty, and he responded because he was closest? That must be it. Why didn't I think of that sooner?"

Gretchen tried to speak, but her words stuck in her throat. She cleared it, emitting a croaking frog sound. "What color was the truck?"

"Hmm . . ." Janice paused, and Gretchen drew Nimrod closer to her chest.

"Green," Janice called out, like she'd remembered the winning Trivial Pursuit question. "It was green."

Gretchen sighed in relief, louder and longer than she'd ever sighed before. If Janice had said blue, Gretchen would have keeled over in a dead faint.

Albert Thoreau had seen Brett's killer step from a blue truck.

Green was a nice, safe color. It meant life, growth, and good health. The green grass of home, forest green. It also could mean jealousy and envy and green money, which could come from a doll full of diamonds.

She shook her head to change her train of thought. She'd been a little nervous lately, not feeling quite right.

Yes, green was very, very good.

31

"Nina, pick up the phone. I know you're home." Gretchen said under her breath, having been reduced, thanks to Nina's antics, to holding conversations with herself.

Gretchen disconnected and punched in Nina's cell phone number.

"Nina, I called your house, and you wouldn't answer. Also your answering machine didn't turn on, so I assume that you shut it off. You know I'm worried about this killer, and I'm worried about you. Refusing to talk to me is making my fears worse. Where are you?"

Gretchen struggled to keep the frustration out of her voice.

"If you don't respond to this message within the next two hours, I'm calling the police."

That ought to fire her up. Obviously, Nina wasn't taking overt threats by a maniacal killer seriously. Hadn't Gretchen just received a "you're next" threat hidden inside a Kewpie Doodle Dog? If Nina wasn't concerned about herself, the least she could do was pretend to show a little concern for Gretchen's welfare.

Gretchen ended the message to Nina and speed-dialed her mentor in the Michigan Upper Peninsula.

"Aunt Gertie, I need more advice." She related all the happenings she thought might be associated with the three murders, leaving nothing out. "I'm at a dead end, a brick wall," she finished.

Gertie laughed. "You sure do give up easily. There's lots that you can do. This Chigger —"

"Chiggy."

"Whatever. That woman has some answers, if you can get to her."

"It's impossible."

"Nothing is impossible. You can infiltrate that nursing home if you put your mind to it. Find a time when all the staff are watching some popular soap opera in the nurses' station and crawl right past. That works every time."

Gretchen decided not to ask her aunt how she came to know this.

"But first, you have to find the bozo who's sending you the messages."

"Impossible."

"I don't ever want to hear you say that word again. It's a sorry excuse for refusing to think your way through a situation. I'm going to help you this time because you're new at this, but after this time, you're on your own. Listen up. Are you listening?"

"I'm listening."

"Sometimes you're dopier than a dwarf. Every single one of those cupid dolls came in the same wrapping. Right?"

Cupid dolls?

Gretchen let the misnomer slide. "Right."

"Then why haven't you been down to that liquor store?"

"How many people would you guess buy alcohol from a liquor store? Hundreds?"

"Stake it out. You'll know the culprit the minute you spot him."

"Aunt Nina thinks it might be a woman."

"Your aunt Nina is one stop short of the nearest loony bin, and the train is leaving the station soon with her on board. Last stop: Nutsville."

"That's a little harsh," Gretchen said in defense of her temperamental aunt. The only reason the two women disagreed so often was because they were exactly the same. Strong, independent females, used to running their own shows, their own ways.

"It's a man, all right," Gertie said again. "Mark my words. I'd hop a plane and help you out, but I've got an investigation going on here that I can't leave. Three murders." Gertie whistled. "That's a handful. Watch your back, dearie."

Gretchen had enough trouble watching her front and flanks. She felt naked as a Kewpie doll but not nearly as happy. Still, she felt better having spoken with her Yooper aunt.

When the doorbell rang and she found April standing outside, Gretchen almost kissed her. Finally, someone to commiserate with.

"I hear you and your shadow are fighting," April said. "Want some company?"

She noticed Gretchen staring at her outfit. "You like it?" April twirled in a blaze orange sundress the size of the state of Michigan, where wearing orange was the height of fashion. Aunt Gertie's hometown seemed to have one hunting season after another, and everyone wore blaze or ange. In Arizona, well, April looked like a retro Volkswagen Beetle.

"Lovely, as usual," Gretchen said, grabbing her purse and calling Nimrod. He charged in, ready to go.

Wobbles strutted behind him, graceful and

lithe even without his back leg. April bent to pick him up, but he gave her a warning glare and flattened his ears.

"That's one ornery cat," April said, settling for running her hands over his lean back and swiping at his tail.

"He doesn't like to be held," Gretchen said, opening a phone book and running her finger down the list of Albrights. "We have to find out where Matt Albright's wife lives and get the Kewpie dolls back. I'm not sure that they mean anything, but I want them all the same."

April sighed. "Still thinking inside the same old box."

"And then we're going to find Duanne Wilson and get my box of Ginny dolls."

"That's more like it. Do you have a plan?"

"I don't have a clue how to find him, so we'll start with the Kewpies." She checked her watch. Eleven thirty a.m. "I gave Nina a two-hour warning. She's not answering my calls."

"That's easy. You want me to get her to respond?"

"Sure."

April picked up the kitchen phone and dialed. "By the way," she said to Gretchen, eyeing the phone book. "The Albrights aren't listed in the directory. Detectives don't usually advertise their home addresses, too many dissatisfied customers. But I know where she lives. Kayla has the house, and he's staying at . . . Nina, pick up. It's me, April . . . We're tracking down evidence, and we hope to crack the case today. If you want in on the apprehension and fame and glory, you better pick up the phone."

April paused as though listening and grinned at Gretchen.

"Yes," she said smugly into the phone. "We'll pick you up on the drive-by, and I'll give you the details then."

"See?" she said, hanging up. "You have to appeal to the adventuress in her. Let's go."

32

Peter Finch moves aside and grudgingly allows the uniformed police officer to enter his apartment. The cop eyes him suspiciously, or so Peter thinks, and he hopes he isn't some sort of suspect.

Don't let on that you know, he reminds himself. If Gretchen Birch hadn't told him that Brett might have been pushed, he would still think it had been an accident, that Brett had stepped out into the street without looking. Like everybody else thought.

What a shock, if it is true. Then again, it must be true. Why else would this cop be standing in front of him, saying he is confiscating Peter's equipment?

Don't let on that you know, he says to himself again. For some reason, he instinctively knows that won't be wise. *Play dumb.*

Unless the cop is here about Ronny Beam. Just his luck to be at Chiggy's house at the same time as Brett and Ronny, and now both of them dead and the cop with a search warrant and eyeing him up like he's a common criminal.

But didn't he hear that they caught the guy who killed Ronny? The cop should pay more attention to the news.

Peter spreads a hand across his gaunt face and rubs his temples with his thumb and forefinger, a dull throb pulsing under his fingertips.

"I can make copies of anything you want," he says again, grasping desperately for alternatives. "This is my lifeline. You take it, I don't have any income. I'll get you copies. What's the difference to you if it's originals or copies?"

The cop brushes past him, a little roughly, pushing Peter against the wall, stalking across the room, arms swinging loose and alert, elbows bent slightly in readiness, prepared for trouble.

Why me? Peter thinks.

And don't these guys travel with backup, other cops?

Before closing the door, Peter sticks his head out. No other uniforms outside.

The cop looks vaguely familiar. Where has he seen him before?

Peter looks at the name on the badge.

Never heard of him.

The cop begins bagging Peter's camera equipment, his flash cards, his downloaded discs. Taking everything instead of sorting through and taking only the photos from the auction. Although the cop has given no explanation for seizing his possessions, Peter knows it pertains to last week's auction and the dolls.

"Let me do it," he says, aghast when the cop starts throwing things haphazardly into plastic bags. "I have padded camera cases. You'll ruin everything that way."

Dumb cop.

Peter gently places his digital camera in a bag.

Most of the doll pictures are already on the Internet, already a commodity, but the pictures taken at the auction are gone now. He wonders if he'll ever get them back.

Then he remembers the woman and the extra copy he made for her. What a relief.

He recognizes this cop from someplace recently. The auction, perhaps, or the doll show.

That's it.

The doll show.

Peter opens the door for the officer, who has an armful of bags and a camera case slung over his shoulder. Peter watches him store the equipment in his vehicle.

He returns, and Peter's heart drops a little lower in his chest when he sees what else the officer plans on removing.

"You can't take my computer." He watches him disconnect the cables and heave the heavy processing unit into his arms. He's strong, like a body builder.

Peter is scared, but he'll file a complaint as soon as the officer leaves. "You can't take a man's only source of income."

The officer doesn't reply. Can't the cop talk?

And why's he putting everything in the back of a pickup truck? Don't cops usually announce their presence better, drive squad cars with flashing lights and sirens?

Peter can't see any lights mounted on top of the truck.

The officer adjusts his holster and comes back in.

Now what? Peter wonders. *There isn't anything left to take.*

"Wait a minute." It suddenly dawns on him where he's seen the cop before. He's even photographed him. "I know you."

The cop's eyes narrow. Staring into them, Peter realizes how brutally cold they are and what a deadly mistake he's just made.

Or maybe nothing he said would have made any difference anyway.

33

Detective Albright's estranged wife, Kayla, lived in the Fairview Place Historic District in Central Phoenix. Taking directions from her two backseat drivers, Gretchen drove along McDowell Road and turned on Sixteenth Avenue.

"Slow down. That's it right there," April announced, pointing at a Tudor with a For Sale sign in front of it. Garbage cans lined the curb up and down the street.

Nina undid her seat belt when Gretchen stopped the car. She leaned forward. "I never noticed how small your Echo was until I had to sit in the back."

"You'd have a lot more room if you'd leave the dogs home," April said, voicing what Gretchen thought but was afraid to say. Communication with her aunt was still tenuous.

Nimrod, Tutu, and Sophie, the Yorkie trainee, bounced back and forth across

Nina's lap, smearing the windows with wet nose goo. It looked like doggie day care in the backseat.

"Cozy," April said, gazing at the house.

"Unpretentious," Nina added. "Bonnie told me that Matt's staying with a cop friend until the house sells. Bonnie wanted him to move home, but he refused. Probably all those dolls in Bonnie's house. Even though he's working on his phobia, that would be hard. Besides, who wants to move home with their mo —" She clasped a hand across her mouth.

Gretchen pretended not to hear. She had to look for her own apartment ASAP.

"We're in luck," she said, pulling to the curb. "It's garbage pickup day, and there it is."

How lucky could she be? The box sat right out in the front yard. No need to confront Matt's wife over it. She'd simply swipe it back.

That is, if the dolls were still inside the box.

"Everyone stay here," Gretchen said, unlatching the trunk from inside the car. "We'll make this as quick as possible."

"I'll get it," April said, making a move to open her door.

"No," Gretchen said firmly. "I made the

336

mistake of giving it to the wrong person, and I'll fix my own mistake."

What she didn't say was that the words *April* and *quick* created an oxymoron, impossible to use together in the same sentence. Even on a good day, April moved with the speed of a tarantula.

Gretchen popped out of the Echo before April could react, ran around the front of the car, opened the box flaps to make sure that the broken doll pieces were still there, and picked up the box.

"What do you think you're doing?" an angry voice shouted from the house.

"Just salvaging a few things before the truck hauls it away," Gretchen replied, keeping her back to the woman in hopes that she wouldn't be recognized. "For our church rummage sale."

"Get out of my yard, Gretchen Birch. Haven't you done enough damage?"

Gretchen turned and risked a glance at the enraged woman. She was everything Gretchen wasn't. Wispy thin, fine bones and features, silky brunette tresses featuring both highlights and lowlights. With the right gown and necklace, she could have been the lead model for the stacks of paperback romance novels sold in every airport.

Gretchen felt chubby, awkward, mousy,

and a multitude of other unattractive adjectives.

Kayla picked up a decorative stone from the base of a prickly pear cactus and flung it toward Gretchen. It bounced off her car, and a small scratch appeared in the finish.

"Drop the box," Kayla said, picking up more stones. "Or I'll hit your car again." She cocked her arm like she thought she was Joe DiMaggio.

Gretchen dropped the box and heard the porcelain pieces inside rattling around.

Kayla marched up with a fistful of stones and stopped when she saw Gretchen's bodyguards rising from the Echo.

April emerged in her orange regalia, followed by Nina with her out-of-control canines lunging at the ends of three dainty leashes.

"Back off," Nina said, threateningly, "or I'll let them go, and it won't be pretty."

A loud snort burst from April, and she and Nina started laughing hysterically.

"Get out of here, or I'll call the police," Kayla said, whirling on Gretchen. "You can have him. You did me a huge favor, you know."

"I really don't know what you're talking about." Gretchen sized up the distance from the box to the trunk and thought about making a run for it. She could always leave the comedy team behind. The only thing that stopped her from abandoning her convulsing sidekicks was Nimrod. She couldn't leave without him.

"Act innocent all you want," Kayla snarled. "Just be careful what you wish for. He's not what he seems on the surface, that golden boy fake front. He's been threatening my life, you know. I have a restraining order to keep him away. The man is insane."

April lumbered over and picked up the box, still trying to stifle her giggles, and Kayla didn't move while she stowed it in the trunk. Who could blame her? April could have been a sumo wrestler in her younger days. "Let's go," April said, slamming the trunk closed. "Everybody in."

Kayla stood glaring at them as they screeched from the neighborhood. Two blocks away, Gretchen glanced in her rearview mirror. Kayla still stood motionless, watching.

"Good thing you had us along," April said.

"Well, that confirms it," Nina said. "Bonnie's right. She needs to be heavily medicated."

Gretchen didn't respond. Kayla was certainly bitter and vengeful and could be making up things about Matt. She wasn't an entirely believable source, but her comments about Matt drove another wedge in the small crack of mistrust that already existed.

Gretchen glanced into the backseat and did a head count. Three women, three dogs. The trunk held a box of broken Kewpie dolls poorly crafted by Chiggy Kent.

All accounted for.

"You should have seen the swirl of dark colors whirling around her. It was like the middle of a dust storm," Nina said from the backseat. "That woman's dangerous."

Nina seemed back to normal, entourage in tow and energy fields spurting all around her. "Have you been practicing with your aura glasses?" she asked.

"I haven't had time."

"What glasses?" April asked.

"Check them out. They're in Gretchen's purse."

"Mind if I find them?" April said, picking up Gretchen's purse. "This thing must weigh twenty pounds." She looked inside. "Jeez."

"They're in the side pocket," Gretchen said, turning toward the senior center that housed the evasive doll maker.

April extracted the cardboard glasses.

"What are they supposed to do?" she asked, putting them on.

Nina explained auras and the practiced ability to see colors emanating from people.

April turned to study Gretchen, squinting through the aura glasses. "I see something, kind of like yellow light."

"Wonderful," Nina clapped her hands. "You're very advanced for a novice."

"Nina," Gretchen said, "isn't light normally yellow?"

"The reason you can't see anything is because of your skepticism," Nina retorted. "You have to let go of your rigid thinking, learn to use your third eye, and embrace the visual that doesn't necessarily follow human logic. Logic, I will remind you, that is flawed to begin with."

"Here it is." Gretchen turned into the driveway of an institutional building that was well-disguised as a senior community for well-heeled Arizonians. She pulled up to a guard station and lowered her window.

"We're here to see Florence Kent," she informed the man when he stuck his head out of the door. "Please open the gate."

He poked his head back inside, pulled a radio from his belt, and spoke into it. He returned the radio to his belt and opened the door wide, framing it with his considerable bulk. "No visitors," he informed them. "No names on the list for Florence Kent today, so you can't go in. Call for an appointment. Then your name will hit the list, and I'll open up. That's the way it works."

"Can I call and talk to her?" Gretchen asked.

"You have to pass it through the switchboard, but I think she's restricted."

"Is this a prison or what?" April called through the open window. "I never heard of a lockdown like this in all my life."

The guard hiked his pants and leaned over to peer in at the passengers, taking in April, Nina, and the festival of canines crowding the car window. "The privacy that our residents receive at Grace Senior Care is the exact reason they come here. They don't want every Tom, Dick, and Harry rolling in whenever, like you women are trying to do."

He frowned when another car pulled in alongside of the Echo. "Now back up and pull away before I get annoyed. You're blocking traffic."

Gretchen backed out of the driveway and drove out of sight of the guard station before finding a parking space. "Now what?" she asked. "Either Chiggy doesn't want company, or someone else is making sure she doesn't have any."

"We can walk in," April suggested. "They probably don't have much security inside because of the guard at the gate. We can walk down that sidewalk over there," she pointed along a walkway. "And go right in."

"Okay," Gretchen agreed. "What do we have to lose? But . . . you'll have to stay in the car, April."

"Why?"

"Because you look like a mutant orange tulip." Gretchen saw April's face caving in and beginning to register a look of anguished hurt, so she added quickly. "Beautiful and vibrant and totally memorable. The last thing we want is to stand out."

April glanced down at her dress and beamed. "I see what you mean." Then, a little sheepishly, "I didn't want to go anyway."

"I suppose you think I should do this instead of April?" Nina piped up. "What you're planning is probably against the law. Since when did you start sneaking around?"

"I guess since I started getting threatening letters."

"That's melodramatic." Spoken by Nina, queen of the dramatic actors association. She crossed her arms over her chest. "I'm staying here, too. If you're in jail, somebody will have to take care of Nimrod and

Wobbles."

"Fine," Gretchen said, opening the car door.

"Leave the air-conditioning on," April suggested. "It's hot as French fry oil out there."

"This sounds like something that bumpkin aunt of yours would come up with. You haven't been getting advice from Gertie Johnson again, have you? I bet —"

Gretchen slammed the door and stalked off.

How does your aloneness feel now? she asked herself, as the building loomed ahead of her where Chiggy, aka Florence Kent, resided.

Sometimes life really was a very lonely venture. Once you veered from the safe and familiar path, no one wanted to follow anymore. Instead, they stood on the sidelines hoping you'd trip over a rattlesnake so they could say, "See? I told you so."

She refused to look back at the parked car loaded with former followers.

34

Doll collectors are perceived by some as crazy old ladies who have nothing better to do than talk to dolls. In reality, this stereotype constitutes a very small percentage of serious collectors. Typically, doll lovers come from all walks of life and backgrounds. They can be biologists, high school principals, lawyers, nurses, novelists, computer programmers, or actors. Occasionally, however, you will still run into the crazy old lady.
— From *World of Dolls* by Caroline Birch

Gretchen walked along the side of the building, making sure she wasn't visible from the guard's station. Once she neared the main entrance, she stopped and wondered what to do next. Her answer magically appeared in front of her.

Today might be her lucky day.

She spotted the car that had pulled up

beside her when she tried to get past the guard. Its occupants were walking from a parking lot on the opposite side of the building, a man, a woman, and two small boys about four or five years old. The man opened one of the massive doors leading into the building, and Gretchen slipped in behind them as they gave their names and the name of the resident they were visiting through an intercom system. She heard the door lock click, released remotely by someone inside the building, and the group moved past a reception desk.

One of the boys glanced at Gretchen, and she looked away, trying to keep the right amount of distance between them — far enough not to arouse the parents' suspicion, close enough not to alert the receptionist to the fact that she wasn't part of the visiting group. She was careful not to make eye contact with anyone.

You certainly are clever, she thought, her heart beating as fast as a revved-up jet about to take off, excited and afraid at the same time. The same feeling she had at the doll auction when she was bidding on the Ginny dolls.

Gretchen waited for the receptionist to call out to her and demand an explanation and the proper credentials, but soon she was past the desk and approaching a long corridor. The only sound was hushed voices from the family she had infiltrated.

Gretchen was inside.

Not that it helped her much, since she had no idea where Chiggy was staying in this vast senior complex.

As soon as she was out of sight of the entrance, she turned a corner, disengaging from the group ahead of her.

She dug her cell phone out of her pocket and called Nina's cell. "Find out what room Chiggy's in," she said.

"Humph," said Miss Suddenly Righteous. "You should have thought of that before you so brazenly flaunted the center's rules."

"Just do it."

Nina must still have had some residual anger over her broken date with Eric and planned on punishing her for the rest of the day in subtle, annoying ways.

"And how am I supposed to find out?" Nina said curtly.

Gretchen could hear April say something in the background. Then while Gretchen walked briskly down another hallway, Nina filled April in. Gretchen hoped no one would stop her if she looked as if she knew where she was headed.

Nina came back on the line. "April says

she'll call and pretend she's with UPS and has a package that requires a room number."

"Whatever works. I'll call back in a few minutes."

She forced herself to wait several long and excruciating minutes before calling back, all the while striding down one corridor after another. When she did call Nina back, she learned the room number.

Gretchen had been noting room numbers on the doors as she turned another corner. Not only was she inside, but she was moving in the right direction.

Aunt Gertie would be so proud.

At first, Chiggy Kent thought she was one of her caregivers. Gretchen figured the bottled air running from the tank to her nostrils wasn't doing the job it should. The lack of proper oxygenation was affecting her mind. Then she realized that Chiggy had a vision problem.

Blind as the proverbial bat.

"It's Gretchen Birch," she said, identifying herself. "Caroline Birch's daughter. We met two months ago at Bonnie's house during one of the Phoenix Dollers Club meetings.

"Oh, yes. I remember." Chiggy sat up straighter in a chair next to her bed.

"It wasn't easy getting in to see you. We were worried that there was a conspiracy going on to keep you secluded." She laughed lightly.

"I specifically said no visitors," Chiggy said, annoyed. "I thought I was firm about my requirements when I moved here." She brushed back a few gray strands of hair falling on her face, and Gretchen thought that, at one time, she must have been a beautiful woman. Nicotine and excessive Arizona suntanning had taken a toll. "No matter. I'll take it up with the staff later. You're here now."

Chiggy spoke slowly, pausing to wheeze and allow the extra oxygen to kick in.

"I have a few questions about your dolls." Gretchen took a seat beside her and glanced around. The room was stark, containing only the essentials, exactly like a hospital room.

"Do you mind talking about your dolls?" Gretchen prompted.

"Ah." Chiggy forced a weak smile. "You were at the auction?"

"I was, along with half of Phoenix. I thought your dolls moved well. There was quite a turnout." Gretchen didn't mention Brett's death. If Chiggy didn't know about it, Gretchen didn't want to be the one to tell her.

"I had admired your handmade Kewpies," Gretchen lied. "But they were sold before I got there."

Chiggy looked surprised. "Really?" she said.

"April Lehman said she appraised your collection for you before you planned to auction them off, and she didn't remember any Kewpie dolls."

"That's right."

"But some were sold at the auction."

"I thought they were some of my poorest work." Chiggy shook her head. "I couldn't get the reproductions right, so I didn't include them with the dolls I decided to have appraised. Basically, I wanted April to tell me which dolls I should keep and which I should sell. In the end, I kept very few. You liked the Kewpies?"

"Very much. I was hoping you had more."

Chiggy shook her head. "That was the last of them."

"I also received several Kewpie dolls in the mail. Did you send them, or do you know who might have?"

"No. I hardly know you. Why would I send you anything? And I don't own a single Kewpie anymore."

Gretchen watched Chiggy's impaired eyes carefully and saw something . . .

Had the old woman sent the dolls? What would have been her motivation? And why, if she had, wouldn't she admit it now?

Chiggy slid further down in her chair, appearing weak and helpless.

How could her condition have deteriorated so quickly? According to Howie Howard, Chiggy was supervising her own move from her home less than a week ago. What had happened to make her suddenly infirm? A stroke?

"How are you doing?" Gretchen asked. "I hear you just moved from the assisted living section over to this area."

Chiggy waved a dismissive hand. "I'm fine. I like the security better here; we have the guard at the gate and a locked door. But look how easy it was for you to get in. That disturbs me." She squinted at Gretchen, appraising her integrity. "You seem like a nice person."

Chiggy held up an object that looked like a remote control, which had been buried in the folds of her dressing gown. "But if I press this button, I'll have someone in this room in thirty seconds flat. I didn't get that level of care in the apartment. Want to see how it works?"

"No thanks. I believe you."

Gretchen recalled the letter found among Ronny's papers, the one addressed to Florence. Don't double-cross me, it had said, or you'll become prey for a hungry predator. Had Chiggy ignored the warning? After the recent deaths, was Chiggy next on the killer's list? Did she know it? That would explain her preoccupation with heightened security.

She wasn't isolated because of any administrative rules.

She was hiding.

"I bid on a box of your Ginny dolls at the action and —" Gretchen stopped when she saw the expression of shock and disbelief on the old woman's face.

"Impossible," Chiggy managed to croak. "That box wasn't supposed to be sold. I gave strict instructions on the handling of my Ginny dolls. That box should be in storage along with several other personal belongings that I chose to keep. Where is it? Tell me." Chiggy was rising from the chair, her face turning red from lack of air. "What are you after? Why did you come here?"

"I . . . I don't have it. It seems that the boxes were mixed up somehow, and I ended up, accidentally, with the Kewpie dolls. I'm looking for the person who bid on the

Kewpies. I think he has the Ginnys. His name is Duanne Wilson."

Chiggy hesitated, her face frozen in a horrific grimace. It crossed Gretchen's mind that she might be out of oxygen. She quickly looked down at her feet to be sure she wasn't standing on the connecting tube. Maybe the machine that was Chiggy's lifeline had run dry, and she was strangling to death from lack of air.

But the horror on her face contradicted that theory. No one would have the energy for that kind of fear if they were running out of oxygen.

"What's wrong?" Gretchen moved closer to the woman.

"Get away from me. Tell him to leave me alone."

Chiggy screamed at the top of her wasted lungs.

A canister of pepper spray appeared in her left hand.

She stopped screaming abruptly, gasped for air, and screamed again.

Then she jammed her right thumb down on the security button and let loose with the pepper spray.

35

Gretchen scrambled for cover before the troops arrived, grateful that Chiggy's poor eyesight had resulted in a direct miss. She burst through a fire exit door and ran as though her life depended on it. Hearing the alarm wailing behind her, she cleared the senior center grounds and sprinted to the curb where she'd left the getaway car.

She whirled and looked down the street in both directions.

The car was gone.

Worse, Detective Albright sat in a blue unmarked police car in the exact spot where her Toyota Echo should be.

"Where is my car?" Gretchen demanded, hands on hips, when he climbed out of his car. "Did you have it towed away?" She was breathing hard. "And where are Nina and April?"

She saw a gleam of amusement in his eyes, a hint of Chrome cologne infusing the air, his smile as dazzling as ever.

"You set off the security alarm system," he said.

She glanced sharply up and down the street. No sign of her traitorous cohorts. His deceptive good looks failed to impress her today. She had learned that his heart was cold.

"Where are they?"

"So you think I had your car towed away with your aunt inside? And with all those critters? The pet protection groups would be all over me for animal abuse." He laughed easily. "It's much less dramatic than that. It seems that April needed something to eat. I, public servant that I am . . ." He placed his right hand over his heart as though pledging allegiance. "I offered to escort you home to join them, where they promised they would have a fine dining experience waiting for you. But if you want to stay here . . ." He dangled the end of the sentence like a fisherman setting the hook, "and face the consequences . . ."

The alarm continued to screech.

She watched the gate guard run for the main entrance, abandoning his station.

"It's entirely up to you," Matt said, leaning against his car.

Gretchen wrenched the car door open and

got in without another word. Talk about choosing between two evils. At least she had some experience with this one, who used his position to brutalize his victims. The other — she glanced back as they sped away — was a complete unknown. She had no wish to meet the guard again, or Chiggy.

If she had wanted to trip Chiggy's trigger, she couldn't have done better. She just hoped that next time, when the gun, or in this case the pepper spray, went off, she'd be safely out of the way.

Gretchen understood why the doll collector might be upset that the Ginny dolls had been sold if she'd made it clear that she wanted to keep them. Gretchen's mother had a vast collection of dolls she kept for sentimental reasons, and Gretchen knew how her mother would feel if they were lost. She had a few herself that were very special.

But the reaction when Chiggy heard Duanne's name was a big surprise.

What was the story with that guy?

"Your aunt Nina said you'd be hungry," Matt said. "How about I take you out for a late lunch? It has the potential to be much better than what awaits you at home. I think April was headed for a Big Mac and large fries."

"No thanks, I have things to do. Take me

home." If Nina wanted to get back at her, she certainly picked an effective way.

"Have it your way. But first I need to talk to you."

"Then talk."

He kept his eyes on the road and didn't reply. She let the silence hang and watched the familiar scenery through her window. Date palm trees lined the boulevards, and, as always, Camelback Mountain towered over the city, its red clay humps assuring her that they were headed in the right direction.

As they approached her mother's house, Matt abruptly turned toward the canyon and the trail leading up Camelback Mountain. He drove into the visitors' parking lot at the base and stopped. "I want to talk to you alone," he said, laying a hand on her arm when she grabbed for the door. "Without your entire ensemble hanging on every word. I'll take you home in a minute."

"I can walk from here." Or run if she had to.

"Peter Finch was attacked this morning."

Gretchen jerked her head in his direction. "What? What did you say?"

"I think you heard me." He watched her with an intense gaze.

"What happened?"

"Shot in the chest."

"Is he dead?"

"No, he'll live, but it was close. He's unconscious, so I haven't been able to talk to him. All of his camera and computer equipment is missing. Whoever did this took the entire computer."

"Why are you telling me this?" Gretchen felt like she might faint. "What do I have to do with Peter Finch?"

"Gretchen, you have to tell me what's going on. Every time I follow a lead, you've been there ahead of me. I've started carrying a picture of you around. I show it to people, and they recognize you."

"Who recognizes me?" Gretchen demanded. "Tell me who."

What was the point of the picture? Was he going to arrest her for Peter's murder?

Through the car's window, she stared at the mountain. No, he would have taken her in to the station. He wanted information to use against someone. Her . . . or . . .

"Ronny Beam's neighbor in the trailer park recognized you instantly," Matt said. "The security guard at the senior home we just left had a few choice words to describe you. And a tenant in Peter Finch's apartment building saw you entering there yesterday."

"That's ridiculous. And where did you get a picture of me?"

"You forget that my mother is the president of the doll club. She gave me one that she took at the last meeting. Very flattering."

Good old Bonnie, always helpful. That must be going over well with the doll club members. It would make a particularly choice topic for Curves. She didn't know which was worse — the doll collectors thinking Matt was interested in her romantically or thinking he considered her a murder suspect.

"The person who identified me at Peter Finch's made a mistake."

After what had happened to Albert Thoreau, how could she trust Matt enough to tell him anything? Albert had been beaten, and she hadn't forgotten that a cop was responsible for it. Matt? Or one of his partners?

Why was she always attracted to the wrong men?

"If your fingerprints show up in his apartment," Matt said. "You'll have some explaining to do." He got out, walked around the front of the car, and opened her door. "Come on. Let's go for a walk."

Gretchen glared at him but got out and

looked up at the mountain. By the ripple of his muscles, he obviously worked out, but in a gym. Aerobically, he wasn't up to her level, thanks to her years of serious hiking.

She could beat him any day in a climb up to the peak, and she could probably outpace him in a race. She felt safer out in the afternoon sunshine with a number of hikers traversing the mountain above her.

Still, if Matt wanted to grill her, he shouldn't have stopped the car where she could see her house. No wonder he couldn't catch the killer; he couldn't even catch her. She hated to think what would happen if she waited for him to protect her.

She started out, headed for home instead of up the mountain. "Have it your way," he called out behind her. "But I'm warning you, Gretchen, and this is a friendly warning that's about to become less so if you don't heed my words. Stay out of this. You don't know what you're getting into. And stay away from Percy O'Connor's sister. You're interfering with an investigation."

Gretchen almost stopped in her tracks, but, with a lot of effort, she willed her leaden legs to continue moving toward home.

Percy O'Connor's sister?

Chiggy?

Nooooo.

Nina and April sat at the kitchen table sur-rounded by mounds of McDonald's bags.

"Hey," April said. "Sit down and eat." She moved her chair to make room. "You should have invited that handsome detective in."

Starving, Gretchen dug in, but she didn't taste the food. It could have been kibble, and she wouldn't have cared.

All the connections and all the deaths. Three people who had been at Chiggy's house before the estate auction were dead or injured: Brett, Ronny, and Peter. Two of them gone, the other barely alive. And Percy, connected by family to Chiggy, also dead.

How did Steve fit in? Steve valued money above everything else, and diamonds would be a huge motivator. Was he the killer, or wasn't he? Her feelings vacillated exactly as they used to whenever she tried to decide whether or not to leave him. Yes, then no, then . . . The same teeter-totter effect.

Since Chiggy's poor health precluded pursuing and killing large men, the only suspects left seemed to be Steve and Howie. But wasn't Howie at the auction block when Brett was shoved into the street? Howie *did* take breaks, but Gretchen thought for sure he had been auctioneering when it happened.

She needed to talk to Steve, find Duanne Wilson, and discover who was sending her cryptic threats inside of Kewpie dolls.

"Is Daisy back yet?" Gretchen asked, seeing no sign that the homeless woman had returned.

"I peeked in her room, and she's not there," April said. "What a disaster. Have you seen it? She has piles of trash from that shopping cart lying everywhere."

"She gave me strict orders to keep everyone out."

April slurped the last of her soda. "I can see why."

"She's pretty demanding, for a guest," Nina said.

Gretchen and Nina made their first eye contact.

"I'm sorry I was so angry," Nina said suddenly, as if she had been working up to an apology and needed to get it over with quickly before she backed out. "April helped me realize that you were trying to protect me because you love me. I love you, too."

"And I'm sorry if I ruined your date. At the time, I didn't care. I only cared about your safety. As it turns out, I don't think Eric had anything to do with the murders."

"Now, before this gets any mushier," April said, "tell us what happened with Chiggy."

Gretchen related the story, ending with Chiggy calling security and trying to blast her with pepper spray.

"I knew going to see her was a bad idea the minute I heard it," Nina said, joining the I-told-you-so association.

"It was worth questioning her just for her reaction." Gretchen chewed a cold French fry. "Duanne Wilson has something to do with this."

"I wonder why she attacked you," April asked.

"She was afraid," Gretchen said. "Very afraid. I don't think she's directly involved, though."

"She does have terrible health," April said, as though her poor health eliminated her.

Gretchen leaned forward. "Wait till you hear the rest."

"There's more?" April exclaimed. "You've been busy."

"Chiggy is Percy's sister."

Nina squealed. "How do you know that?"

"Matt Albright told me."

"Percy's sister," April said. "Imagine that."

"I'm so glad you're working with the police," Nina said, brightly. "Detective Albright will figure it out. He has resources."

"You're not kidding," April agreed. "His buns, his . . ." She started giggling.

"Does he have any suspects yet?" Nina asked. "I mean besides Steve, who we know didn't do it."

"Suspects? Ah . . . not yet." Gretchen couldn't say for a fact, but *she* was pretty sure *she* was the latest suspect. And she wasn't about to tell I-told-you-so that news.

Nina and April waved goodbye, leaving a vacuum of silence in the house. Gretchen called Information from the workshop bench and waited for the connection to go through.

"Don't hang up," Gretchen said quickly into the phone. They were the first three words out of her mouth. She said them again from the stool she perched on inside the workshop. "Please don't hang up."

"I'm paying my attorney a lot of money to advise me," Steve said. "And he insisted that I stay away from you."

"You're far away from me. Lots of air-waves between us. Your attorney can't complain. Anyway, I'm glad they released you."

He sighed heavily into the phone. "What do you want?"

"Just wondering how you are," Gretchen

said. Partly true. She did wonder.

"Considering that I have to stay in Phoenix until this is resolved and consequently had to find other attorneys to handle my clients and caseload — and considering that I've been charged with murdering Ronny Beam in spite of the lack of evidence and glaring proof that the knife in his back belonged to you — and considering that your new boyfriend happens to be the one gathering evidence against me, I couldn't be better."

No bitterness there.

"At least you're free for the time being," she said. "Things could be worse."

"Things could always be worse. A boulder from the mountain could fall and crush me. I'm not sure, though, that crushed bones would be worse. Death might, but even that's starting to sound more appealing."

An awkward silence fell between them, their once-upon-a-time comfortable familiarity a distant memory.

Gretchen cleared her throat. "Steve, I'm really sorry about what's happened."

"About my legal situation or about us?"

"Both. And I'm trying to help you. I discovered some things that might clear you."

"Like what?"

"I don't want to tell you right now because I have some loose ends." *An understatement, if I ever heard one.* "Let me work on it a little longer. But I need to know if you were at Chiggy Kent's house the day before the auction."

"Why?"

"Were you?"

"Why do you want to know?"

"It could be important."

"I haven't told the police that I was there. The only one who knows is my attorney. I don't know how you found out. But I suppose you shared that information with your detective?"

"I haven't. Why don't you want him to know?"

"Because Ronny Beam was at the house that day, too. I wasn't introduced to him, and we didn't exchange words. I didn't even recognize him on the day of the doll show until afterward, but the police will try to use that against me if they can."

"I'll keep your secret, if you tell me what I need to know."

"What?"

"I need to know why you were at Chiggy Kent's house."

Gretchen fiddled idly with her repair tools.

"Why do you want to know?" he asked

again reluctantly.

"Please, tell me."

"Okay. It isn't a big deal. I was delivering a doll to her."

"A doll?"

"Yes, some kind of Kewpie doll from her brother."

She almost dropped her tools on top of Nimrod, who slept curled nearby. *Stay calm,* Gretchen thought, her heart beating to the band.

"From Percy O'Connor?" she asked.

"Yes, how did you — ?"

Gretchen interrupted him. She had to know the rest. "What kind of Kewpie was it?"

"Gretchen, you should know better than anyone that I don't know the slightest thing about dolls. I wouldn't recognize a Kewpie doll if it wore a name tag, let alone figure out what kind of specific Kewpie it was. I didn't even know there were different kinds. Besides, it was inside a sealed box."

"Then how did you know it was a Kewpie?

"I met Percy through one of the attorneys at the firm. The three of us had lunch one day, and the subject of the Boston Kewpie Club's expedition to Phoenix came up. When I told him I was planning a trip to Arizona, he asked me to deliver the doll to his sister. She lived in Phoenix, and he said he couldn't go to the show himself — health reasons — and he didn't trust the postal service. He said I should tell her it was his favorite Kewpie collectible."

Favorite, like a million dollars favorite? Gretchen was sure that Steve had delivered a doll filled with diamonds, or at least one that the killer thought was filled with diamonds. After killing Percy and failing to find the gems, he must have suspected that Chiggy had them.

But if she did have them at one time, they must be missing now. Why else would she be so skittish?

"You know that Percy was murdered?" she asked Steve.

"Yes. No one knows why; nothing was missing, and he didn't seem to have any enemies. Quite a likable fellow, really." Steve continued. "The police thought Percy must have surprised a burglar in the act, the burglar killed him, then panicked and ran away without stealing anything. What a tragedy." He paused for a respectable moment of silence. "Chiggy was beside herself with joy when I presented the doll to her."

"I bet," Gretchen muttered.

"A final parting gift from her brother. She seemed to recognize it."

"What makes you say that?"

"She said something like 'at last, I thought it was lost.' Then she cried."

"Do you remember what she did with the doll?"

"I'm not sure."

"Think, Steve. It might be important."

"I think she may have added it to another box of dolls. Yes, she did. One she planned on keeping, because she made a big deal out of it, pointing out to everyone that they shouldn't take that box."

Gretchen stared at the Kewpies on the worktable. Chiggy wanted to throw out the badly reproduced Kewpies. They really were worthless.

Chiggy had hidden Percy's Kewpie doll inside the box of Ginnys.

36

Bert's Liquor Store was located in a run-down neighborhood in central Phoenix. Its less-than-distinguished features included a cheap rectangular facade, an enormous yellow sign with exposed gray metal where the paint had peeled away, and questionable clientele at the store's drive-through service window.

Gretchen arrived in the late afternoon when she hoped the store's most loyal customers would be thinking about that first jolt of the evening. She sat in her car with the doors locked and thought about her next move.

An hour passed while she considered her options and watched a steady stream of people arrive at the store empty-handed, and leave clutching brown paper bags.

The three liquor store bags that the Kewpies had arrived in were lying on the seat next to her. Not that they would do her any good. She couldn't march into the store and demand to know what they had contained and who the alcohol had been sold to. Although, if she acted slightly off, she would fit right in with the current clientele.

She was wasting her time. She'd give it another half hour and then leave.

What had Aunt Gertie said to her on the phone?

Something like she'd know him when she saw him. Well, she didn't know anyone coming or going. No one even remotely familiar.

You'll know the culprit the minute you spot him, that's what Aunt Gertie had said.

Or her.

The only familiar character Gretchen had seen so far was approaching the liquor store this minute and was about to pass right by the Echo.

She sat up straighter.

With her shopping cart, Daisy would have blended right in with the rest of the street people. But Daisy's colorful attire stood out from the crowd, and Gretchen was able to spot her at a distance. She wore her red hat and purple sundress, and she sashayed along the sidewalk as if she was the queen of her very own Red Hat parade.

What was she doing near the liquor store? She didn't drink, as far as Gretchen knew.

Daisy didn't have to drink to escape reality. She had her own source of hallucinations.

Daisy curtsied to a passing pedestrian, a wide smile on her face.

"Hey, Daisy," Gretchen called out the window when she came even with the Echo.

Daisy started, jerking quickly around, panic flickering across her face. Then she saw who it was. "Gretchen, you scared me. I didn't see you." She moved closer. "What are you doing here? Hey, little doggie."

Gretchen thought quickly while Daisy reached in and let Nimrod lick her hand. "I . . . ah . . . stopped to buy some wine. How was the audition?"

"Same as always. They were looking for a younger actress. That's my problem." Daisy leaned one arm on the car, the other on her waist. "When I was young, they said I was too young. Now that I'm older, they say I'm too old. I can't win. One of these days my star is going to arrive. That's the thing. I can't give up. All the famous actresses had to go through tough times."

"I'm sure you'll make it." Gretchen got out of the car and stood on the sidewalk next to Daisy, who didn't seem in any hurry to move on.

Gretchen pointed to the liquor store. "Are you going in?"

"Oh, no, I don't drink." Daisy adjusted her hat. "Never touch the stuff."

"How's Nacho?" Gretchen asked. "Is he still mad at me?"

"Ask him yourself. Here he comes."

They watched Nacho approach. When he spotted Daisy, his face lightened from his standard scowl, but when his eyes slid to Gretchen, he looked the other way, passed right by them, and entered the store.

"Yep," Daisy said. "He's still mad. You'll have to go away in a minute. You shouldn't have told the cops about Albert. It puts me right in the middle, and I don't want Nacho mad at me, too." She peered through the liquor store door. "He's coming out soon. He asked me to meet him here, but he won't come near me if you're still around. You have to go."

Lately, it seemed Gretchen had a knack for alienating people. Steve, Nacho, Nina. She opened her mouth to deny the allegations against her, but maybe she *had* been directly responsible for Albert's assault.

At least she and Nina had made up, and Steve was on speaking terms with her. Sort of. He hadn't hung up as soon as he'd he heard her voice.

"I didn't know that Nacho shopped at Bert's Liquor," Gretchen said.

Could Nacho have sent the Kewpie dolls to her? The thought was too far-fetched to consider. He had no means to purchase the dolls, no opportunity to find out enough about the murders to write the messages, and no apparent motive to do so. The same went for Daisy.

Of course, Chiggy could have sent the dolls and the cryptic messages, but this dilapidated liquor store in this questionable neighborhood wouldn't be the kind of place Chiggy Kent would frequent. Even if she could.

Daisy struck a haughty pose. "Bert's Liquor Store, I'll have you know, is where all my friends purchase their alcoholic beverages. Bert has the best prices and friendliest service in all of Phoenix. Everybody who's anybody shops here."

Gretchen looked at the litter lying in piles against the buildings: windblown newspapers, empty bottles, and cigarette butts. Some of the nearby stores had been boarded up and abandoned. Daisy's immediate circle of friends wasn't particular.

"Go, now," Daisy said. Gretchen saw Nacho at the cash register, paying the clerk.

She got into the Echo and pretended like she was about to start the car and drive off, slowly digging through her purse for her keys.

Nacho swung the door open and joined Daisy without any apparent concern over where Gretchen had gone. The two homeless friends wandered away together, arm in arm.

Gretchen was about to follow them, but she paused with her hand on the gearshift and the car still in park.

Albert Thoreau, sole eyewitness to Brett's death, limped across the street directly in front of her car and went into the liquor store.

When he came out with a bagged bottle under his arm, she was waiting for him on the sidewalk with Nimrod peeking from her shoulder bag.

She saw recognition in Albert's eyes. He glanced away and moved around her.

She held out an arm to stop him. "You know who I am," she said decisively.

Albert's face was swollen and blackened, and she noticed that his limp was more pronounced than when he'd entered Bert's. He looked exactly like the picture Daisy had shown her. If he'd had time to heal, she probably wouldn't have recognized him.

He stopped, looked directly at her, and nodded. "I've seen you with Daisy," he said through cracked and puffy lips.

"What happened to your face?"

"Wrong place at the wrong time. It's nothing to you."

"I heard a cop did it."

"You heard wrong." He stared at her defiantly.

Gretchen knew he wouldn't talk to her because she wasn't from the street, she wasn't one of his kind. Or perhaps Nacho had shared his anger at Gretchen and the reason why. Albert might blame her for his abuse at the hands of the Phoenix police.

"I'm sorry about what happened to you," she said. "If I am in any way to blame —"

"You're not." He cut her off. "It's got nothing to do with you. You go home and stay out of trouble."

"You saw the man at the auction, the one who was pushed? Tell me who did it."

"Go home," he said roughly. "And watch out." His face softened. "You remind me of my sister."

"Your sister?"

"Same hair, same lots of things. She moved away. Maybe you know her. Susan Thoreau — well, its Mertz now that she's married."

Gretchen shook her head.

"Hey Thoreau," someone called out, and

376

a man came up and high-fived Albert. "What's happenin' man?"

"Coppin' a little friendly comfort." Albert held up the Bert's Liquor bag. "This here is one of Daisy's friends." He gestured toward Gretchen. "Meet BJ."

Gretchen reached out to grasp the offered hand, a hand coated with grime. She forced herself not to flinch. He was a two-handed shaker, working his left hand over the top of their clutched right hands.

After giving her an appreciative stare, BJ broke the shake and popped Albert lightly in the chest. "See ya later." He looked at Gretchen. "Don't follow this guy's lead when you cross the street. He's color-blind, ya know. He'll have ya crossing against the light cuz he can't tell red from green."

"Catch ya," Albert said, and he limped away, crossing in the middle of the street and heading back the way he came. BJ bee-lined for the liquor store.

Gretchen watched Albert go. How could these people live like this? Scrounging for basics like food and shelter, living for their next cheap bottles of booze, rejecting offers of assistance. Gretchen couldn't imagine what their lives must be like in July when temperatures remained in the triple digits, day and night.

Not all were alcoholics, but most of those Gretchen met were. Many who remained on the street for any length of time had psychological issues. Like Daisy. Sweet and harmless but unbalanced and unwilling to accept treatment.

Maybe living in the make-believe world Daisy had created was easier than facing reality.

Gretchen felt as if she could use a little escape from it herself right about now.

How did Albert escape from the reality of his life? The booze, of course.

With one hand on the car door, a thought struck her.

Color-blind?

Did BJ say Albert was color-blind?

Gretchen started running down the street. Nimrod let out a yip, and she slowed slightly, readjusting him against her side.

She ran two blocks and stopped at a corner, looking both ways. There he was. She could see him up ahead. The man walked fast for someone with a bad leg who was going nowhere.

Getting closer, she called out his name, and he turned and waited for her to catch up.

She stopped in front of him, her breath fast and ragged, more from the discovery than the physical exercise. "You're color-blind?" she said.

"A little."

"What's a little?" Gretchen wanted to know. "You're either color-blind or you aren't, right?"

"Okay, I'm color-blind, but it's no big deal. I forget about it all the time."

"So . . . do you confuse all the colors?"

Albert shrugged. "What's this about?"

"I'm curious. For example, if I see blue, what color do you see?"

"What is this, some kind of test?" Albert frowned at her.

"Humor me, okay? What color would you see?"

"Daisy tells me I see purple."

"What color would be blue?"

"What?"

Gretchen wasn't communicating well. She knew it. "You see blue, I see . . ."

She waited.

"I see blue," Albert said. "You see green."

Gretchen stared at him. According to Nacho, Albert had seen someone get out of a blue truck and push Brett into the street.

But Albert hadn't seen a blue truck. He'd seen a green one.

37

A green truck.

Gretchen had watched Howie get into a blue truck and drive off after the auction, after Brett had been killed.

Albert had seen a man get out of a truck that, it turns out, was actually green.

Gretchen blanched.

The cop at her house. Her neighbor said the police officer who had been at her home, looking for her, was driving a green truck.

A cop had beaten Albert, and, judging by Albert's physical condition, the attacker meant business.

Why would she be a target? She didn't have the Ginny dolls, and she didn't know anything significant about hidden treasures or murder victims.

Wait a minute.

She knew plenty.

Was someone really after her?

Far-fetched, Gretchen reminded herself as she picked up her cell phone.

She still had Chiggy's broken Kewpie dolls in her trunk. To her, they weren't worth two bucks, but they were the only things that connected her to whatever was going on.

She had to ditch the dolls as fast as possible and get out of this circle of murdering thieves.

Howie Howard's answering machine turned on after the sixth unanswered ring.

"It's Tuesday at five o'clock," Gretchen informed the recording. "When I spoke to you last, you offered to take the box of Kewpie dolls and find the owner. I assume that offer still stands. If anyone's been inquiring about them, please let them know that I'll be returning them to you tonight at Brett's memorial service. Getting the box of Ginny dolls back is no longer important to me." She stressed the next sentence. "*I'm returning the box. No questions asked.* See you then."

Gretchen hung up, threw the cell phone on the passenger seat, and headed home. She had a few hours before the service, an event she was dreading but knew she had to attend.

As the broad side of Camelback Mountain

came into view, her mother called.

"What's new?" Caroline said, unsuspecting in her cheerfulness.

"Not much," Gretchen said, keeping her eye out for a green truck.

If only her mother knew! But it was too late to hit her with all Gretchen's problems.

What had she gotten herself into?

"I need you to look at something," Gretchen said, when Janice Schmidt opened her front door. "It's in my workshop."

"I'm making dinner right now," Janice said. "I'd be happy to come over afterward."

"It's kind of important," Gretchen insisted.

Janice hesitated. She must have seen the seriousness on Gretchen's face because she said, "Let me turn the stove off and get the kids."

"Don't bother knocking," Gretchen said, walking away. "Come right in when you get there."

"Give me five minutes."

Gretchen was cautious about approaching her mother's house, careful to make sure the doors and windows hadn't been wrenched open. She walked around to the back of the house and opened the gate leading to the pool. Nothing seemed tampered with, at least on first sight. She hoped she was astute enough to detect sights of forced entry.

As she opened the front door, Nimrod perked up, and his tail thumped against her side. Gretchen relaxed. He might be pint-sized, but he was street smart. If danger was close by, he'd be the first to announce it. He'd be the first to know.

The second to know, actually. Wobbles had intuitive skills Nimrod could never touch, but Wobbles wouldn't even think of Gretchen. He'd protect his own feline skin by slinking into a private hole someplace safe and leaving her to fend for herself.

She relaxed further when Wobbles greeted her at the door.

After letting herself in, she turned on lights, greeted her two favorite animals, and started the computer in the workshop, shoving piles of doll clothing and paperwork to the side to make room.

Glancing up at Camelback Mountain through the workshop window, she saw twilight approaching. Shadows fell across the face of the mountain as the last stragglers made their way down to the trailhead. They looked like small, black spiders from this distance.

Gretchen shuddered, remembering the

scorpion found in Nimrod's traveling purse and her own close escape from the dreaded arachnid.

By the time the computer booted, Janice and her kids had shown up in the workshop. The boys, still too young to understand their stereotyped future of imposed role-playing in society, lit up at the sight of all the dolls. Gretchen settled them at a table with dolls and clothes and left them to dress and undress them at will.

They promptly took all the clothes off every doll.

"What a fascinating room," Janice said, wandering from corner to corner, picking through the open bins and handling some of the dolls and their accessories. "It must be a treat to go to work every day."

Gretchen laughed. "It's like working in a candy store but without the temptation and added calories. I was a graphic designer when I lived in Boston. This is my mother's profession. I'm helping her now that the business has taken off. It worked out well for both of us."

Janice held up a Barbie doll that needed a new leg. The toes of the damaged leg had been chewed off. "Pet problems?" she said.

"Happens all the time. Dogs love to chew on plastic dolls."

Gretchen sat down at the computer. "Come and look at these pictures," she said. "I'd like to know if any of the people in these pictures are familiar to you."

Janice sat down at the chair in front of the computer screen and glanced at the display of one of Peter's photographs. After a puzzled glance at Gretchen and scrolling through some of the pictures, she looked up.

"This must be about the cop yesterday. The one who was at your house, talking to Lilly Beth."

"Why do you say that?"

"Because . . ." Janice pointed at the screen. "That might be him."

Janice went home to finish making dinner, dragging two boys who wouldn't leave until Gretchen gave each of them an old doll that she had been saving for parts. It was a small price to pay for the valuable information she had received from Janice.

Gretchen turned off the overhead lights to reduce any glare on the screen and stared at the photograph.

The cop was out of focus, on the periphery of the action that Peter was intent on capturing. The officer must have realized that the photographer was shooting toward him because he had turned his face away. His movement blurred part of his body and he had one arm raised as if to ward off a blow.

Or that could be Gretchen's imagination.

Something about the man seemed familiar to her now that she was really studying him. The way he stood, the tilt of his head . . . think.

Imagine him without the uniform.

Gretchen put her hand up to the screen and covered his body so only the back of his head was exposed.

Nina had accused her of inflexibility, insinuating that she couldn't see auras because of her inability to let go of what she thought reality should be.

Feeling slightly ridiculous, she found her purse and put on the aura glasses. Returning to the computer, she saw nothing different except for a change in the colors created by the indigo lenses.

She wondered if Nina would tell her that no one could see auras emanating from pictures. She also wondered if Nina made up the rules as she went along.

Gretchen removed the glasses and thought about another of Nina's comments. She needed to use her third eye. She sighed heavily before going back to the picture.

Then she saw it. The bushy eyebrows. In the picture his hair was a glossy black, not white, as it had been during the auction.

At the time, Gretchen had thought him odd with white hair and black eyebrows, but suddenly it made sense. It's much harder to disguise eyebrows than hair. He wasn't nearly as old as he'd pretended while bidding so fervently on the Kewpie dolls.

The cop in Peter's photograph was Duanne Wilson.

Was Duanne Wilson impersonating a police officer? Or was he actually a cop? Gretchen didn't really care whether he was or not.

She really didn't care if her third eye had helped her or not.

Because she knew what had happened, and that's all that mattered.

She felt surprisingly calm as she stared at the man she knew had to be the killer. But why so many deaths? And why hadn't he been seen?

Dressed in a cop's uniform, that's how he'd done it.

He could kill Ronny Beam in broad daylight without witnesses. He could bide his time using the Phoenix Police Department as camouflage. And Peter must have let him into his apartment because of the uniform.

Brett was the biggest puzzle. Why push him in front of a car? Unless he was part of the scheme. What if Brett had told Duanne to bid on the Kewpies, knowing all along that one was concealed in the Ginny box? Maybe he had tried to steal the Kewpie for himself. It was a possibility.

Then there was Ronny Beam. He planned to write a story about the diamonds. That would give the police a motive in the investigation of Percy's murder. If the reporter hadn't dug through Chiggy's personal boxes, he'd probably be alive today, although his big mouth may have doomed him anyway.

Peter Finch had taken a picture of Duanne in his uniform. When she looked again at the photograph, Gretchen could see more clearly that Duanne was attempting to hide from the camera. Peter had been attacked and left for dead because of the pictures. That expained why Duanne had removed Peter's computer and camera equipment after shooting him.

She still thought it was more than a coincidence that most of the men who had been at Chiggy's house before the auction were now dead. Had Duanne been there? How else would he have known who his targets were?

Peter had told her who had been present before the auction started: Peter, of course, Howie, Brett, Ronny, and Steve. That was it. No one else . . .

Gretchen saw the light for the first time.

Of course! There must have been one more person at the house. The killer would've blended into the background, but he was there all the time.

The mover.

None of the others would have known who he was. Only Chiggy. But she hadn't recognized him because her eyesight was as bad as a rhino's.

He must also have been the person who wrote Chiggy the letter with the veiled threats. What had it said? *So nice of you to help me find my treasure, just don't double-cross me.*

Everything made perfect sense now. Except the final question, the one she didn't have an answer for: Why was she next on his list?

38

"Nina, I need to find Daisy," Gretchen said into the phone. "Have you heard from her?"

"You sound rushed. What's going on?"

"I'll explain later."

"Have you tried her cell?"

"Daisy has a cell phone?" Technology was changing even the street people. "She's homeless. How did she get a phone?"

"Beats me. Here's the number."

"Daisy, this is Gretchen."

"Oh, it's you." Gretchen could hear the disappointment in her voice. "I thought it might be my agent with good news."

"Sorry. I need to know who told you to find a safe place to stay."

"Why?" Wary. "You haven't told anyone that I'm not at your house, have you? If he knew, he'd be angry."

"Who would be angry?"

"I promised not to tell."

"Come on," Gretchen said. "I won't tell anyone." She felt like she was back in seventh grade. Back then, she remembered, no one really kept a promise.

"It was Detective Albright," Daisy said.

"What does Detective Albright have to do with this?"

"He came downtown the other night and warned me."

"What did he say?"

"He said bad things were happening in downtown Phoenix, and I should get away for a while."

"I thought Detective Albright was the one who beat up Albert."

"Why would you think that?"

"Because I'm the one who told him about Albert."

"Well, Albert was attacked by someone else."

It hadn't been Matt.

Gretchen hung up the phone, leaned her elbows on the doll worktable, and stared out the window at Camelback Mountain.

She'd been wrong about Matt, and she was relieved. He hadn't beat up Albert. Instead, he'd warned Daisy.

If Gretchen had shared more information with him, maybe the real killer would be behind bars right now.

If only she'd trusted him more . . .

April appeared at the door.

"Why's the front door locked?" she asked when Gretchen let her in.

"I've been a little nervous lately. I can't see who's at the door. I need to install a peephole."

"Let's go," April said, missing the significance of Gretchen's comment about locks and bolts.

"Go where?"

April had stuffed herself into a black, clingy number, and Gretchen could see every ripple and ridge. "To the Phoenician. We're having a goodbye reception for the Boston Kewpie Club. They're going home tomorrow. Well, all except Steve, who has to stay in Phoenix."

"I have to go to Brett's memorial service," Gretchen said wistfully, wishing she could celebrate life, renewal, and friendships with April and the doll group rather than mourn a tragic death.

"I don't know who else will be at this service," April said. "No one I know has been invited."

"I think the gathering is for the people who were at Chiggy's auction when Brett died. Howie must have arranged it."

"Where is it?"

"Someplace on McDowell Road."

"Do you need directions?"

Gretchen shook her head. "I'll find it. We have to talk later about the murders."

"I'll call you after the party," April said. "Right now, I'm running late."

"Lilly Beth, I know you're in there," Gretchen said, after knocking until her hand hurt. "I can see you through the window."

She backed up and peeked in, her eyes adjusting to the darkening night. Lilly Beth stepped farther back into the shadows.

Gretchen pointed at her and their eyes met. "See, there you are. Let me in."

Finally the door opened a crack.

"What do you want?" Lilly Beth asked.

Gretchen thrust a printout of a photograph through the crack. "This police officer came to my house," she said. "And you talked to him."

"That's the back of a head. Even if I did, so?"

"So, what did he want?"

"That's private information under the federal homeland security law."

"I demand to know under the freedom of information act, and that supersedes homeland security."

The ridiculousness of the conversation wasn't lost on Gretchen. Lilly Beth had more screws loose than Daisy ever would.

"He didn't tell me," Lilly Beth said. "It's on a need-to-know basis, and I didn't need to know."

Translation: Lilly Beth never stopped talking long enough to find out.

Lilly Beth, once started, took off like a buzzard smelling carrion.

"I don't know what's going on over there," Lilly Beth said. "But whatever it is, the police are on notice. That nice police officer has a job to do and I'm going to see that he accomplishes it. I'll help him in any way I can." Lilly Beth looked Gretchen up and down. "I'm on the side of the law."

"He's driving a green truck, not a squad car," Gretchen said. "Don't you think that's suspicious?"

"He's undercover." Lilly Beth frowned. "Although, you'd think he'd hide it better. If he shows up in the same truck every time, people are going to start noticing."

Gretchen felt cold. Every time? "How many times has he been here?"

"Three. I watch for him at the window because I want to support the police, and I tell him that every single time. I think he appreciates my efforts. Last time I took out some of my chocolate chip cookies. I had just baked them."

"What did he do? Did he knock on my door?"

"Lucky for you, you haven't been home even once, and I tell him that. I think he's going to arrest you if he can pin you down. What you did, I don't even want to know. The goings-on in this neighborhood are ruining the property values."

"What did he say?"

"Like I told you, he kept it to himself, as he should. Quiet man." Lilly Beth thought a second. "Humph . . . now that I think of it, he didn't say more than a word or two."

Lilly Beth wouldn't have given him a chance.

Gretchen was pretty sure that her busybody neighbor, in her own conniving way, had unknowingly saved her from the same fate as Brett and Ronny. Lilly Beth was like the neighborhood watchdog. She also had pit bull jaws. Once she latched on, there was no getting away.

With any luck, she'd driven him off for good.

"If you see his truck again," Gretchen said. "Stay away from him."

"Oh sure, like I'd listen to you. Whatever you did, you'll have to suffer the consequences."

Gretchen hurried back to her house.

It was time to call Detective Albright and fess up.

39

Gretchen called Bonnie Albright for Matt's private phone number. Belatedly, she remembered that Bonnie would be on her way to the Phoenician for the Boston Kewpie Club's bon voyage party. She thought about calling Nina's cell phone, but their repaired relationship was still delicate, and she wouldn't disrupt Nina's good time with Eric again unless she had to.

She called the police dispatch nonemergency number and was told that Detective Albright was unavailable.

"I need his phone number," she said.

"I'm afraid I can't give that out."

"Can you get a message to him?" she asked.

"Certainly."

"I have important information involving a case he's working. He has to call me immediately."

"We'll see that he receives the message,"

the dispatcher said, dispassionately taking her cell phone number. Gretchen wondered if he really would be informed and, if so, when. She couldn't wait much longer.

She dressed in somber clothes — black pants and a beige top with decorative black buttons — and ran a brush through her hair. *Brace yourself,* she thought, *this is only the beginning.* Ronny Beam's funeral was also upcoming, and she knew the next few days would be as sorrowful as the last. Even though she hadn't known either of the victims well, Brett and Ronny meant more to her than mere statistics and canned obituaries in the Phoenix newspaper.

Nimrod and Wobbles followed her into the kitchen. As always, she was amazed that their internal clocks were so accurate, telling them exactly when dinner should be ready. She fed them and nibbled at leftovers in the refrigerator. The invitation hadn't mentioned food.

She scooped up Nimrod, locked the door, and drove toward McDowell Road, scanning the traffic around her for signs of the green truck. She hadn't realized how many Arizonians drove pickup trucks until now. On this moonless Phoenix night, every truck seemed dark and potentially dangerous.

The Sky Harbor Airport lights grew

brighter as she continued. She wound her way to the far west side of the airport and began to check the street signs, searching for McDowell Road.

A plane came in directly overhead, wheels visible in preparation for landing, and it reminded Gretchen that the Boston Kewpie Club would be returning home in the morning. She hadn't spent much time at all with them. If not for the memorial service, she would be at the party at the Phoenician this minute, sipping expensive red wine and nibbling French cheeses.

Maybe she could swing by on her way home if it wasn't too late.

Right now, as she turned onto McDowell and realized how dark and desolate the area was, she longed for Aunt Nina and the spectacular lights of the elegant Phoenician Resort.

What was she thinking to come over here by herself? She flipped on an overhead light and checked the address on the invitation. The 1500 block.

"We just passed Fourteenth Street," she informed Nimrod. "So it has to be in the next block." The teacup poodle wagged his tail.

She crawled along McDowell looking for the address, then turned the car around and slowly edged back along the other side.

She stopped the Echo and looked at the address on the invitation again.

That was the house where the memorial service should be starting, a one-story with a swamp cooler on the roof.

But something was wrong.

No lights illuminated the interior of the house, no cars were parked in front, no mourners congregated inside waiting to hear comforting words to ease their grief.

The house was totally dark.

She looked at the invitation for the third time. It was the kind you could buy in any store that carried greeting cards. The details of the memorial service had been handwritten. She'd automatically assumed that Howie Howard had organized the event because the handwriting was distinctly male. No graceful loops or careful lettering to denote a feminine hand.

Gretchen double-checked to make sure the doors of the Echo were locked and pulled quickly away from the darkened house, circling the block one last time. The house with the swamp cooler on the roof remained dark.

The more she thought about it, the more unlikely it became that the service would be here, next to the airport, and that no one else from the Phoenix Dollers Club had been invited. Absolutely no one that she knew would be in attendance.

Not only that, it had coincided with the Boston Kewpie members' farewell party, so she wouldn't have Nina or April or any of the other club members to attend with her.

Convenient for someone who might want to get her alone. Hadn't she seen this exact scenario in enough thrillers? Hadn't she laughed cynically at the hapless victims and their incredible lack of forethought?

"Gee," she said, talking to Nimrod again. "Wouldn't you think we'd stay out of dark alleys when a killer is on the prowl?" His ears twitched as he listened.

Gretchen drove toward the bright lights of the airport.

She asked herself again, *Why?*

That had been the three-letter word of the day, of the week.

Why, why, why had she received a bogus invitation?

Maybe because someone wanted to lure her away from her home by inviting her to an event she would feel compelled to attend. Gretchen Birch's whereabouts could be guaranteed for Monday night at eight o'clock.

So much for varying her routine to throw

off the bad guys.

Several blocks ahead, the street she was on would end abruptly, the overpass into the airport directly in front of her. Bright lights and safety. Looking into the sky, she could see planes lining up awaiting clearance to land.

But the invitation had arrived several days ago. If this was premeditated, the sender knew even then what he wanted her to do and where he wanted her to be.

He also could have known that the Boston visitors would be having a party and that her friends and family were not likely to attend the memorial service with her. They would opt for the opulence of the Phoenician over a service they hadn't been invited to.

Gretchen felt manipulated and angry with herself for blindly following the predictable path she'd been so artfully steered along.

Was he at her house right now? Waiting for her?

No — not for her. If she was the target, he could have waited for her on this lonely street. Gretchen stared into the few parked cars scattered along McDowell and was relieved to find them empty.

He must have wanted her house vacant tonight when Lilly Beth's prying eyes wouldn't be able to see him. He would have parked the truck down the road and crept in under cover of night.

Would he wear his police uniform?

Probably.

He'd want to fall back on his image of authority if any of the neighbors became suspicious.

What was inside the house that he wanted, if not her? The only thing she could think of were the Kewpie dolls that had been sent through the mail. They, along with the messages she had found inside, were in the workshop in plain view.

Gretchen picked up her cell phone to call the police again, wondering why Matt hadn't returned her call yet. She would ask the dispatcher to send a squad to meet her at her home. Gretchen tromped on the accelerator and, with one eye on the road as she steered, she searched through her recently called numbers for the right one.

At the stop sign, she signaled to turn left and hit the Send key on her cell phone.

As soon as she turned the corner, another vehicle came up rapidly behind her. It must have been parked close to the intersection and had started up when she passed by.

The car was following close behind her, too close.

Her cell phone flew from her hand at the first impact.

If she hadn't grabbed Nimrod to protect him, she would have had both hands on the steering wheel and might have stayed on the road. Instead, when the second blow struck the driver's side of the car somewhere close behind the front seat, the Echo careened into a shallow ditch that separated the street from the airport on-ramp.

It happened so quickly that she didn't see the vehicle until it appeared in front of her after striking her the second time. Now it forced her car away from the street and toward the fence.

A green truck.

She slammed on the brakes and came to a stop, with the pickup truck wedging her next to a concrete pylon. Before she could throw the car into reverse and make a run for it, she saw the blur of a uniform.

And a gun.

And a familiar face.

40

Duanne Wilson of the bushy eyebrows and gleeful bidding tried to wrench the car door open. The jolliness was gone.

"Unlock the door," he snarled, the barrel of the gun up against the glass.

Gretchen had never looked into a gun barrel before, and if she survived tonight, she hoped it would be the last time.

She'd never thought of herself as a particularly brave person, and she wasn't out to win any medals right now.

Brave and smart weren't the same things.

You could be brave and foolish and dead.

Not having a lot of options to choose from, she chose to go with cowardly, alive, and still foolish.

Gretchen unlocked the door while scanning the seat and floor for the cell phone that had flown out of her hand.

No such luck.

"Moonlighting as a Phoenix Police officer?" she said as he opened the door. The badge on his uniform seemed to mock her. The Phoenix bird adorned it. The mythical bird that could never die. "Halloween is still a few weeks away," she said.

What a card she was.

"Move over. NOW." The threat in his voice was enough to make her spring across to the passenger seat and wedge Nimrod into her purse.

Gretchen gulped air through an obstruction in her throat the size of a Gila monster.

Maybe he didn't kill women. That would be good news for her. He'd take what he came for and leave.

Gretchen didn't believe that for a minute.

Duanne took the wheel. The car lurched backward and sprang from the ditch.

"Finally, I've got you," he said, slamming the gears into drive. "Captured."

Captured? Like a flag?

It's strange what goes through your head when you're paralyzed with fear, Gretchen thought.

"Where are we going? To the farewell party?"

"Not even close."

Gretchen slid her hand closer to the door. Next light, and she'd make her escape. She'd take her chances that Duanne wasn't a sharpshooter. She'd risk a bullet in her back.

As if reading her mind, he said, "Try it, and I'll make a point of eliminating every single thing you value, starting with that ragged, floppy mutt and ending with your devoted aunt."

He'd established enough motivation to keep her inside the car.

Gretchen felt Nimrod shudder inside her purse, and she reached in and gave him a reassuring pat.

The airport lights dimmed behind them as they sped toward Camelback Mountain.

Gretchen's cell phone rang from someplace on the floor, and she automatically stooped to retrieve it from under the seat.

"Get up," Duanne screamed, digging the gun into her side. "Sit up. NOW!"

She eased back into the seat, careful not to startle him, and listened as the phone rang several more times before stopping.

Was it Matt finally calling her back? Like every other man in her life, he offered too little, too late. This seemed to be a recurring theme.

She glanced down between her feet but didn't see the phone.

Help as close as the floor mat yet as far away as the stars.

A few minutes later, they pulled into her carport. Duanne turned off the car and, waving the gun, motioned her out.

Tied to a leg of the doll workbench, Gretchen contemplated life.

It was extraordinarily complex, with unexpected plot twists. Her situation at the moment was a perfect example.

She strained to lift the bench to free her hands, even though she knew it was built into the wall. She couldn't feel so much as a millimeter of movement.

She had managed to slip the cell phone into her pocket, a feat she was proud of at first, but what good was it doing her now?

With her hands behind her back, she couldn't reach her pocket, let alone bring the phone to her ear. And with her legs bound together with her own doll restringing elastic, she wasn't going anywhere soon.

She could hear Duanne ripping through the house, pulling out drawers and overturning furniture. Wobbles, true to form, was nowhere in sight. Nimrod, wisely sensing random chaos within his domain, remained inside her purse. It lay next to a bin filled with dolls' underpants.

Once Duanne left the room, Nimrod boldly ran over to Gretchen, crawling over

408

her bound body hunched on the floor.

"Hide," she commanded him after a moment of intense puppy love. He rushed back across the room and burrowed inside the purse.

More banging, and Duanne came around the corner and entered the workshop.

"Where is it?" he said, enraged, his face the same color as the red clay from the darkening mountain framed in the window.

"I don't know what you're talking about."

"The box. Where is it?"

"It's in the trunk of the Echo." She should have told him where the Kewpies were stashed earlier, but she'd been frozen with fear.

Duanne smiled, a cruel tilt to his lips.

"If that idiot auction creep hadn't pulled a fast one," he said, "none of this would have happened."

Gretchen tried to stretch out a cramped leg but only made her position on the floor more uncomfortable. "You mean Brett?"

Without answering, he stomped away, and she heard the door leading to the carport close. Then it opened again, and he reappeared with the box of broken Kewpies in his arms.

He dumped the contents on the floor and kicked shards at Gretchen, stomping on the larger pieces. Bits of porcelain flew in the air, and a powdery silt fell over Gretchen's legs.

"Wrong box, silly girl." He clenched both fists.

"It's the only box I have."

"You're as obstinate as Florence. She wouldn't help me, either." He continued to slam through rooms, and Gretchen shifted her body and stretched her fingers toward her pocket. She felt fabric with her fingertips and continued to stretch, straining as far as she could.

She felt the edge of the cell phone and adjusted her body again. Picking at the pocket and shifting her shoulders and legs, she finally managed to palm it.

The easy task was over. She flipped it open. Stage two, keying in a number without being able to see the phone, was under way when she heard Duanne's footsteps.

She jerked into her former position, the phone behind her back.

Duanne had a cardboard box in his arms and a sneer on his face.

"Bingo," he said, gently placing it on the floor and squatting over it. "Let's see what we have here. If my calculations are correct, my quest is over."

He held up a Ginny doll, and Gretchen's

mouth dropped open in surprise.

"Where . . . did . . . you find that box?" she stammered.

"You think you're so cute," he said. "Still playing dumb. But you're smart. Smart enough to hide it in all that junk, and the smell in that room . . ."

Daisy.

Daisy had the box of Ginny dolls all along in the spare room she occasionally called home?

Gretchen remembered the day that Nina had arrived with Daisy and the contents of her shopping cart. She and April had been preoccupied in the doll repair room and hadn't noticed. Daisy must have carried in the box of Ginnys right in front of an oblivious Nina.

"I didn't know the Ginnys were here."

Duanne shrugged. "It doesn't matter anymore. I have them now." His face darkened. "It was that derelict sitting on the curb. He made off with them when I wasn't looking."

Duanne began to empty the box, throwing the dolls onto the floor.

Gretchen cringed at his harsh handling of them and was glad that each came in its own small box. Hopefully the damage would be minimal.

She must be a certified nutcase or a full-fledged rabid doll collector to be thinking of doll preservation at a time like this.

He dug down to the bottom of the cardboard box and extracted a small white rectangular box, quite different from the others.

Gretchen intuitively knew what was inside.

Duanne rubbed the white box lovingly between his hands.

"This whole thing has been a series of missteps," he said. "One mistake after another. But this . . ." He held up the box. "This is what it was all about."

He opened the box and removed a Blunderboo Kewpie doll. The genuine article, Gretchen noticed. Not one of Chiggy's reproductions, but a fine example of Rosie O'Neill's early work.

Blunderboo, always the clumsy, tumbling, laughing Kewpie.

Duanne rummaged through the doll tools on the workbench, almost stepping on Gretchen in his rush. She heard the doll break open.

The room was silent while Duanne looked over his treasure.

Then Gretchen's cell phone rang.

She stabbed at the key pad, blindly searching for the one that would connect the call.

The ringing stopped when Duanne kicked her hands.

The pain was excruciating, and she struggled not to cry out as the phone skidded across the room and hit the wall.

Gretchen let out a frustrated gasp and closed her fingers together, ignoring the throbbing.

"You stupid . . ." Duanne backed away from the table and glared at her. The top of Blunderboo's head was missing, and, by the tender way he held the doll, Gretchen knew he had found what he was looking for.

"Diamonds?" she asked. "Did you find diamonds?"

He held up a large, sparkling stone. "The finest there is. My cousin Percy would be alive today if he had shared with me. Instead, he was greedy. Too greedy for his own good."

"You killed Percy, and then you killed Brett and Ronny?"

"Couldn't be helped, now could it?" He fondled the diamond and returned it to the Kewpie. "People are exceedingly stupid."

"You make it sound like they deserved to die." Gretchen stared at Duanne, searching for any sign of compassion, but finding cold, lifeless eyes staring back at her instead.

"If Chiggy had given the Kewpie up . . .

but no, the sentimental fool insisted it was the last gift she'd ever receive from her brother. She even tried to trick me with those ridiculous Kewpie reproductions. But I knew what she really had."

"Ronny Beam was writing a story," Gretchen said, all the time working her fingers through the nylon that bound her hands. Her captor was insane.

"Ronny Beam was a parasite. Too bad his newest fantasy was a little too close to the truth."

Nimrod chose that moment to forget his "hide" command, and he bolted out of the purse and ran to Gretchen. *No, no, no,* she wanted to scream.

Duanne's face registered cunning. "Ah, the mutt with multiple lives. I had forgotten all about you. Did you like the scorpion?"

"Why would you try to harm a little dog?"

"You stole what was mine."

"This is so ridiculous," Gretchen blurted. "Take the diamonds and go. Leave us alone."

Duanne grinned. "You have to pay for what you've done. Let's start with the dog."

He came toward her, and she knew he was going to reach down and grab Nimrod.

Gretchen could have killed him with her bare hands if they were free. She struggled to loosen the string wound around her legs to give him a good solid kick, but all the mental strength in the world couldn't budge the cords.

"Nimrod," she called loudly as Duanne bent over to pick him up, keeping her voice as firm as she could, hiding the fear. "Nimrod, parade!"

The tiny dog turned abruptly and bolted for the kitchen doggie door, his toenails making clicking sounds on the tile floor. He skidded around the corner, and Gretchen heard the sound of the doggie door flapping open.

Duanne was right behind him. Then Gretchen heard Nimrod barking sharply as he raced around the perimeter of the fence, as Nina had taught him to do. The kitchen door slammed.

Alone in the workshop, Gretchen struggled to break free, using the resources she had learned in her doll repair business. Didn't she work with restringing cord all day long? Untangling and unknotting should be second nature to her. Her agile fingers worked on the tiniest of knots every day.

She felt the binding loosen slightly. She closed her eyes and concentrated on the task, working without sight and at an awkward angle.

Nimrod stopped barking just as her hands came free. She pulled herself up to the worktable, grabbed a pair of scissors, and cut the cord binding her legs.

Her eyes fell on the headless Kewpie with the hidden treasure of diamonds. In his haste, Duanne had left it behind.

She grabbed it and raced out the door.

Duanne had Nimrod backed into a corner of the privacy fence on the far side of the pool. Nimrod was growling, and his tiny teeth were bared. Duanne heard her coming and turned.

She raced directly at him and threw the Kewpie toward the pool. His eyes left her, and he watched it fly, diamonds exploding in the air and dropping like scattered pebbles into the blue water.

His momentary distraction gave her the seconds she needed, and she lunged onto his back, wrapping her arm around his neck, tightening as she searched for a tender spot on his neck, hoping to shut down his air flow.

Duanne bucked like a bronco, and Gretchen knew it was only a matter of moments before he found the gun in his pocket and used it.

She squeezed hard and held on.

Gretchen felt him pitch sideways and lose his footing. They were falling backward. Water closed in around her as they sank into the pool.

She instinctively let go and kicked away from him, and they each came up sputtering.

Nimrod leapt from the edge of the pool and swam toward her.

Duanne turned to her with a menacing grimace, but before he could say or do anything, a voice called out from behind them.

"Look at that," Howie Howard said in his big Texan accent. "We were worried about her, and all along she's having a pool party."

"Nobody invited me," April said.

"Me, either," Nina added.

But Matt Albright, Gretchen was relieved to see, had a steady bead on Duanne.

41

"I got your message," Howie said after Matt escorted Duanne to the nearest squad car and deposited him in the backseat. "Didn't know anything about a service going on for Brett. The whole thing smelled of ripe road kill to me, so when the detective came over to ask me some more questions, I mentioned it to him."

"We came here," Matt said. "But you weren't home. I knew about the party going on for the Boston group and went over there looking for you."

"I helped out, too," April said. "I told him the service was over on MacDowell."

"Right then," Matt said, "we knew something was really wrong. That's a rough neighborhood. So I called your cell. When you didn't answer, I kept trying, and the four of us drove up and down MacDowell looking for your car."

"No luck," Howie added. "But we found

an abandoned truck with stolen plates."

Gretchen sat poolside wrapped in a towel, attempting to control her shaking limbs.

"She's freezing," Nina exclaimed. "Let's get her inside."

"I'm fine, Aunt Nina. Just a little shook up." Gretchen burrowed into the towel. "When the phone rang Duanne found out I had it and kicked it away."

"Yes, but the call connected before he did that," Matt said. "I could hear him talking to you."

"You heard him admit that he killed Brett and Ronny? And that Brett had been helping him?"

Matt nodded somberly. "But we needed to know where you were. We'd already been here to your house. He could have been holding you anywhere."

"Then," Howie said, "you yelled, 'Parade' to Nimrod."

Nina grinned. "No place else that would work except right here where you have that doggie door."

"Nimrod saved you," April said. "Just like Lassie. I loved Lassie."

"So where are the diamonds?" Matt asked.

Gretchen gazed at the pool.

"I think it's a fine night for a pool party," she said. "Anyone for a dip?"

42

Gretchen sat on a bench on Central Avenue. The scorching heat had vanished, leaving Phoenix ready for November's perfect weather. Another month or two, and the snowbirds would flock in.

She watched Steve walk toward her and braced for the inevitable.

"Why are you here?" he said, stopping and sitting down beside her. "Neutral territory?"

She nodded, biting her lower lip. She had picked the center of Phoenix for that very reason.

No tears! she reminded herself sternly.

"My plane leaves in two hours," he said. "I don't have much time. Are you sure you won't change your mind and come back to Boston with me?"

Gretchen stared at the concrete sidewalk. "I'm sure. It's over for us."

"I'm sorry," Steve said. "For everything."

"I know. So am I." Gretchen raised her

eyes and met his. "Have all charges been dropped?"

"Yes. My reputation has been restored. But I've lost you. My pride has been damaged beyond repair."

That was the old Steve she knew best. He'd pursued her all the way across the country because of hurt pride, not real love. He'd get over it the first time a pretty woman strolled by and showed interest.

"Did you find out why Duanne Wilson stuck the knife in Ronny's back?" Steve asked.

"He saw it lying on my table," Gretchen replied. "It was an afterthought, to cast suspicion on the doll dealers."

"It certainly complicated my life."

They sat in silence for a few minutes, then Steve rose. He didn't try to kiss her goodbye, for which she was grateful.

Gretchen wiped away a tear as she watched him walk away.

Someone slid onto the bench. "Hey, doggie."

Gretchen looked over at Daisy as Nimrod pounced on the homeless woman's lap.

Swathed in her red and purple regalia, Daisy went about her business of feeding tiny crumbs of bread to a flock of pigeons. Nimrod sat contentedly on her lap watching the birds waddle beneath him, pecking at the ground.

"Come home with me," Gretchen said. "My mother invited you."

"It's nice to have her home," Daisy said.

"I really missed her," Gretchen agreed. "She could hardly believe what happened while she was gone. I'm glad everything was resolved before I had to tell her."

Daisy looked down the street. "There he is," she said. "Told you he'd show up."

Albert, his limp less noticeable today, joined them on the bench, scooting next to Gretchen.

"You look like you're healing," she said.

"It's not bad."

"You're the one who sent the Kewpies to me." She studied the fading bruises on his face.

"How did you know?"

"Your sister gave you some of her dolls and tools."

Albert looked surprised. "You *do* know Susan."

"No," Gretchen said. "I guessed after I looked her up on the Internet. That's how I found out she's a doll reproductionist."

"She used to pay me to help her in her shop before she moved away," Albert said.

"I told you she was famous," Daisy said.

"The ground-off Kewpie feet were clever touches. What if I'd missed it?" Gretchen asked.

"You wouldn't have."

"You knew what was happening when Brett and Ronny were killed. You tried to warn me with the note on a napkin."

Albert nodded. "Ronny had a big mouth. He liked to sound important, even to me, so he told me the diamond story. And I was at the auction and saw things. It was easy to figure out what was happening." He threw an arm over the back of the bench, and the smell of body odor drifted toward Gretchen.

Albert Thoreau was one of the city's invisible residents. No one paid any attention to Phoenix's homeless. Albert had been in the background all the time, and no one had noticed.

"I saw those two men arguing at the auction," he said. "And I took the box of dolls. I couldn't help myself. I took it."

"And he asked me to hide it for him after that guy pretending to be a cop beat him up," Daisy said.

"Did you know what was inside?" Gretchen asked her.

"I was pretty sure."

"Albert doesn't care about material things," Daisy said. "But he's a very sentimental guy."

Gretchen studied Albert. "Why didn't you just tell me what was happening?"

"You would have believed a drunken bum?"

"Of course."

Albert snorted, and Gretchen was silent.

"I didn't want to see you hurt," he said. "You look so much like my sister. Same nose, same hair . . ."

Gretchen sat awhile on the downtown bench, sandwiched between Daisy and Albert, and watched traffic go by.

So much for intuition and first impressions.

Milt Wood had given her the creeps, and he'd turned out to be nothing worse than pompous and arrogant.

Brett, the faithful auctioneer's assistant, had been part of the scheme to steal the diamonds.

The cold, heartless killer was the jolly old elf with the twinkle in his eyes.

And the homeless alcoholic sitting next to her, exuding ripe, unsavory odors, had tried to save her life the only way he knew how.

People were full of surprises.

A pigeon landed on the back of the bench. Nimrod yipped, and it flew down to Daisy's feet.

At the moment, life was good.

Tonight, Gretchen would have dinner with Matt Albright. He'd asked, and she'd accepted. She planned to keep it casual and friendly. After all, he *was* still married.

Howie, ten-gallon hat and all, would continue to call his auctions, and Nina's new friend, Eric, had promised to keep in touch with the psychic diva.

Nina might have a special gift for reading auras, but Gretchen would stick to what she knew best: restoring treasures.

She stood up and hoped she could find her way home without getting lost.

A workshop filled with dolls awaited her.

ABOUT THE AUTHOR

Deb Baker collects vintage Barbie dolls and contemporary Zawieruszynski Originals, and can be found haunting doll conventions and shows. Originally an enthusiastic researcher with only two treasured childhood dolls, she is proud to announce that she is now irrevocably hooked on dolls and doll collecting.

Visit Deb and her dolls at www.debbaker books.com.

The employees of Thorndike Press hope you have enjoyed this Large Print book. All our Thorndike and Wheeler Large Print titles are designed for easy reading, and all our books are made to last. Other Thorndike Press Large Print books are available at your library, through selected bookstores, or directly from us.

For information about titles, please call:
  (800) 223-1244

or visit our Web site at:
  www.gale.com/thorndike
  www.gale.com/wheeler

To share your comments, please write:
  Publisher
  Thorndike Press
  295 Kennedy Memorial Drive
  Waterville, ME 04901

CORE COLLECTION 2007